CW01597701

Praise for Liz Fenwick

'Vivid and beautifully written, Liz Fenwick is a gifted storyteller'
Sarah Morgan

'Beautifully descriptive, unashamedly romantic and evocative, Liz Fenwick has nailed the sweeping escapist read'
Veronica Henry

'What a treat *Flora's Day* is. Cornish joy swaddled in an exquisite story of secrets, love and revelations as Liz Fenwick does best'
Pernille Hughes

'Poignant and intensely atmospheric, *Flora's Day* is a joyful celebration of the heart and soul of a town and the power of love'
Linda Wilgus

'Pure escapism at its best'
The Sun

'Full of emotion and mystery'
Hello

'Full of warmth, wisdom and compassion... Liz Fenwick's writing is vivid, satisfying and descriptive'
Daily Express

'With a gifted storyteller's talent for crafting compelling characters and putting them in alluring locations, Liz Fenwick's books invite readers to open the covers and explore a dramatic terrain of love, family, and friendship...'
Deborah Harkness

Also by Liz Fenwick

<u>Novels</u>

The Cornish House

A Cornish Affair

A Cornish Stranger

Under a Cornish Sky

The Returning Tide

One Cornish Summer

The Path to the Sea

The River Between Us

The Secret Shore

The Secrets of Harbour House

<u>Novellas</u>

A Cornish Christmas Carol

Delivering Christmas

Flora's Day

A Cornish Love Story

Liz Fenwick

First published in 2026 by EMF Press

www.lizfenwick.com

Copyright © Liz Fenwick 2026

The right of Liz Fenwick to be identified as the author of this work has been asserted in accordance with the Copyright, Designs and Patents Act 1988.

All rights reserved. No part of this publication may be reproduced, stored in a retrieval system or transmitted in any form or by any means, without the prior permission in writing of the publisher, nor to be otherwise circulated in any form of binding or cover other than that in which it is published without a similar condition, including this condition, being imposed on the subsequent purchaser.

No part of this book may be used or reproduced in any manner for the purpose of training artificial intelligence technologies or systems.

This novel is entirely work of fiction. The names, characters and incidents portrayed in it are the work of the author's imagination. Any resemblance to actual persons, living or dead, events or localities is entirely coincidental.

ISBN: 978-1-7384170-4-9

Printed and Bound in Cornwall, UK, by TJ Books
Cover by BerniStevensCoverDesign.com

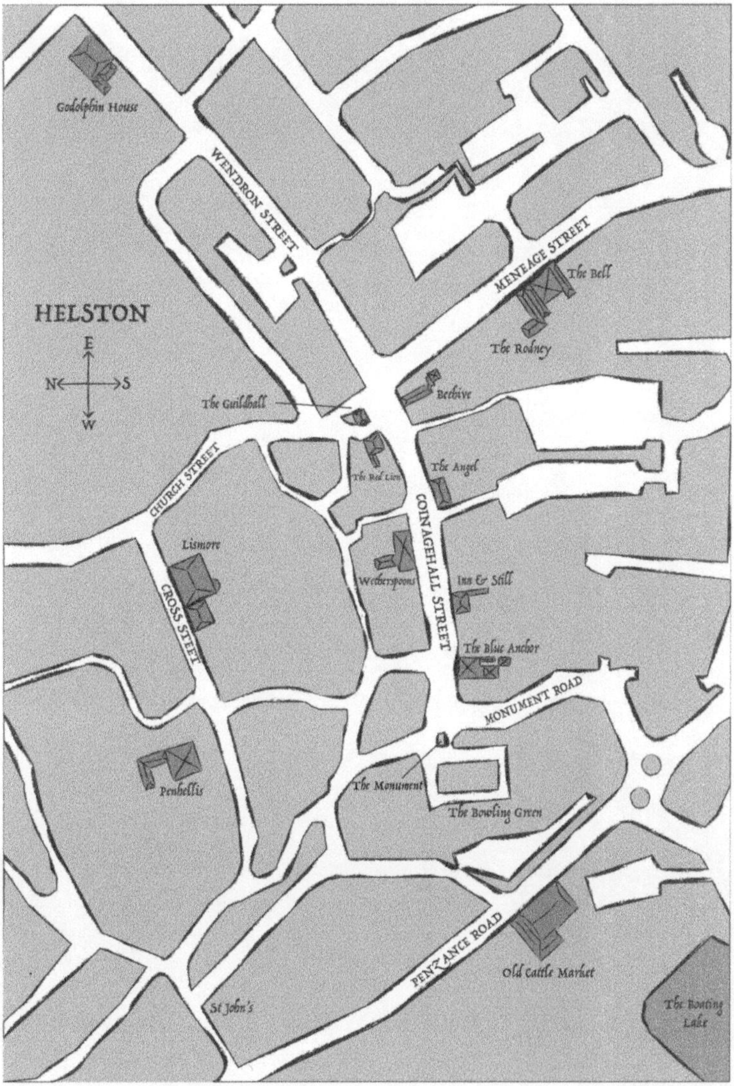
HELSTON
E
N
S
W
Godolphin House
WENDRON STREET
MENEAGE STREET
The Bell
The Rodney
Beehive
The Guildhall
The Red Lion
The Angel
CHURCH STREET
COINAGEHALL STREET
Lismore
CROSS STREET
Wetherspoons
Inn & Still
The Blue Anchor
MONUMENT ROAD
The Monument
The Bowling Green
Penhellis
PENZANCE ROAD
Old Cattle Market
St John's
The Boating Lake

For

Annabel Harper-Fenwick

At Helstone, a genteel and populous borough town in Cornwall, it is customary to dedicate the 8th of May to revelry (festive mirth, not jollity). It is called the *Furry-Day,* supposed Flora's Day; not, I imagine, as many have thought, in remembrance of some festival instituted in honour of that goddess, but rather from the garlands commonly worn on that day.
Gentleman's Magazine, Vol 60, Part One (1790)

* * *

Helston Flora-Day – This strange annual jubilee, which has existed from time immemorial, and which it is supposed to have originated from the Roman custom of paying an early tribute of respect to the goddess Flora, was kept up with great spirit on Friday, the 8th instant.
Sun (London) – 19 May 1835

* * *

In short, the town has nothing to offer to attract the stranger, but a public festival – sort of barbarous carnival – held there annually on the 8th of May. This festival is said to be of very ancient origin, and is called "The Furry"– an old Cornish word, signifying a gathering; and, at Helston particularly, a gathering in celebration of the return of spring. The Furry begins early in the morning, with singing, to an accompaniment of drums and kettles. All the people in the town immediately leave off work and scamper into the country; having reached which, they scamper back again, garlanded with leaves and flowers, and caper about hand-in-hand through the streets, and in and out of all the houses, without let or hinderance. Even the "genteel" resident families allow themselves to be infected with the general madness, and wind up the day's capering consistently enough by a night's capering at a grand ball.
Rambles Beyond Railways by Wilkie Collins (1851)

The Early Morning Dance

BEFORE BREAKFAST DANCERS MAKE AN EARLY START

The haunting Furry tune resounded in the streets as early as 7:20 a.m., when 15 couples of young people assembled in the Corn Exchange to participate in the opening dance.

Western Morning News, 9 May 1928

* * *

FURRY-DAY AT HELSTON – PICTURESQUE WELCOME TO SUMMER

The time-honoured ceremony of the Helston Furry-Day took place yesterday in glorious weather. From the windows of the houses hung gay streams of bunting, and crowds poured into the town.

At 6:30 a.m. a peal of the bells from the church tower announced the opening of the day's proceedings, and the townspeople arose to spend the whole day in giving a hearty welcome to the summer. The younger element went to the moor to collect sycamore boughs, and returned waving them aloft as they marched through the streets.

Western Morning News and *Daily Gazette*, 11 May 1932

One

2025

Thursday
8 May, 6:30 a.m.
Forecast: Sunny intervals

Furry, Faddy or Flora? That was the question.

All of them sounded strange if you weren't from Helston or Cornwall, but to those who lived in the town it was the best day of the year. The eighth of May had been marked by dancing through the streets and houses of Helston for hundreds of years, while the dispute or discussion about its name had probably been going on for just as long.

Of course, for me it had always been Flora Day, because my name's Flora. It is not my birthday. It was the day I was conceived. So, choosing to prefer Flora over the other more historically accurate names was entirely selfish. It had always been *my* day. A day when good things happened, like fun with friends and my first kiss, until one Flora Day changed it all. From then on my annual pilgrimage home had become a penance. Each year it reminded me how easy it was to lose someone you loved, how friendship was more important than anything else, and how I would make different decisions from the women whose genes I had inherited.

I'd been awake for an hour dreading today and had written a plan for it in my diary.

Hold it all together.
Get through the day with as little interaction as possible.
Survive the dance.

Once, this very day had been better than Christmas, but now it was something to endure. Which felt wrong in so many ways. It was Helston's one day of coming together. Spring was here, and it should be a time to thrive.

Outside the church bells rang, alerting the town the festivities would begin soon. For most of my life this had filled me with excitement. But this year was different... not because I wasn't hungover as I had been on so many of these mornings. No, because this would be the last time I'd be here on the eighth of May. This was final.

I swung my feet out of bed and hesitated. Already there would be people downstairs getting things ready for the day. They'd been here late into the night too, festooning the entrances with flowers and greenery. I'd left them to it. They didn't need me. The volunteers' excitement was palpable and if I wasn't careful it might sink into me. That was their plan. They didn't even try to disguise it.

Why was I even here? Of course, the answer was simple. Sir Anthony Peter Sebastian Clemens, otherwise known as Tony. He was to blame, but I couldn't rage at him. He had died two months ago and yelling at the newly installed gravestone wouldn't have the same effect. Nothing could calm my anger, ease my grief or quell my nerves. I, Flora Portia Richards, had been chosen to lead the Midday Dance in less than six hours. This was the highest honour Helston could bestow, and it could only go to those who'd been born in the town. It was meant as a bribe, as an enticement, and as a plea. Thanks to Tony, who'd been my godfather, I now owned Lismore, a Georgian house, which always played a starring role in the celebrations. From the Children's to the Midday and the Evening Dance, Lismore was a key location for the spectacle that was Flora Day.

The whole town was desperate to know what I was planning for my new inheritance. Already I was sitting on three unsolicited offers. As this was Helston, nothing was a secret. Nothing at all. In this former stannary town, where tin had been weighed and assessed for quality, everything was scrutinised with the same intensity. This had always included me, my mother, my grandmother, her mother, and her mother before that. And now I was the owner of a crown jewel. What I chose to do next was important. How could the granddaughter of the woman who should have been better, should have known better, and had died in an alcoholic haze, own Lismore? They clearly thought by giving me the honour of leading the Midday Dance it would stop me in my tracks, and wake me to my responsibilities as a Helstonian – born, bred and raised. But they had miscalculated and made a huge mistake, especially in whom they'd chosen as my partner for the dance.

Ke Dale.

Anyone but him. Even though we'd known each other since we were children, the distance between Ke and I was now far wider than the Cober that flowed through this ancient town.

But to really explain why I was here now, I needed to go back in time. Not just back to Tony's death two months ago but back to Flora Day 1986. The day I was conceived. My mother had never let me forget this fact. In truth, she'd told me this story so many times I thought of it as a fairy tale. But I later realised it was to cement the lie, the lie of omission, to both herself and me, and anyone else who would listen. My mother excelled at telling stories. She was a trained actor and had had a promising career –

in fact, she'd had a shot at Hollywood, until my arrival as a blue strip on a pregnancy test changed all that. She'd always maintained this was the fork in the road that took her on the right path. I didn't agree with that bit, even though I wouldn't have existed if she'd taken the other road. I understood crossroads only too well. We all have them, but some are more life-changing than others.

On the eighth of May 1986, my mother's day had begun early despite her hangover. She'd helped her mother close the bar at The Angel Hotel the night before, then gone out with Tony and the rest of their gang, who'd been drinking and dancing into the small hours. With only an hour's sleep, she was up and on duty to help ready the performers for the Flora Day Hal an Tow. She loved the folklore, legends and otherworldly aspects of this ancient pageant.

To this day I don't know how she could have done the job of corralling everyone for this. But she'd been thirty and in top shape from her last role as Portia in a Shakespearean troupe, which travelled to a new venue every night. The production had finished two weeks before, and she'd come home to Helston to see her mother, her friends, and to surf. No matter where she'd been working, as she constantly reminded me over the years, she'd always come home for Flora Day.

That year, in 1986, she had fixed costumes, reminded the performers what to do, made sure no one was too drunk or too timid to play their role, as the Hal an Tow made its way noisily through the streets of Helston. All went as well as these things do. Something always falls apart, spectators join in, and it was a glorious welcoming in of spring. Winter was dead, and new life could start. Little did she know that mine would begin that night too.

After the Hal an Tow, my mother had then met with friends in The Blue – the legendary Blue Anchor – before catching the end of the Midday Dance. She'd done stints behind the bar at The Angel with Gran, to help with the crush of people. Many had bought her drinks, so by the time it was eleven at night, she'd had no clue who she was, let alone the man she'd met and had sex with, or so she'd said.

This was the part I always found hard to believe. For I'd seen my mother drunk, but never to that degree. She'd always pointed out, when I was old enough to understand these things, that shagging a bloke and ending up pregnant had taught her it was a reckless thing to do. And she, of course, was right. She'd woken the following morning in her own bed with just a vague memory of what had happened. It was only three months later that the consequences of her recklessness had hit home, when she discovered I was on the way.

Gran had said it was fated to happen, as all the women in the family had become single mothers, bearing only daughters. But the truth was more nuanced than that. It involved two world wars and other tragedies, from what I could tell. Whether my conception was fated or otherwise, it was why my name was Flora, even though I've gone by Flo since I was fifteen. It was Tony who suggested my middle name should be Portia, as that was my mother's best role – and her last, since she never took that plane to Hollywood to star with Kevin Costner.

Fate.

Maybe it was fate, but more likely it was the failure of birth control. That was something my mother never mentioned when she recounted the tale of my conception, even though I asked. She had simply said I was meant to be. It was my godmother, my mother's closest friend, Tricia, who eventually told me the condom had probably broken. And she'd only let slip this info after my best friend Micki and I had plied her with wine one night.

As Micki pointed out, my birth had nothing to do with fate. It was all about crap condoms. Less romanticism and more realism was always Micki's modus operandi. I loved her for it. She kept me grounded. Made sure I didn't become too LA or too London after I moved away to pursue my dream career. But as soon as I sold Lismore, Helston would no longer be a part of my life.

Nothing would tether me here, and I could close off this chapter of my life. I couldn't wait. The past was the past and that was where I intended to leave it. This was my last Flora Day. But flickers of my first Flora Day dance still played at the edges of my mind. And all the Flora Days over the years that had made me the person I was today, that had brought me to this point.

Two

Flora Day, 1995

Saturday
Age: 8
Forecast: Sunny intervals

Flora Day was always the best day of the year but now it was the worst. I looked in the mirror. The white dress didn't fit. It was a hand-me-down from Michaela, my best friend, who was taller and, as I realised tugging at the tight top half, smaller than me. This was her dress from last year's Flora Day when we'd had the day off school. This year, it was happening on Saturday because the eighth of May fell on a Monday – market day. Flora Day was never celebrated on a Sunday or a Monday. So, no school holiday and I had to wear this stupid dress. It stunk, both the dress and no holiday.

I picked up my diary. This year it was apple green, and last year's was bubble-gum pink. Every year Uncle Tony gave me a diary to record my world. He told me to tell it all my secrets, hopes and fears. Through writing, he said, I'd create distance from events and people. Then they wouldn't seem as important or even hurt as much. I wasn't so sure. I looked at the words I'd written weeks ago.

No one wants to dance with me. If I had a dad, then I'd have a partner. Michaela has a partner. He's the son of her dad's best friend. That's how it's done.

It still hurt. A lot.

Now it was Flora Day, and I was wearing Michaela's old dress, and I was dancing with Ke Dale. The boy everyone teased about his name, saying that his dad had forgotten the last letter of his name... Kea or Key as in lock. I liked that he and his brothers all had Cornish names. Ke's name meant rejoice in Cornish. His father had just asked Mum but it was obvious we'd dance with each other. Only Ke and I had been left without partners. Even the two new kids whose fathers worked at the naval base, Culdrose, had been chosen. No one had picked us.

In the past, I'd always been in the Hal an Tow with Mum. That was what I wanted to do this year. But it wasn't happening, and now I was standing here looking all wrong. Nothing fit. I didn't fit. Despite what Gran and Mum said, it wasn't right not having a dad.

When I'd complained to Michaela about dancing with Ke, she'd laughed and then said it was because my dad hadn't fixed it, knowing I didn't have one. Her words stung, and I'd said that wasn't fair, and she repeated what her mum always said to almost everything – life wasn't fair. Just because it wasn't didn't mean she had to point it out. I thought about not having a father every day. She knew that.

Looking in the mirror, I heard her voice again. This dress wasn't fair either and would seal my fate forever. Even before the dress, I'd begged not to dance. Last year it had worked.

I clumped down the stairs and into the kitchen, wanting to kick something. 'Please Mum, don't make me do the dance.'

Silence.

'Why Mum? Tell me why?' I stomped my foot like a little kid. She was going to say because she'd done it, Uncle Tony had done it, Gran had done it. Since 1920 everyone who went to school in Helston had danced it. This was what she'd said last week.

She put her tea down and looked at me. 'Because Ke needs a partner.'

I shut up. She knew I felt sorry for him. It was the same for sport too. We were always the last to be picked. He was short, smelly and fat. Or in Gran's words, well padded. Others weren't so kind. His clothes had holes. He had two older brothers who weren't nice. They knocked him around when they thought no one was looking. They even stole his glasses. Ke was the youngest of a bad lot, I'd heard someone say. People always had a lot to say. Especially when they thought others like me weren't listening. When I'd wailed at Gran about who I was dancing with, she'd said, 'He's a fine lad, just wait and watch. That one will surprise everyone.'

I didn't believe her because she also told me I'd be a star one day, like my mum should have been. Mum *was* a star, at least to me. The day before yesterday when we were collecting bluebells to adorn our doorway, she'd told me again the story of the fairies who lived among the trees and how we must ask their permission to pick the flowers, and promise we were only taking what we needed. In the woods she bowed down low, and asked the fairy queen if we could take a few blooms to bring the summer home.

It had been damp, and the scent of bluebells was magical, their fresh smell tickling my nose. We'd danced and spun around. Before long we'd gathered just enough to decorate the front door of our little house. In Helston everyone knew where to find the bluebells and they had permission to pick them, not just from the fairies but the landowners too. Bluebells were protected, except for Flora Day, my day, when Helstonians collected them as they had done for hundreds of years. I loved being a part of something people of my town had been doing forever. It didn't mean I wanted to do the Children's Dance, and I especially didn't want to in this dress. Not that I didn't feel bad for Ke.

'Right,' Mum said, yanking a brush through my hair. 'We

need to go now. I'm dropping you off at Michaela's and I'll see you dancing, if I don't spy you watching the Hal an Tow before.'

I made a face. I really needed Mum to understand I didn't want to do this. The only hope I had was if Ke or I got sick. Throwing up would do it, but I'd eaten a huge bowl of porridge this morning, so I couldn't even try that one on her.

A crown of cornflowers and lily-of-the-valley circled my head. A single stem of lily-of-the-valley was attached upside down to the dress while Ke's flowers were pinned upright on his shirt. He fiddled with his royal blue tie, looking as unhappy as I felt. At least we were the last pair of dancers for our year.

The terrible dress felt hot and itchy when the sun came out. I couldn't manage a good scratch, though, because of the white gloves I'd been forced to wear. Even worse were the awful frilly socks Michaela's mother had also made me put on when I arrived at their house. I hated them more than the dress. Ke wouldn't look at me, and I couldn't blame him. If I felt awful in all of this, his outfit was worse. His trousers were both too short and too tight, causing a wedgie that must have been driving him mad. I'd have been tugging at it all the time, but he stood fairly still.

Would he be able to remember the steps for the dance? He hadn't danced last year either, like me, because he'd been sick. We'd practiced at school, but usually got it wrong more than right. I glanced up and saw Michaela and her partner, Tom Roger, lining up. Both looked happy. I should be too. The sun was out. Last year it had rained, which only the flowers had liked.

Mrs Potts, our teacher, rushed up to us. 'Tim, Susan, Mark and Jen are all ill. Michaela and Tom, you will dance with Ke and Flora.'

Tom groaned and opened his big mouth to complain, but a look from the teacher had him shutting it again. Michaela gave me a thumbs up as Mrs Potts stopped beside us. Ke stared at his feet. There was a big, black, freshly muddy mark across the top of his trainers. Bet one of his brothers had done that. They were dancing too, but being older, were thankfully nowhere near us in the line-up.

'Ke, take Flora's hand.'

His arms stayed down, hands hanging by his sides.

Mrs Potts squished her lips together, making them disappear. 'Ke Dale, do as you are told. Take Flora Richards' hand. We are about to start.'

He glanced up at me, then back down at his feet. 'Sorry,' he said, taking my hand just in time, as the big bass drum sounded and the music started. Michaela looked over her shoulder, grinning at me. After a few stumbling steps, we were off.

Step. Step. Step.

Step. Step. Step.

Step. Step. Step.

Ke and I finally matched steps. The music helped – from the beat of the drums to the clear sounds of the trumpets, trombones and the deep euphoniums.

Step. Hop. Step. Step. Step. Hop.

Step. Hop. Step. Step. Step. Hop.

Change partners.

Tom took my hands.

Step, step, step, hop, as we spun around. Step, step, step, hop.

Then back to spin with Ke.

We processed down the street, as the teacher had described it, because the dance was processional. Michaela's grin grew bigger each time she swirled back to Tom. I didn't like him, and he clearly didn't like me. Even though Michaela thought Ke was the useless one he could actually do the dance, unlike Tom. Despite how awful we'd been in practice, he didn't step on my toes once, while Tom did almost every time. In fact, he was so bad that at one point he knocked Michaela's shoe off and Mrs Potts had to help her.

When the boy in front of them threw up near the end and Tom stepped in it, Ke and I couldn't stop laughing. Michaela hissed at us to shut up, and Ke whispered, 'The best part of today.'

'Yes,' I said, giggling and squeezing his hand.

I saw Mum waiting for me as we finished, and Ke's dad was there for him too but not his mum. She must be there somewhere, like everyone else in Helston. Mum took my hand and smiled at Ke's dad. 'Right John?'

He nodded but didn't reply, turning to push through the crowds with Ke in tow. Ke looked over his shoulder with a small smile on his face and waved. I waved back. Dancing hadn't been so bad after all. Ke had made it fun, and now I could get out of this terrible dress. I skip-walked alongside Mum to rush home, a glow of joy tingling in my stomach.

Three

2025

8 May, 7:00 a.m.

After I'd showered and dressed, I ventured downstairs to grab something for breakfast. Thankfully, the coast was clear. The whole day stretched before me, and even though I knew the timing of everything, I didn't have a script. I couldn't prepare for encounters because I didn't know who I'd see, and that bothered me. Hell, I hadn't even had the necessary rehearsals for the Midday Dance. Micki had said it'd come back to me, but I hadn't done it since Flora Day 2019. Hopefully watching the earlier dances first would help, but I really wasn't comfortable about this. Yet the alternative of a rehearsal with Ke would mean speaking to each other before we had to. Even with a script, that'd be a strain.

With a mug of coffee in hand, I ventured into Tony's study to look at the two letters given to me by the solicitor, Peter Johns. In the pub last night, Tricia only asked me about one letter. When I'd asked how she knew about it, her glance had darted all around The Blue, which was heaving with people. Eventually she looked at me and said, 'Your mum mentioned that she'd written one years ago and had given it to Tony for safekeeping.'

'And did she say what was in it?' I asked.

She nodded. 'I know the subject, but I haven't read it, if that's what you're wondering.'

Now I rubbed my temples. My head pounded, but not from overindulgence, as I'd only had one cider. The pain came from thinking about those letters and probate. Yesterday's meeting with Peter had done nothing but increase the questions I had. Sleep hadn't answered them, and I wasn't sure anything could. I glanced towards the Gainsborough hanging on the wall. It had been one of Tony's favourites. This was why it was here and not on permanent loan to some museum, as most of his family artwork was. The list of all the pieces here and those loaned sat in front of me. It hadn't really sunk in that it was now all mine.

Tony had been the only surviving member of a wealthy, upper-class family in the area. He'd made his own way not by choice but because his father had disowned him when he came out at sixteen, and his mother hadn't intervened. Tony had said that had hurt the most. I still distinctly remember the first time he'd told me about this. I'd wept. It was Gran who'd taken him in and ensured he continued school. Not the private Truro School where he'd been, but the local comprehensive with Mum. The young Tony proved himself to be very smart and a financial wizard, working hard to become a trader in the city, then making his fortune there.

It was with this money he'd bought Lismore from his godmother when he retired at the early age of forty-five, spending the rest of his days as a philanthropist. And that philanthropy had included me, supporting me when I needed it for education and helping me pursue the career I'd set my heart on. But mostly he would listen to me rabbit on about everything in my life. I could tell him pretty much anything – he'd known all my secrets. Even the ones I'd never told Mum or Micki. With both Tony and Mum gone now, I was fully adrift. Nothing to hold me here once this house was sold.

Freedom.

So why did the thought of it make me feel so lost? But this would pass once the sharpness of grief dulled, I was sure of it.

Yesterday, as Paul handed over two envelopes, he'd said, 'I've done as instructed.' He leaned back in his chair, watching me from across the desk.

This seemed an odd comment. Everything else had been handled via email. After studying them, I'd replied, 'Was that the instruction for one or both?'

'Both.' He paused. 'Tony gave me them after he'd had his diagnosis.'

Tony's death had come swiftly after his diagnosis of cancer, as he'd opted for no treatment other than pain relief. This still made me angry. Yes, it was his choice, but it hurt not having him a part of my life anymore. Maybe we could have had a bit more time.

When I'd started to open the one in Tony's handwriting, Peter had said, 'I think it would be best if you wait to read it for when you are alone.'

I'd raised an eyebrow. 'That sounds ominous.'

'In my years of doing this job, I've found that letters from the deceased are always more personal and emotional than you'd expect.'

'Do you know what's in them?' I studied Peter. I'd known this man all my life. He'd been a good friend to both Mum and Tony, with Tony having been best man at both of Peter's weddings.

'No.' He paused, tenting his fingers and asked, 'How long will you be in Cornwall?'

I glanced over his shoulder, looking out the window at The Inn and Still. It had been The Star previously. Things do change here in Helston, even when it feels like they don't. 'Only as long as I need to be.'

He coughed.

'The series I've been working on goes into full production next week and I won't be needed on site after that.' Until probate was finished, I couldn't put the house on the market, but I could still set everything in motion. Photos could be taken for a brochure next month, when Lismore would look at its most beautiful, with the garden in full bloom. I couldn't deny that part of me would be sad to see it go. There had been so many good times at Lismore – from Christmases to Flora Days – as well as memories I wanted to bury. Before my world became complex and spread across continents.

'Probate will take some time. It's a big estate, compounded with all that old man Clemens left Tony.'

The legacy Tony had inherited couldn't begin to make up for the pain his father had caused. Maybe not having a dad hadn't been such a drawback after all. My mother and grandmother had loved me unconditionally. Had I run off and joined a cult, I would have heard their thoughts and, in my grandmother's case, quite colourfully, but they still would have told me to follow my dreams. They'd loved me. They never tried to make me something I wasn't. But the one thing I'd wanted my whole life was a traditional family – mother, father, brothers and sisters. This desire had ached within me constantly, and I'd envied anyone with a family I encountered, even if it was dysfunctional. Micki's was chaotic, and Ke's family was very broken.

Sitting down at Tony's large oak desk with its view of the garden, I paused and picked up Gran's gaudy Welsh bowl. One Flora Day, it had been knocked to the floor by accident, and Gran had been devastated. It had belonged to her grandmother. Being Tony, he'd collected up the pieces and returned the bowl to her mended, repaired in the Japanese style, kintsugi. He hadn't chosen gold but Cornish copper to illuminate the fracture lines. She'd wept as he explained the concept of this to her, and his choice of a Cornish mineral to demonstrate the strength and beauty that ran through her. The metal had now become partially green, complementing the blues and reds of the painted design, making it even more interesting and beautiful than the original bowl had been. When Gran died, Mum had asked Tony if there was anything of hers he wanted, and he'd requested the bowl because it reminded him of her resilience.

With a deep breath, and calling on Gran's strength, I unlocked the top drawer where I'd put the two letters for safe-keeping. There had been no time or space to read them yesterday. I picked up the one with my mother's handwriting on it, leaving aside the one from Tony.

Her handwriting was still so familiar. But why was I only receiving this letter now? Why not just after she'd died? Unease fizzed through me as I speculated about its possible contents. Tony writing a letter didn't surprise me. He'd always liked putting pen to paper, and I'd had hundreds of letters from him, despite the fact that email was quicker and easier. He would write out my full name, Flora Portia Richards, in his favourite teal ink on the envelope. I picked up Tony's fountain pen and played with it. Did I want to read messages from the dead? After Mum had died, I would have done anything to hear from her again. To have one last conversation, to laugh or do something silly, or to cry about some film or book that had touched us both. But right at this moment, with Tony gone too, I wasn't sure I was ready for what this letter might say.

I could imagine what worldly advice Tony might have given had I been twenty at his passing. He'd been filled with life lessons. Most of them good, but some of them crazy. His best one was never to put down or let go of a drink in a club or bar. That was followed by... always drink beer at university parties because no one knew what went into the other drinks on offer. I'd stuck with those rules and only once fell foul.

Putting those memories aside, I slipped my finger under the flap of Mum's letter. The glue barely held it closed. Half of me wondered if someone had opened it before, because of the way it came free so easily. But why would someone want to read this? Maybe it had been my mother herself, or possibly Tony.

Metaphorically putting my big-girl pants on, I pulled the sheet from the envelope. It was headed with lily-of-the-valley. The return of happiness. I smiled. She would have chosen this with care. The date at the top of the page was 16 February 1987.

That was two days after I was born! I'd always hated having my birthday on the day that celebrates romantic love. No one had paid attention to my day, being too busy chasing dreams of hearts and flowers. Maybe that was why Flora Day had always felt more important when I was young. As the years ticked by, Valentine's Day then became the loneliest day of the year, as I watched other people with their loves and I remained alone. Mum had always insisted I brought true love into her life. I took a deep breath and began to read.

My dearest darling Flora,

I am so glad you are here in this crazy world. My heart swells with love I didn't think was possible. Only now that I have you do I know how much my mother loves me. It's funny how becoming a mother changes you. Suddenly my eyes are open, and I see things differently, better, more clearly. You are the most precious gift I've been given.

My hand shook so much I could barely read the words. I'd ruined her life and chance of stardom. That's what everyone had said. There goes Maria Richards. She could – and should – have been someone.

You won't be reading this letter until I'm gone. I hope you can forgive me, for I will be lying to you always. Not about Father Christmas, although I will preserve that magic for as long as I can.

But I will lie to you, and it's important I do so. You'll want to know who your father is. I wanted to know mine as well, and my mother told me. No one else knew. But he was married to another and wouldn't leave his wife. This has slowly been eating away at her, even if she pretends otherwise. I hate him for what he did.

Unlike my mother, I won't tell you who your father is.

But I want you to know you were born of great love. You need to understand that. Of course, by lying to you, you won't know this until I'm gone. I love your father more than any man I have ever met. He loves me too. And he loves you. He always will, but there are reasons why I can't say who it is.

So, my darling Flora, you are a product of love made on Flora Day.

I hope you can forgive me for keeping this knowledge from you. It was to protect you.

Love you always,
Your mum xoxoxoxoxoxox

I put the letter down.

She lied.

She *had* known who my father was, despite swearing to me she couldn't remember. All the times I'd asked, pleaded, searched, desperate to know.

Protect me? From who? Him?

All those years she'd maintained the lie. Living with secrets was hard. This I knew. They ripped at you, tearing your heart to pieces as you kept up a front to the world.

The Flora Day volunteers' feet clunked on the wooden floors as they moved through the house. The early morning dancers must be nearing, ready to dance down Cross Street and past Lismore. I stuffed the letters back in the drawer and locked it just as there was a knock at the door.

'They're almost here,' Polly Tonkin, who ran the sweet shop, said, beaming with enthusiasm. 'My son Johnny is dancing with Sarah Hopkins.' She took a breath. 'Do you remember your first early morning dance?'

I nodded. How could I forget?

'Are you coming?' she asked.

'In a minute.' The distant sound of the Helston Town Band drifted in.

'OK,' she called over her shoulder as she dashed away.

Sunlight flickered through from behind a cloud and filled the room. *Mum had lied.* There was nothing I could do about it, and I couldn't prepare for today either. I'd have to wing it. And, as I knew from the few acting classes I'd taken in uni, I not only hated improv but totally sucked at it. Taking a deep breath, I reminded myself that once today was over I could return to the job I loved, and one where I was in control.

The music grew louder, and my heart started racing – from which emotion it wasn't clear. Was it excitement, fear, or dread? Once the sound of those notes would have lifted me immediately. My feet knew their steps, and my inner voice shouted 'summer is coming', so it should have been joy. But in this moment, something darker flooded through me. Leaving the study, I went to watch the dance, the thought still repeating through my mind like a heartbeat: *she lied, she lied.*

Four

Flora Day, 1996

Wednesday
Age: 9
Forecast: Sunny

It was six in the morning on Flora Day. I sat on my bed with my diary, scanning my latest entry.

> *There are so many things to do, and I can't wait. The noise from people already in the streets woke me and in just half an hour the church bells will ring, then it will all start at seven. I hear the music already in my head. While I waited for Mum to come out of the bathroom, I practiced my steps so Tom wouldn't crush my toes this year, even if he tries to. I could take smaller or bigger steps and... evade Tom's big, mean feet.*

I closed the diary.

Evade was a new word Uncle Tony had taught me. We talked and wrote to each other about words. Sometimes his partner Angus suggested new ones for me too. Angus was a lot older than

Uncle Tony, but he said Tony kept him young. Not sure how that could work. It wasn't like the creams Mum put on her face that she said were anti-ageing. Why was she against ageing?

Tom. There had to be a special word for him, but I could only think of bad ones. He'd made fun of Ke and me all the time during rehearsals. Michaela didn't say anything to him about it, which really bothered me.

'Tell him to shut up,' I'd said through gritted teeth last night.

She frowned, then, seeing him staring at us, changed it to a smile. 'No.'

'I'm your best friend,' I reminded her.

'I know.' She wasn't looking at me but at him.

'He's mean.' I looked over at him too – he was watching us so closely it felt creepy.

'I like him.' She smiled again at him and suddenly seemed like a different person – not the one who'd been messing around with Ke and me just ten minutes ago. This Michaela was acting like her older sisters, even walking differently when she was near him. Mum said boys didn't tend to like girls in a loving way at our age – that happened later. Which I was happy about. When I also asked her about boys liking boys that way, thinking about Uncle Tony, although I didn't know of any others like him, she'd smiled and told me to ask Uncle Tony that question. So, I planned to when I saw him later. He was down from London for Flora Day, and this alone was reason to celebrate. Uncle Tony was the best. He wrote me a letter every week, even though we spoke on the phone too. I'd asked Mum why he wrote letters, and she'd said because he thought better on paper – weird. He also liked getting them back, so I always replied, even if it was just a short note.

'Why do you like Tom when he's so mean?' I asked Michaela because I didn't get it. Maybe he was OK, but nothing special.

She sent me a look and crossed her arms.

'It's not a stupid question,' I insisted.

'Totally stupid.' She drew a deep breath. 'He's... sexy.'

I rolled my eyes. What even *was* sexy? The Backstreet Boys

were, according to the magazines in Merritts. Tom had nice hair, I suppose, but his eyes were small and unkind. Cute or sexy, he was not. But I couldn't deny that Michaela was excited to dance with him. Even though she could have had her pick of any of the boys except Ke because she didn't want him.

No one wanted Ke or me, that hadn't changed. But we'd hatched a plan at the end of last year. We would always choose each other, and so we had again. Each afternoon this week we'd met secretly and practiced. I'd brought Mum's homemade saffron buns too, as Ke was always starving. Tom and others made fun of him for being fat, and he was always given a bit more food by the lunch ladies. Mum said she didn't think he was fed very well at home. Apparently his mother had a problem. Although Mum never said what the problem was.

I guessed from things Ke said that he was never given anything that hadn't come out of a packet. When his dad came home from work, he would sort their dinner. 'Sort' was the word Ke used. It was something I did with the socks and the rest of the laundry for my pocket money, not what Mum ever did with food – she cooked or made it, like she did the saffron buns.

Mum finally came out of the bathroom and ran a hand through her long brown hair. She was so beautiful. I must look more like my mystery dad, my hair was lighter than hers, and my eyes were green like Gran's, while Mum's were brown. She had long arms and legs that moved in such a pretty way. Mine were long too after my growth spurt, but this meant I was taller than everyone else, and I tripped over a lot. Half the class called me a muppet or an elephant, with my nose being long and thin. Mum said kids could be cruel and not to listen to them. That I'd grow into my looks, like she had. She'd been bullied too.

'Excited for today?' Mum asked, slipping on her sandals. Each of her toenails was painted a different colour. I'd done them for her, and it reminded me of a rainbow. We'd had lots of rainbows recently, with all the rain. It had been very muddy when we went to pick bluebells yesterday, but at least it wasn't raining now.

'Put the kettle on for me my darling, while I finish getting dressed.'

'Be quick Mum,' I yelled, heading to the kitchen.

Our little home was perfect. We had two bedrooms, a sitting room, a tiny kitchen, and a bathroom that was the same size as my room. Outside the kitchen was a courtyard, which Mum had packed with pots filled with flowers and herbs. I always loved sitting in it and breathing deeply. It smelled so good, like now as I opened the door.

I put the kettle on and took down her favourite mug with the lily-of-the-valley on it. It was like the bouquet she'd painted on the door number plaque of our house. She'd told me the flower meant the return of happiness. I'd asked if hers had gone, but she said no. It reminded her every time she used it how lucky she was, and how I filled her life with happiness. Uncle Tony had given it to her. If she and Uncle Tony got on so well together, I wondered why hadn't they married. He was her best friend. I knew he was gay and had Angus, but Michaela's mother said that Michaela's dad was her best friend, so best friends did marry each other. If Mum and Tony married, I'd have a dad and we could be a proper family, even if he had to be in London for work. Lots of dads and mums in Helston worked for the Navy, and they were away for long periods, which was hard. I got that, but at least they existed, even if they were away on some ship half the time. My father didn't.

Only yesterday I'd asked again, was he someone from far away and exciting? She'd laughed, asking, 'Do you look exotic?' I'd crossed my arms and made a face, and she laughed even more as she kissed the top of my head. I didn't look exotic. I looked like half the people in Helston. But then I didn't know who my grandfather or great-grandfather were either.

I put the tea bag in the mug, but didn't pour the hot water into it as Mum might get cross – I could spill something on my dress. This year I loved the dress. It wasn't a hand-me-down from Michaela, and it was prettier than hers. Mum had found it in a charity shop in Truro, and it was just the right size, plus it had what Mum called an overskirt that was covered in small white daisies. I twirled about in the kitchen, feeling like a princess.

'You're so beautiful,' Mum said as she walked in. She was now dressed head to toe in green, ready for the Hal an Tow. I would have loved to have seen her in a ballgown like the other ladies in the Midday Dance. Uncle Tony was dancing in it this year. She should have been his partner, but she preferred the Hal an Tow always. Today was going to be the best Flora Day ever.

We were at the top of Meneage Street and well into the dance. Tom hadn't stepped on my toes once, and Ke was smiling and his blue eyes sparkled behind his glasses. It was all wonderful. I'd even waved at a few people along the way and still felt like a princess. Michaela wasn't happy for some reason, though, scowling whenever I looked over to her. It could have been that, since Tom couldn't stamp on my toes, he was doing it to hers. Whatever it was, her face was puce and her mouth a flat line – she wasn't looking her best.

I watched her whisper something to Tom. Then, as we began the bit of the dance when I had to leave Ke and twirl with Tom, Tom grabbed my hands, spun me violently, then pushed me to the ground. He laughed as I lay there, winded and shocked. I fought back the rising tears – I wouldn't let him see me cry. Ke dropped Michaela's hands instantly and rushed over to help me up, soon followed by a teacher. My dress, my beautiful princess dress, was covered in muddy streaks. The day was ruined. The teacher brushed me down, trying to clean the dirt off, but only made it worse.

As I stood up again, I looked over to see Michaela laughing with Tom. Had she asked him to do it? Why would she do that? The music changed, and we automatically went through the steps of the dance again, Ke squeezing my hand a little tighter each time. And whenever he did, it felt like coming home. I hated Tom so much I trod on his toes for every single partner change we went through after that. If I'd had my way, he wouldn't be able to walk again. But Michaela's laughter stung the most. Why would she want to bring me down? Was this what happened when a girl chose a boy over their best friend?

Five

2025

8 May, 7:45 a.m.

It was a surprise to find I was slightly lightheaded as I walked to the gate. But then maybe it wasn't. The story of my life had turned upside down. My father was a known entity, at least to my mother, and not the stranger she'd always insisted. How could she have lied to me and for so long?

The sound of the brass horns snapped me out of my thoughts as I stood by the side of the road to watch the band file past. These musicians were the heroes of the day. They played and walked through the town, sparking joy in Helstonians and visitors alike. Behind the horns, euphoniums, trumpets, and coronets were some familiar faces. There were new ones too, marching proudly alongside the old hands who had been keeping the dancers moving through the streets for decades.

Bringing up the rear on the big bass drum was Wilf Shaw. It was a balm to see his familiar face again, with his now broad shoulders matching his giant hands and feet – he'd always been a dependable friend in our once close group. He grinned at me as they passed, still making sure he didn't miss a beat. Behind him were the stewards and the mayor in their bowler hats and suits. They all smiled broadly at me too, and I couldn't help but smile back. There was too much history here, and now I was looking at every older man I'd known for years, wondering if he might be my father.

I scanned the faces, searching for traces of myself, but none of them had ever seemed more than minor friends and acquaintances of my mother. Over the years she'd had the odd boyfriend, or more like passing fancies, but nothing ever stuck. Loneliness had concerned me – hers and mine. My grandmother had been so isolated, despite working at the bar at The Angel for so many years. There wasn't anything she didn't know about everyone, yet from what my mother had said in her letter, I doubted she'd confided in Gran about my father's identity.

Maybe I should take a DNA test and see what it reveals. That could, as Gran would have said, put the cat among the pigeons. Part of me wanted to do just that. Thirty-eight years of longing. Longing to know my father, to know that other side of me which wasn't a Richards. A memory returned of when I'd had a gentle go at Gran regarding our last name, as I helped her in The Angel one day.

'Richards is a good Cornish name,' she'd declared.

'Sort of,' I said, crossing my arms and fizzing inwardly. 'It's not like Tremayne or Penrose. It's patronymic which, considering we're a family of women without fathers, is a bit ironic or even wrong.'

'Who taught you such things?' She was smiling now.

'Me, I was looking up Cornish surnames.'

'Well, yours is a good one whether it came from a man or not. Be proud, my chick, be proud to be a Richards, to be proper Cornish.'

I could tell I wouldn't be able to convince her we should change our name by deed poll to something more female focused, or at least really obviously Cornish. We remained the Richards women. 'How do we know we're Cornish when we don't know who half our DNA comes from?'

'I know, and you know it in your bones too.' She went to hand Thomas Hocking his pint and left me to fester. How could I know who I was if I didn't know who my father, grandfather, or great-grandfather were? Yes, I was Flo Richards, a good student, a hard worker. But that really said nothing about me. But those two things, I'd later learned, had proven to say a great deal about me.

The big bass drumbeat brought me back to the here and now. What would Gran have thought of me owning Lismore? She'd have loved it, but would she have understood my decision to sell it? And had my mother known that Tony intended to leave it all to me? Gran and Mum had been like family to him, and I was his only godchild, so I suppose it made sense, even if it was unexpected.

The dancers came into view. They looked far brighter than I'd ever felt at this hour of the morning, facing the longest dance of the day at nearly four miles. The riotous night before always impinged on the Early Morning Dance, yet looking at them I couldn't see it. Maybe I hadn't shown it either, back in the day. The men in their crisp white shirts and the women in pretty frocks twirled to the beat of the music. The tune reverberated through me until it hit my heart.

Spring.

Life.

Survival.

What were the silly words of the song written in 1911 by Katie Moss? Bloody Terry Wogan had made a hash of it as well, leading everyone to believe it was Helston Floral Day or Floral Dance.

I thought I could hear the curious tone of the coronet, clarinet and big trombone, fiddle, cello and big bass drum, bassoon, flute and euphonium.

You had to wonder if she'd seen the band at all. A cello? Really? Fiddles did feature greatly in the historic accounts of the day and were still used in the Hal an Tow, but once the town band took over, fiddles were out. As for all dancing together, well, that didn't happen either. This early dance was the traditional one for the workers or servants, who'd then head off to do their jobs, before returning at the end of the day to dance again. The familiar steps of the dance, the faddy, spoke of joy, with its spins and hops.

This day had so many possible roots. It was clearly a pagan thing. Bringing in the greenery and flowers to welcome the spring, and the period of abundance which followed it. The dancing had at some point been corralled by the church, who set the celebration on the eighth of May, the feast of the apparition of St Michael. As a child, I'd loved the story of St Michael fighting the devil over Helston, until St Michael had thrown a large rock at the devil, who then sank into Loe Pool. This had been enough to keep me out of that dangerous body of water. I remembered being paralysed with fear watching the weeds gently sway below the surface, thinking it was the devil in there trying to tempt me in. When we'd come back from walks around there, my mother had lectured Gran on not scaring me to death. Gran had replied that plenty of people had gone to their death in that pool and left it at that.

Much of Cornwall had some sort of May celebrations. Padstow had its Obby 'Oss Day, Penryn and St Ives had their May Day and Penzance had its May Horns. The Helston of my childhood had been filled with magic and folklore. Anything could happen, like falling in love with your dance partner. But I soon learned this was just a fairy story or legend of old. Real life was far different from girl meets boy and they walk off to a happily ever after. And fathers didn't magically appear because you wished them into being, however hard – just like the story that the massive stone used in the courtyard of The Angel was actually part of the stone which had sunk the devil and saved the town.

It was all tall tales, like the legend that St Michael still comes to sit on his chair in St Michael's Mount, where he'd been seen by some fishermen a few hundred years ago. The child in me had believed it all. Happy ever afters were as real as the stories of the saint. But, as any scriptwriter would tell you, the happy-ever-afters depended on where you ended the story. Continue it for just one more day, or even just an hour, and the ending could be less than happy. The adult in me was very sure the fisherman hadn't been fishing, but on the lash, so had needed to explain why they hadn't caught a damn thing. Dreams, fairy stories, and wishes didn't come true.

40A Bywater Street, London SW3

---

3 May 1997

My darling girl,

I can't wait to see you on Flora Day. Your mother tells me you look beautiful in your dress and that you are dancing with Ke Dale again. Remember to enjoy it. So many things can trip us up on the day, from other people's feet in the wrong place to our own feelings. It is feelings that are the most dangerous.

Sometimes we keep these emotions hidden and they can eat at our insides. And sometimes they reveal themselves even when we don't want them to be seen or can't even find the words to describe them. Keep using your diary to record what you are feeling, and why you think you are feeling that way. Does that make sense? Then, once they are on the page, you can see them. I find that looking at them written down makes it easier. Sometimes I can pretend they are not mine, more like a friend's, and that allows me to see the way forward.

I'm sad to report Angus can't make Flora Day this year. He sends his love and I'm to give you the biggest hug from him. Shall we go out for dinner just the two of us while I'm down? I cherish our last meal alone, when you beat me at every game of hangman. I still think of the poor waiter's face when we kept asking for more and more paper napkins.

See you soon.

All my love,

Uncle Tony xxxx

Six

Flora Day, 1997

Thursday
Age: 10
Forecast: Sunny

Mum's alarm went off and I crept out of bed, putting the radio on. 'I Believe I Can Fly' was playing as I heard Mum in the shower. I pulled out my diary, and its bright orange cover glowed in the sunlight.

8 May 1997

Flora Day. My day. Not everyone can celebrate the day they came into existence or, as Mum says, was conceived. People line the streets for me. Not really, but like the song 'I believe I can fly', or I can dance on this day. Ke's my partner as usual, and that means it'll be fun. And best of all, Michaela won't be dancing with horrible Tom this year, as his gran died in Devon and it's her funeral. I've forgiven her for last year after she eventually confessed. She's dancing with a new kid, Harry. He's cool. He's lived all over the world with his dad in the Navy. It's just so interesting. I mean, he's lived in the Middle East, with deserts, camels and so much more. So jealous. Maybe my dad is in a country like that? He's an explorer, or a nomad like the gypsies, and travels around helping endangered animals? Maybe a filmmaker or a spy like James Bond. I wish I knew. I mean, do I have his eyes or Gran's? Will I ever know him? This makes me really sad, especially today, Flora Day.

My dress this year is another hand-me-down but that's ok. It fits and it doesn't itch or smell. Ke's clothes were sorted by Mum, so they fit him too. His mother is in hospital, and Mum being like she is offered to help. His poor dad looks so tired, but I think that's 'cause he's trying to keep Ke's brothers in line. One has been in trouble with the police for fighting all the time. But I kinda get why. Someone was slagging off their mum. If anyone said something about mine, I'd hit them too.

They say stuff about Gran all the time, but Gran says just to ignore it. It makes no difference to her, none at all. That sort of talk would hurt Mum, though, even if she wouldn't show it. These days she's working as a teacher's assistant in the secondary school and also giving them a hand with any productions. She seems to enjoy it. I wish she'd go back to acting. I've looked through her old photo albums, and she was amazing. The newspapers wrote nice things about her too. I hate that she stopped because of me, even though she keeps telling me it was the best thing, and that she's happier now. I try to believe her.

The doorbell rang, so I closed my diary, shoved it under my pillow, and then raced to the door. Ke was there with his dad, fidgeting with his tie.

'Your mum?' his dad asked.

'Just coming.' I smiled and stepped aside so Ke could come in. I heard Mum walk up behind me.

'Thanks Maria,' Ke's dad said.

'A pleasure,' Mum replied, and then he was gone to the

hospital to visit Ke's mum. I didn't know where his brothers were, but no doubt someone had them.

'I'll make breakfast while you get dressed, Flora.' Mum smiled. 'Ke, why don't you sort the toast for me?'

'Of course, Miss,' he said.

I snickered. Mum had told him to call her Maria, but he never did. He wouldn't call her Miss Richards either, just Miss, which was kinda weird but sort of sweet. Michaela thought it was odd. She called Mum Maria now, having jumped at the chance when Mum offered it to her a year ago. Michaela had always put her foot in it before by calling her Mrs Richards. Ms would have been better than Miss, but Mrs really didn't apply. Gran had explained that women in our family lived in the no-man's-land of not having a defined place in society, as it was currently sorted. But we worked in the older one, with the roles of maiden, mother, and crone, which didn't rely on men to define our role. She said she liked being a crone, it suited her. In her words, I was the maiden.

Looking in the mirror after I'd put on my dress, I wasn't sure that maiden best described me. I looked nothing like Maid Marian, but it was obvious I'd grown a lot recently. Mum had a photo of Ke and me tucked into the corner of her mirror. We'd both been the same height last year, but I was taller than him now by a bit. No doubt his brothers probably hassled him about this. I hated the way they were with him. It was almost enough to make me not want brothers or sisters – almost, but not quite.

Michaela's sisters weren't so bad. They gave her a hard time only when she nicked their stuff. Usually they told her things, lots of things, and most of it was true. I'd checked some of it out with Mum a while ago to see if they were lying about things like Father Christmas, and more recently about kissing. Kissing wasn't something I was interested in doing, but I was still curious to know more. And they were full of this information about it. Michaela said they were full of shit, but that's what they said about her.

To be honest, some of the time Michaela was, and she could do things I really didn't like, but mostly she was the best. When she was around boys like Tom, she was different. Thankfully, she wasn't weird around Ke. The three of us spent a lot of time together at my house watching films, and imagining we were in the films, or we made up stories to carry on from them. I usually sorted who was playing which role, and what needed to happen, like the sword fights. Ke loved those the most. We never did the kissing bits, although Michaela was always eager. We were the Three Musketeers, we had decided. Not that we dared to tell anyone else this. No one else was like the three of us.

I peered into the mirror and studied my mouth. Kissing. It was an OK mouth. It spoke, it yelled, it ate, but was it kissable? I pouted like Michaela's sisters did and looked so funny I laughed.

'Breakfast is on the table,' Mum called from downstairs.

After one last glance in the mirror, I ran down to join them. It was clear Ke was already on seconds, as he grinned at me with a mouthful. I'd better catch up.

Ke and I were back at home in normal clothes again. Our dance had gone so well. No one had been sick, been pushed, or lost their shoe in our group. The sun had been hot, which'd been the only problem, but a good one. The Evening Dance had finished an hour ago, and Mum was at the pub with Tony and Angus. Mrs Hoskine was watching Ke and me.

We were watching *The Three Musketeers* again and listening to the noise outside. It sounded fun out there, but it was just as fun here with Ke. He liked the same stuff as me. We sat there in the cloaks Mum had made for us and practised our sword fighting.

'Take that!' I charged and managed to get in a good hit. Ke fell dramatically onto the sofa. He threw his legs in the air like a dying bug and gasped loudly.

'You got me,' he croaked.

I fell over in a fit of laughter. He quickly rose and stabbed his sword between my arm and my body, killing me! We couldn't stop giggling. Mrs Hoskine wasn't so sure it was a good film when she popped in to check on us, but she let us continue as the video was nearly done.

By the time we put on *The Princess Bride,* we were both yawning. Mrs Hoskine had given us pasties for tea, and crumbs covered us and the floor. We had school tomorrow, and Ke's dad was due to pick him up at nine. I knew Mum would be home by then too, as she had work.

Once the film had ended, we sat staring at the blank screen.

'Do you want to find true love?' Ke suddenly asked, imitating a character in the film.

'Yup, I do. Don't you?' It was a funny question – surely everybody wanted to find true love, didn't they? But thinking about it I guessed most people didn't, since Mum hadn't, though Tony had with Angus.

He cocked his head to one side, and then to the other, before starting to chew his thumbnail.

'Well?' I asked.

He drew a big breath and stood a bit taller. 'Yeah, I do, and I know who I want to be with.'

I opened my eyes wide, then wider still, staring at him, waiting, but I gave in and asked, 'Who?'

He looked towards the door and then at the TV.

'Who?' I ran through all the girls I knew, and then, thinking of Tony, I ran through all the boys. Or maybe he was thinking of a celeb? That would make sense. I mean, I was in love with Leonardo DiCaprio.

He cleared his throat, then looked down at the floor. He was afraid to tell me. I placed a hand over his to reassure him, like Mum did with me.

'Don't worry, I promise not to tell a soul, especially not Michaela, who we both know can't keep a secret.' Michaela still had a bruise on her arm where her oldest sister had bashed her after she blurted out to Johnny Penrose that her sister wanted to kiss him. I was certain she'd learned her lesson from that, but she hadn't. She next told Mrs Rogers that her mother thought she was cheating on her husband, repeating her mother's words exactly. That had seen Michaela grounded, which was why she wasn't with us tonight.

'Promise?' He glanced at me, then back to my hand on his.

'Promise.' I crossed my fingers on my other hand and held them over my heart. 'Who?'

He looked me directly in the eye.

I couldn't move. No one liked me. But his eyes said he did, and his mouth lifted in a half smile. My stomach did a funny flip.

I looked down at my hand on his. I felt the same way about him.

Hal an Tow, Jolly rumble O

REVIVAL OF HALANTOW

An innovation this was the "Halantow," which has been revived by the Helston Old Cornwall Society, after 35 years. The march started at 8:30 a.m. A crowd of youth of the "village" went on to the Moor and there procured branches of sycamore. Returning, they marched through the town, stirring all with their lusty shouts and songs as they waved their branches in the air.

The "Halantow" is an ancient custom, and was practiced by the inhabitants of Helston for many years, up to 35. It is symbolical of the rejoicing of the coming of spring. In the olden days they went out into the moors and picked sycamores, and returned singing the song 'Bringing in the May-O!' Then they went to the grammar school in Wendron Street, and asked for a holiday for the boys, which was usually granted. Then they marched to the chief houses and public houses of the town.

The Cornishman and *Cornish Telegraph* – 15 May 1930

Seven

2025

8 May, 8:30 a.m.

Once the dancers had passed and the band was a distant sound, I returned to the house weighed down with sadness. The Hal an Tow was about to begin. This part of the day was so closely connected to my mother. I walked through it all in my head. From Epworth Hall, the performers made their way to the first stop, which was on the site of what had once been a medieval religious hospital, St John's. The pageant would then move noisily through the town, telling the story of St George and the dragon and a few others, including the puzzling Aunt Mary Moses.

Everyone asked who the hell she was. A reference to Mary, the mother of Jesus, or a reference to Charles II returning to power after the Civil War? Or, more controversially, Queen Mary? We would never know now. The words to the song had altered little and were sung elsewhere. There were written accounts of it being sung in Cornwall since the 1600s. Like all oral traditions, things evolved. Robin Hood and St George had little connection to a town whose patron saint was Michael, therefore additions had been made over the years. Now he gets a shout-out, as does St Piran.

Back when I'd volunteered at the museum in Helston, I was a fount of knowledge about such things. In my head, it had been so I could hand it down to my children, as my mother and my grandmother had done, but I was the end of the line of Richards women. That thought stopped me in my tracks as I began to climb up to my room. Tony and I had talked about being the end of the tree. It was the last conversation we'd had. It was typical of him to find some dark humour in it, going on about questionable genes and back-alley shenanigans.

Had my mother and my father engaged in that? Or had it been something else? She'd said in her letter I was born of great love. Had they crept back to Gran's flat while the whole of Helston partied and created me there? Or had it been a drunken, impulsive decision? Those happened, but I had to accept I'd probably never know now what my mother's actions had been that night. Tony's letter wouldn't tell me. He was good at keeping secrets. He'd held mine close when I needed to talk, to think, and to grieve. So, if Mum had told him in confidence, I could be sure he wouldn't have written it down. He would have taken it, like mine, to the grave.

I walked back downstairs and heard, 'Hey, Flo.' I turned to the front door to see a flustered Gina, costume designer extraordinaire, carrying a garment bag. My dress for the Midday Dance had arrived, as had Vlad, hairstylist and makeup artist to the stars. Along with Micki, they were my closest friends. Gina was based in LA and Vlad in London. Since I'd introduced them ten years ago, they had worked their magic together many times. Thanks to them, not only was I to dress the part, but they intended I should look my best.

'Wow, this place,' said Vlad, as he moved into the hall.

Seeing Lismore through his eyes, it really was a wow in its Georgian splendour, reflecting all of Helston's past glories gained from the mineral wealth that was found in the land around. But looking at Helston now as a whole, and specifically The Angel Hotel, it was hard to picture that wealth. The Angel had once been the town house of Lord Sidney Godolphin, who'd been first minister to three monarchs, as well as a serving member of parliament for Helston.

Helston's prosperity had grown and grown to the glory days of mining money and three members of parliament. This borough town had punched far above its weight, considering its distance from all the seats of power. Once it had also boasted one of the top grammar schools in the country, and a train station. These days most people just drove around the town on their way to the Lizard, or to Penzance. They had no idea what they were missing, though – the architectural gems which lived beyond the superstores lining the ring road. The high street had suffered thanks to those big stores. Once Meneage Street had been home to three butchers and a greengrocer. All gone now, and the most heartbreaking of all, Eddy's, where all my childhood dreams of toys had come from. Thankfully elsewhere in the town there were still a fishmonger, a butcher, and a greengrocer. And the pubs had survived. Each with its own unique history. The Blue Anchor being the most famous, or infamous, and the unofficial heart of Flora Day. It had always been my personal favourite. I loved that it had begun life as a monks' rest, brewed its own beer and even had a skittle alley.

'I didn't take you seriously when you said to get here before six this morning,' Gina said as she dashed up the stairs. 'It's mad out there, and I had to sweet talk my way through to where you'd told me I could park.'

'Are you heading out to the Hal an Tow, Flora?' Mrs Wearne asked, another of the volunteers busy around the house.

I hesitated, still not sure I could bear to watch it.

'Hal an Tow?' asked Vlad, lugging his makeup trolley up the stairs. It looked like he'd brought the full works, and maybe I needed it to face Ke. God knows what his thoughts were about partnering me again, after everything.

'Hard to explain,' I replied, leading them up to my room. Gina hung the garment bag on the wardrobe door. 'This is quite the place, and the artwork must be worth a fortune.'

I nodded, thinking of the list in the study.

'Can we see this Hal an Tow?' Vlad asked. He wasn't one to let something go, and it would be right up his street. Could I face it? It had been such a key part of who my mother was, and my heart ached when I thought of her getting ready for it. Her green costume, her rainbow toes. Part of me wanted to scream at the performers for continuing it without her.

My grief for her remained a tight ball inside me, fighting for space with all the other things I kept hidden within, other grief I didn't show the light of day. At this moment they bumped up against each other, leaving little space for me. The me who'd survived it all and become hollow, despite the stones of pain filling my soul. I was merely a vessel these days, and I was OK with that. My career was my passion. I loved what I did, working as a casting director in the film business. The alchemy it took to match a role to an actor, the right actor who would bring the flat words on the page alive. I was a key part of that creative process, of making something entirely new. This lifted me and filled the emptiness around the granite weights inside.

'Of course we can go.' I glanced at my watch. There was plenty of time before I had to get ready. How long would it take to transform me from a tired, disillusioned woman into one ready for the ball, as it were? It would be my Cinderella moment, ready to face the prince I'd already lost.

Eight

Flora Day, 1998

Friday
Age: 11
Forecast: Light rain showers

I'd never told a soul what Ke and I had talked about last Flora Day, and he never mentioned it again. But we spent more time together, especially as his mum had become meaner now she was 'clean' as my mother phrased it. So, he took refuge at our house much of the time. He didn't do the same at Michaela's, though, as her mum wasn't too keen on him. I couldn't figure out why. He was always polite, far nicer than me, and certainly better behaved than Michaela. So, we hung out at my house on wet days and around the boating lake on dry ones. And when acting at being the Musketeers, Helston's opes would become the alleys of Paris. Adventure lurked around every corner, like the murder in The Blue or the grand balls of past Flora Days held in The Angel.

Today was Friday, and because that meant no school the next day, we could enjoy the Flora Day fun fair for longer this year – Mum wouldn't be so stressed about getting me to bed in good time. I couldn't wait.

I was wearing last year's dress because it still sort of fit. And I wasn't much taller than Ke now. We'd both grown, but he'd grown more. Mum had sorted his clothes for him again this year, and he'd be arriving any moment.

I opened my diary. This year's was the blue of a summer sky.

Flora Day

I've been wearing my new shoes every afternoon this week so I don't get blisters. Michaela said it was silly but Mum insisted. If I got blisters, then I wouldn't be able to enjoy everything, and I really wanted to. I've been saving my pocket money for weeks, and Tony gave me ten pounds on my birthday that I've kept just for this too. So I have fifteen pounds for the fair.

Ke won't have much of anything, but I'm happy to share. He needs to have some fun. I still don't get his mum. She's not on drugs now so she should be feeling better but when Michaela and I go round to get Ke she's horrible, shouting at him and making him feel awful. He doesn't say but I can see it. He always races us away from his place and I totally get it.

It's going to be the best Flora Day ever!!!! Just hope it doesn't rain.

Outside Ke was chatting to his dad, and I raced downstairs before the doorbell could ring. Ke was staying at ours tonight, as would Michaela. It was going to be epic.

The rain held off until halfway through the dance, and my new shoes, once wet, cut into my heels. Before long Ke whispered that my socks had gone pink. I carried on twirling and hopping through the steps, wincing, and thought the dance would never end. When it finally did, Michaela's mum was waiting for us and looked at me in disgust when I asked to take my shoes off. She immediately went to get Mum in the Passmore Edwards building, which wasn't far but I couldn't walk any further in these shoes. This ruined the plan, which had been for Michaela's mum to watch the three of us for the start of the Midday Dance, then give us lunch while Mum sorted the Hal an Tow costumes. Only after that was Mum meant to come to take over.

Once she was back, Mrs Williams said, 'Flora, you stand there by the museum until your mother arrives. She said she won't be long. I'm going to take these two to watch the dance.'

'But...' I started.

'Don't make a fuss. You'll all see each other later.' She pushed both Ke and Michaela along, who gave me sympathetic looks, and left me by the cannons outside the museum in the rain with bleeding heels. It was all I could do not to cry. The band struck up, and normally I'd have been practically dancing just listening to it, but my heels throbbed too painfully.

I leaned against the cannon to take the pressure off my feet. I instantly regretted it, though, as my dress absorbed the raindrops pooling on the metal. Things couldn't get worse than bloody feet and a wet bum. My tears mixed with the growing rain. With my head down, I prayed no one would notice.

Suddenly in front of me were rainbows. Mum's toes. As I looked up, I saw she was still head to toe in green stuff, including the flowers and leaves in the wreath on her head. She loved the Hal an Tow so much, and I knew it couldn't happen without her. I looked down again. My stupid bleeding feet had taken her away from the important task of regathering all the costumes so they'd be available for next year. I swallowed.

'Oh, my poor girl.' She wrapped me in a hug. 'We hadn't counted on the weather, had we?'

I shook my head, sniffling. She handed me a tissue and helped me take off my shoes. We walked home hand in hand, and I pretended I wasn't just in my socks.

. . .

Once I'd had a bath and she'd put plasters on my heels, we went back out to meet up with Michaela and Ke. From the look Ke sent me, I think I'd had the better time. Michaela's mum was tricky. Whereas my mum was nothing but lovely, even when we had to help her with the costumes until Tony and Angus could collect us. They'd promised to take us to the funfair at the Fairground Car Park opposite the boating lake.

Once there, the rules were laid down. We were to check back in with Tony and Angus every half hour. They were taking shelter from the light rain under a tree and drinking coffee.

We rushed to the candy floss stall. Not our best decision, as candy floss and rain don't mix well, but we ate it faster because of that. After this, we put our funds together and bought tickets for the rides.

'I want to go on the Ferris wheel first,' Michaela said, looking up at the swinging baskets above us. My stomach turned. I wasn't sure if it was the height or all the candy floss I'd gobbled down.

'OK,' said Ke, and we walked over to join the queue. But we couldn't avoid passing Ke's brothers, Jorin and Pawl.

'Hey, Jorin, how is it that your fat little brother pulls two birds and you can't even pull one?' called Matt Spence, one of the coolest and meanest guys in Helston.

Ke picked up his pace as his elder brother Jorin moved towards us to reach Matt.

'Hey, mate you aren't doing any better than me,' Jorin replied.

Ke grabbed my hand as I glanced over my shoulder to watch his brothers. Ke's eyes were full of dread. I wanted to fix it, but I knew I couldn't. He hated drawing any attention, unlike Michaela, who loved it all – good or bad.

Once in the queue, Ke hid behind Michaela and me until Jorin and Pawl had moved away, towards the dodge 'ems, the ride next to us. As we got closer to the front, it became clear that one of us would have to go alone. If it was me, I realised I'd need to back out – there was no way I could go up there on my own.

'You're all white,' Michaela said.

I nodded.

'What's wrong?' she asked.

'Not sure I want to do this.' My stomach rolled over.

'Come on, we're the three Musketeers, remember?' She nudged me. 'All for one and one for all.'

I nodded. 'We are... but three of us can't go in one basket together.'

'Oh,' she said.

I swallowed.

'You're scared,' she whispered.

'Yup,' I whispered back.

'I'll go on my own,' Ke said.

'Really?' I watched his face.

'It's cool.' He shrugged and stepped aside for me and Michaela to go first. I still wasn't sure about this, but with her next to me, I would try it.

Once we were locked in, and the wheel had turned a bit, I was desperate to get out. Michaela turned to wave at Ke behind us and the basket we were in wobbled. I grabbed her hand, and she sent me a funny look.

'It's *OK*,' she said. The wheel turned again, and we moved higher. I tried to focus on what I could see, but it didn't help my stomach. I grasped Michaela's hand tighter.

'You really are scared.'

'Yes!' I released her hand and gripped the bar in front of us so tightly I couldn't feel my fingers. With every move of the basket, my stomach dropped to the ground, then rushed back up, making me feel like I was going to puke.

'We're safe,' she reassured, turning to wave to Ke again. 'That's the last basket to fill, and once we start moving properly you'll feel better.'

'I'm not so sure.' As the wheel gradually rotated fully, we were soon at the top. I could see the whole boating lake and all the people dodging the light rain. Tony and Angus were still standing under a tree. We then moved from the top, and I felt a little better.

Ke waved down at us. He was rocking his basket, and I could see Michaela wanted to do the same, but she didn't dare when she glanced over at me.

'Look, there's Matt with my sister. I wonder if she's kissed him yet?' She pointed, and I peered down. That was a mistake.

Michaela kept looking all around, and each time she did, we rocked. 'Sorry, I really am. Maybe if you close your eyes, it'll be easier.'

I tried that. It felt even worse, and the next thing I knew I was heaving up pink-coloured sick. It flew through the air, splattering down below, and I heard someone start swearing. This was my worst nightmare.

'Don't panic,' Michaela said, stroking my back. 'You didn't get any on us.' She peered down and grinned. 'But you did manage to hit Ke's brothers standing in the dodge 'ems queue.'

Despite my misery, a giggle erupted from me, and Michaela laughed too.

Thankfully, once our basket reached the bottom on its cycle, the guy running the thing stopped it to let us jump off. We then stood by the side together, watching everyone else continue to go around and around. Ke called down to me, asking if I was OK.

'Stupid little shit!' yelled Jorin, coming up to us while trying to brush globules of pink off his shirt.

'Watch what you say, she might just do it again.' Michaela crossed her arms and glared at him. I began to make a retching sound. Both of them fell silent and backed away.

'You feeling OK now?' she asked.

I nodded, still a bit wobbly, but happy that Michaela was my friend and had my back, as well as my front in this case. She wasn't with a mean boy laughing at me this time.

Nine

2025

8 May, 9:30 a.m.

Weaving our way through the throngs of people outside the house and lining the streets, Gina, Vlad, and I reached the Guildhall. Spectators packed the pavements and spilled onto the streets. Movement through them was tricky. Known faces mixed with complete strangers, pushing forward to catch the spectacle of the Hal an Tow. We found a spot behind a woman with a buggy and two small children, which meant the three of us had a clear view of the street. I tried not to think too much, but the weight of grief in my stomach roiled uncomfortably.

The sounds of the bells and whistles reached us before the troupe could be seen. Branches of sycamore swept through the air as the crier rang his bell and the crowd cheered. My mother had loved this so much. This was always her moment. The connection of the past to nature and the joy of acting – acting out, being bigger, louder and better, while being a part of something ancient.

'Oh my God,' Vlad said, catching sight of St George and the dragon. 'I'm not sure I've ever seen anything more camp, except maybe Pride in LA. I love it. *Robin Hood: Men in Tights* meets the pantomime.'

'Oggy, oggy, oggy,' the crier shouted.

'Oi, Oi, Oi,' the crowd called back.

'Oggy!'

'Oi.'

'Oggy.'

'Oi.'

'Oggy, oggy, oggy.'

'Oi, Oi, Oi.'

'What the hell is oggy?' Vlad peered at me like I was from another planet, and maybe I was.

'It's slang for a pasty,' I replied. There was a longer explanation, but now wasn't the time to go into linguistics. We were penned in as the crowd joined in with the noise of the bells, whistles, and tambourines.

'Oggy'

'Oi'

'Oggy'

'Oi'

The crier's bell then settled the crowd before he handed it over and unrolled his scroll. He welcomed everyone in Cornish first, followed by English. The singing began almost like a chant.

Hal an Tow, jolly rumble o

For we are up as soon as any day o

The dancers covered in leaves from head to toe moved rhythmically in and out, while women and girls dressed in frocks, with wreaths of flowers adorning their heads, twirled in pairs. I couldn't watch this. I couldn't. It was all too close, too much.

And for to fetch the summer home

The summer and the May, O

'Is that Friar Tuck?' Vlad pointed to Phil Tonkins, who'd been playing this role for as long as I could remember.

'Yes,' I managed to say, though my mouth and throat were dry. It was one thing to watch this on videos from afar, as I had done recently in LA, but another to stand here and feel the music, the beat of the drums, the voices together. The ancient words swelled up and around, moving through me.

Summer is a come, O

And winter is a gone, O

'Good God, is that Robin Hood? Maid Marion and the Merry Men?' Vlad beamed. 'I love this place. Camp and filled with charity shops. I've died and gone to heaven.'

Robin Hood and Little John

They both are gone to Fair, O

Watching Friar Tuck bless the couple brought all the memories back of when I'd stepped in once to be Maid Marion, with Ke as Robin Hood. That had been a Flora Day of both joy and heartache.

'What's happening with those three?' Gina asked.

'They're supposed to be Spaniards from the Armada.' I listened to the words.

Where are those Spaniards

Who make so great a boast, O?

Heaven knew what Gina and Vlad would make of St Piran. The verse for him had been added in 2005.

'Is that supposed to be a millstone?' Vlad stared hard at the local MP with a paddle and papier mâché millstone about his waist, surrounded by women with shells in their hair and floaty blue dresses representing the sea.

The crowd sang out.

St Piran showed his care for us

And all our sons and daughters, O

Each time they reached the chorus, the pain of losing Mum hit. This had been her thing, always. And once the dance had finished, she'd been like a child at Christmas, already looking forward to the next one. Had she danced this with my father all those years ago? Could he have been part of the troupe too?

'What does St George and the dragon have to do with Helston?' Gina asked as we watched the saint slay the dragon.

'Nothing.' I shrugged.

As for that good knight, St George

St George he was a knight, O

'Great sword play,' said Vlad, his head swivelling as though he was watching a tennis match.

'Wait until what comes next.' I watched the dance of the chorus.

'Don't tell me: the Virgin birth.' Vlad arched an eyebrow in the most dramatic way.

I laughed. He and Gina were good for me. As friends from my life far outside of Helston, they helped me step away, put distance between me and the past.

But to a greater than St George

Our Helston has a right, O

St Michael with his wings out spread

'No, tell me that isn't the great Michael?' Vlad looked on in dismay as the battle ensued between the tall Michael and the small devil. This had been added in the 1930s, making it more Helston specific.

But I knew with everything in me I couldn't watch the end and see someone else do it. I tugged on Gina's and Vlad's hands, pulling them away, and we worked our way to the back of the crowd.

God Bless Aunt Mary Moses

And all her power and might, O

I should have known better. I shouldn't have come at all.

Ten

Flora Day, 1999

Saturday
Age: 12
Forecast: Light rain showers

I don't want today to happen. I shouted at Mum I wouldn't go. Michaela sprained her ankle on Wednesday, and I was told I'd now be dancing with Tom, not Ke. Tina would dance with Ke. I said no and was told off. When Mum said it wouldn't be too bad, I reminded her what he'd done three years ago. But she pointed out boys can be stupid, and Tom was older now. It wasn't stupid, it was cruel, and he'd done it deliberately, after Michaela told him to. I'd forgiven her. She was sorry, but not him. I begged Mum to talk to my Miss Bell, but she wouldn't. Normally she fights for me at school if something goes wrong, but there's some reason she wouldn't this time. I think it's because the teacher is new. There's something about her that Mum doesn't like. She's an OK teacher, but she told me not to fuss when I mentioned Tom had pushed me to the ground before.

And it's raining, which will make everything worse.

I put my pen down and waved my hand like my teacher's as I looked into the mirror, repeating her words. 'You are both the right height. It will work better this year. Ke is too short to dance with you.'

I'd noticed Ke's shoulders slump, and it'd taken everything in me not to kick off – he'd heard what she said. He may not be as tall as the other boys in the class, and was more round than tall to be truthful, but there was no need to say it. It made him feel terrible, and he felt bad most of the time. During breaks at school I'd usually stay with him, or sometimes Michaela would, because otherwise he'd sit alone. Tina was angry about the change in partner too. She said to me she didn't want to dance with Ke. He didn't need to hear that. No one did.

There was only one thing to do. Once we were lined up, I'd either faint or punch Tom. Both could work. I'd told Ke my plan, and he'd said I'd just get in trouble if I did that. Maybe he was right, but either one would make sure I didn't have to dance with him. Ke would still have to dance with Tina, though, who wouldn't even talk to him. Maybe I could tell her to swap with me at the last minute instead, so she went with Tom and I went with Ke? Once the dance was going, the teacher wouldn't be able to do anything.

My feet dragged on the way through the rain to watch the early dance. My godmother Tricia was taking part, despite being pregnant. She'd said it would be fine, but Mum was concerned. 'Two long dances carrying twins isn't exactly what the doctor ordered,' Mum had warned her last night. Tricia had laughed and said, 'Sometimes you have to do what feels right.' Mum shook her head, saying, 'There's no telling some people.' Tricia had laughed again and replied, 'You mean there's no telling me.'

Mum was already prepping everyone for the Hal an Tow, which began in an hour. The drumbeat sounded, and the early dancers began their way through the streets. Michaela hobbled up to stand beside me. Her mother wasn't far away. Maybe I could just disappear and not show up for the Children's Dance. And, when discovered missing, I could say I'd been helping Michaela and lost track of time.

Michaela needed to be on board for this plan, though, and her face was stuck in a firm scowl. How could I suggest this to her if she wasn't talking to me, let alone listening to me? It was like she was still blaming me for her ankle. But I'd been by the back door of her house, nowhere near her when she'd fallen. All I had done was say that Tom was on the street, as I'd just seen him standing outside of Michaela's sitting room. So she'd turned and dashed away to look through the window. Next thing I heard was a yelp of pain, followed by screaming, which got worse as I moved closer to her. Her mother had come through to see what was wrong.

Somehow both Michaela and her mother thought it was my fault, even though I'd done nothing other than point out Tom. That was enough, it seemed, and they were sure I'd made it up to trick Michaela into falling over. None of it made sense, but when they kept insisting, I just said I was sorry and promised not to point out Tom again. Either Mrs Williams didn't believe me, or she was cross about something else.

'Just remember Michaela, don't let her pull you down,' she'd said as she wrapped Michaela's ankle.

I'd opened my mouth to say again that I'd been nowhere near her when she fell, but then closed it. Something told me the comment wasn't anything to do with the sprained ankle.

Once her mother was chatting to a friend, Michaela looked at me and said, 'You did this,' she pointed to her ankle, 'so Tom would have to dance with you, not me.'

I was speechless. How could she even think that? Michaela was my best friend, but sometimes I felt as though she didn't even like me. I wasn't sure why she'd be jealous anyway. She was prettier and had more friends, while I had only her and Ke. One minute she was our third Musketeer, and then she'd flit off, especially if a boy was involved. Sometimes I thought this was her trying to keep up with her sisters, and sometimes I wasn't sure. One thing was certain – she was funny about Tom. I couldn't even talk about him without her thinking I liked him. This was so wrong. I hated that boys had to mess things up. At least Ke was different.

I sighed. 'Look, I don't even want to dance with stupid Tom, I want to dance with Ke, as always.'

Mrs Williams turned to Michaela now. 'You stay here and you'll have a good view of the Hal an Tow. I'm going to get a coffee. Flora, fetch her anything she needs. She shouldn't put weight on her ankle.' She handed me her umbrella.

I nodded, although I had no money, so couldn't get Michaela anything if she asked. We both called out to Tricia as she danced past, giving us a little wave and a big smile. Mum had been worried for no reason. Had she and Tricia had the fights that Michaela and I did? Ke and I didn't fall out, and I didn't think Mum did with Tony either. Boys were different, I supposed.

With the early dancers gone, I was itchy to move on and catch the start of the Hal an Tow, rather than watch it from here, but looking at Michaela's face I could see that wasn't going to work. She wouldn't even move as far as Cross Street. Hopefully her mother would return soon, and I could race off to see part of it at least. The atmosphere between us wasn't normal. I felt guilty, even though I hadn't done anything.

'Fine, I believe you. But to make it up to me,' she said, tapping her leg, 'you better make sure Tom doesn't start to like Tina.' Michaela shuffled to lean against a post. There went my plan to swap partners.

'She's dancing with Ke,' I pointed out.

'But you are paired up with them.'

God, I'd tried to forget that.

'Cut in as quick as you can when they spin.'

I frowned. That would just cause a crash. And I wanted to dance to the music, not Michaela's orders.

'You'll get more time with Ke that way,' she pointed out.

I shook my head, still frowning. 'No, I won't.'

She stared at me coldly, but I wasn't budging on this. If I were cutting in quickly, then I'd be leaving Ke more quickly. No way she could make this plan of hers appealing.

By the time we all gathered to dance, everything was in chaos, not helped by the heavy downpour. Several kids were down with a puking bug. Tina refused to dance with Ke and I wanted to hit her when I saw Ke's face.

Miss Bell looked at me with her eyes narrowed. This was my chance.

'I will, Miss.' I dashed to Ke's side, taking his hand and gave it a squeeze.

'Fine. Tina partner Billy Jenks and Emma can dance with Tom.' She sighed loudly and I grinned. This was perfect. Tina wasn't even in our foursome.

Ke and I had so much fun dancing together again, laughing through the rain, not caring our outfits had become soggy and heavy with water, our hair plastered to our faces, our shoes squelching with every step, and unlike last year's shoes, these don't rub.

Michaela was furious with me, though. Emma was even prettier than Tina, the prettiest girl in the class. No matter what I said about the puking and teachers changing things, it didn't make any difference – Michaela wouldn't speak to me. Her final words at the end of the dance were, 'I thought you were my friend and had my back but no, you only think of yourself.'

That was so unfair, but she wasn't ready to listen. All because of a boy, and one I didn't even like. She was welcome to Tom, and she was far more interesting than Emma anyway. If Tom didn't see that, then he didn't deserve her.

As Michaela hobbled away, I sighed. Ke nudged me and said, 'Don't worry, she'll calm down.' He tilted his head to the side and pulled a funny face until I smiled. 'Come on.' He tugged my soaking sleeve. 'Let's go find a spot to watch the Midday Dance.' He always knew how to make me feel better.

Eleven
2025

8 May, 9:55 a.m.

Back at Lismore, I headed straight for the coffee, wanting something stronger but needing a clear head for later. It was only mid-morning, yet I felt like I'd lived a lifetime since I'd woken up. Every step I'd taken had tripped me up in some way. This wasn't surprising. Coming home always did this.

'That was batshit crazy and I loved it.' Vlad poured himself a coffee, assessing the kitchen. It was strange seeing it through other people's eyes. Tony had updated it over the years but hadn't changed the vibe of this as a domestic space. Now it had all the mod cons, which should help the sale in a few months' time. The bathrooms were all modernised too, but still in keeping with the age of the house. Somehow Tony had made it his in his own unique way, antiques mixed with modern art.

'What's next on the agenda?' Gina asked as we walked into the hall.

'That'll be the Children's Dance which is just starting,' said Mrs Wearne, passing by.

'Will that be so cute it'll break me?' asked Vlad, peering into the study.

'Possibly, but as you see the older kids, you'll squirm with them in their discomfort, and at the same time see they secretly love that they're doing it.'

'What absolutely perfect torture.' He paused and then pointed to the Gainsborough on the wall. 'Is that you in another life?'

I glanced at the painting and laughed. 'Definitely not. It was a favourite of my godfather's.'

'He had good taste,' Gina said as she walked to my side.

'He did.' I led them out of the study and towards the stairs.

'What time do you need to be dressed and adorned?' Vlad asked.

'She needs to be in the Guildhall by eleven thirty, if not a little before that, to catch up with Ke, as you weren't able to be here for the rehearsal last night. It was good of the stewards to give you special permission to just appear on the day,' Polly said, walking through with a tray of cups. 'But you and Ke should be able to do the steps in your sleep, you've danced together so many times through the years.'

I didn't reply. There was no point in saying I hadn't been here to rehearse because I hadn't known I'd be part of the lead couple, or in the dance at all for that matter. The guilty party who'd orchestrated this was a mystery. Everyone I'd asked had denied all knowledge.

'This sounds like the beginning of an interesting story.' Gina took my arm.

You have no idea, I wanted to say, but some things were better not said out loud, or even in your own head. God knows I'd talked too much to myself about Ke and me. Thankfully, Gina knew me well enough not to push. We'd met sixteen years ago when I was an intern in LA, and she'd taken the rookie on set under her wing. Our friendship had been cemented all those years ago when she'd picked up the pieces that were left of me that summer and helped me to reassemble them.

Gina was one of the few I let into my inner circle, which I kept small. My world contained many people, with either huge egos or ones so fragile it was best – as I'd discovered along the way – not to become too invested. I'd made that mistake to my cost, and the price was too high – I was still paying for it, in heartache and self-loathing.

I'd thought I'd freed myself of that baggage back in my late twenties, but I was living proof that sometimes you never learn. Brett, the clever, handsome actor, had seemed to be the opposite of all the men I'd dated or fancied before. Therefore, I believed he'd be perfect. We'd circled each other for months after I'd had him audition for a key role in a film, until we'd finally met a few times for drinks. And it went from there. He'd been forty and looking for a life partner. All good so far. But that was where I got it wrong. He hadn't really wanted a life partner but a manager, and maybe a mother for his offspring. He had two children from previous relationships. Alarm bells should have rung then, but my ticking body clock kept directing me away from the warning signs. And they came thick and fast, like billboards down the strip when you're speeding.

Even before we'd agreed we wanted to make the relationship permanent, he was pushing to try for a child, as if the two he had weren't enough. Month after month of no results became soul-destroying for me. Not for him, though. He studied my cycle as if he were a scientist looking for the secrets of eternal life. Meanwhile, I began to go off sex. When he pushed me to see a specialist, because I must of course be the one at fault, it all came out. I had been pregnant before.

Brett's reaction had been apoplectic. It was as if he thought I'd lived the life of a cloistered nun and never loved before him. He then said it must be secondary infertility. I should have stopped it there, but before I knew it, we were both being investigated. The doctors were thorough, and it was only then that Brett had decided to ask more about this pregnancy. When had it been? Where was the child?

'You have that look on your face, like you're thinking about that arsehole again.' Gina stood me in front of the full-length mirror in my room.

'That look will give you wrinkles faster than the sun,' Vlad added.

I shrugged. This was why I needed to leave the past behind. Brett was now married to another actor, but knowing that he was the infertile one, so those two kids couldn't biologically be his. To be honest, if he'd hounded the other two as much as he did me, I wasn't surprised they'd found other people to get pregnant with. Or maybe just to discover sex was fun and not something that had to be done according to their cycles.

'You're doing it again darling.' Vlad pushed me into a chair. 'Stop.' He pulled a hat out of the large box and stuck it on my head. 'There.'

He lifted my chin and turned my head to the left and then right. 'The hat casts a lot of shadow so we'll need to illuminate. I won't need to do much with your hair.' He looked at his watch. 'What time do the kiddies pass? I don't want to miss a minute of this glorious day.'

'She said it began at nine fifty.' Gina unzipped the garment bag.

'They'll arrive at the house at about ten fifteen,' I added.

'If we wait for them to come to the front of the house, we'll be cutting it fine, unless we transform you now.'

'Transform?' I laughed. 'Are you my fairy godmother?'

'Of course I am darling.' Vlad winked.

'Where's the coach and the horses?' I asked.

'Lucky if you get a pumpkin and a dormouse,' Gina said, beginning to steam the satin dress. It was the colour of bluebells and, like the flowers, the blue changed to purple with each movement. There was nothing that could quite match the carpet of bluebells in a wood with sunlight cutting in through the leafless branches. The sight always took my breath away. But this fabric came close to capturing that.

'This dress.' I whistled.

Gina grinned. 'When you showed me pictures of previous dances, I thought of this dress. It's what Angelina Jolie in *The Tourist* would have worn to Ascot, if she'd gone and they wore long dresses.'

'How did you find it so quickly?' I stroked the fabric. The bodice was fitted but the skirt was full.

'I waved my wand, or... more prosaically, called in some favours.' She held the steamer in her hand as though it were indeed a wand.

'Well, if I have to do this, and I do,' they both stared at me, 'then I'll look fabulous thanks to both of you.'

'While the mistress of the wardrobe finishes the dress, I will work wonders on your hair and face.' Vlad bowed. 'And you can tell me more about this Hal an Tow, or ancient mating ritual.'

I snorted. 'It's not a mating ritual.'

'I've been around the block enough times to know when I see fertility rites, and I saw it today. It positively shouted come shag me.'

'It welcomes the spring and summer and fruitfulness, as in we survived the winter.'

Vlad raised his brush. 'Fruitfulness is just another word for fertility so bring on the shagging, I say.'

I was wasting my breath. It was best not to say anything more.

Twelve

Flora Day, 2000

Saturday
Age: 13
Forecast: Sunny intervals

I had boobs. Not as big as Michaela's, but they were there. Two days ago, I'd insisted Mum and I go to buy me a proper bra, since the 'training ones' as Mum called them didn't give enough support.

Standing in front of the mirror, I frowned. No longer a princess, more of a frog. A large zit filled most of my chin. I wanted to pop it, but Mum had said to leave it. With it there, no one would look at anything else. Maybe that wasn't a bad thing. My bra was sort of visible under the thin fabric of the dress, which wasn't a surprise, as the dress was a tight fit, since it was the same one as last year, and the year before. But as Mum said, needs must.

I scribbled in my diary.

> *I look shit. I feel shit. It's bloody Flora Day, and it's a Saturday. It should be perfect. It won't be.*

The only good thing was I was dancing with Ke, as usual, and Michaela was partnering with another new boy, since she and Tom had fallen out again. Jon was so handsome, and she was over the moon, although he wasn't so great at the dance. It wasn't hard, but I guess we'd been doing it for so long it seemed easy to us now. To be honest, I really wasn't looking forward to it this year.

I would have claimed to be ill if it hadn't been for Michaela and Ke and the funfair. We'd still avoid the Ferris wheel, although I wasn't such a scaredy-cat now. But I'd puke all over Ke's brothers again any time. Ke's eldest brother was doing the Early Morning and Evening Dances this year, and that was what we were looking forward to – being a part of those other ones and ditching all the white clothing of the Children's Dance. Michaela was really desperate to, just like both her sisters had done too. Hardly anyone saw the Early Morning Dance compared to the Children's and the Midday. And that sounded good to me. I'd asked Gran what her favourite part of Flora Day was and she said, 'The day after.' We'd both laughed.

Gran had finished work at three a.m. last night and was opening the bar in The Angel at six this morning. She'd muttered something about thank God this only happens once a year. Mum reminded her she loved it, and that it always provided the biggest takings of the year.

'Hardly worth it for what it does to my old bones,' she'd said loud and clear for all the punters to hear. Besides, as she reminded Mum, she hadn't seen the dancing properly since she last took part in it, back in what she called the dark ages. Gran had a way of saying things that always made me laugh. She saw everything clearly but differently, and took no shit, as she said when she thought I wasn't listening. But I was always listening, and I think she knew that.

If Mum was busy and Michaela and Ke weren't free, I'd help Gran wash glasses and stuff after school. It was during those times that she told me how important it was for womenfolk to stick together. And that our family, the Richards, were a strong lot, going back a long time. I guessed we needed to be strong because the Richards women always seemed to have no husbands to help them, so they found a way of surviving. At least that appeared to be the point of her stories.

Michaela and Jon, Ke, and I were the second set of pairs dancing in our group behind the primary schools. It went pretty well, considering that Jon forgot how to do the dance part the way through, and we all collapsed laughing. Now, the four of us were standing by the boating lake, planning to head back into town. We were supposed to be outside The Blue at five, to check in with Mum, and to watch the Evening Dance. Ke's eldest brother, Jorin, had danced this morning, and by one o'clock he was so drunk it looked like he might be the one to puke this year, which'd be so funny. Except his partner this year, Ginny Jenks, was great, so I'd feel sorry for her if it did happen. And if he was too drunk, they'd have to find someone else to dance with her for the Evening Dance at short notice. Nightmare.

The smell of cooking onions made me hungry, even though I'd eaten a pasty for lunch at three. The food stalls lining the hill were tempting, but we were waiting until after the Evening Dance was finished to get supper. My stomach rumbled loudly but it would have to wait.

We rounded the corner and pressed through the crowds opposite the Monument and outside The Blue. I hadn't spotted Mum yet, but she would be here somewhere. This check-in was important.

'Bleddy beggar can barely stand,' Ke's middle brother, Pawl, said, nodding his head in the direction of where Jorin had staggered off to for the dance. Ke sent a side-eye look to Pawl, who was hiding cans of lager in his jacket pockets, and grinning from ear to ear.

Jorin wouldn't be the only one in that state. There were many adults around us totally pissed, although Mum wasn't, nor were

Tony or Angus. They came and stood behind us just as the sounds of the band could be heard.

'Doesn't seem that long ago since we did this,' Tony said to Mum.

She laughed. 'It was a lifetime ago.' She looked down at me. She'd come home every year while she was in drama school in London. It wasn't just the dance, it was to reconnect with her roots, she said. She'd loved London, but there was something about Helston that always pulled her home. It did the same to Tony too. He never missed a Flora Day. They'd danced their first Flora together, but after the second year Tony had been sent away to school and they hadn't danced together again.

The dancers arrived, and they were chaotic, especially Jorin but, like me, they could do the dance in their sleep.

Step, hop, step, step, step.

Change.

Everyone was having such fun it didn't matter that steps were missed. Soon they'd passed by and people filtered off, into the pubs again. We were heading back to the funfair, with Mum's last words being that I had to be home by eight thirty. It was only then I noticed that Michaela had nicked the lager out of Pawl's pockets. He must have been too far gone to realise.

'Let's go someplace where we can drink these,' she said giggling, once we were halfway down the hill to the fair. Part of me felt this wasn't such a good idea, but I simply nodded along when Jon suggested where we could go. Two lagers between the four of us couldn't do much harm, could they? As long as Michaela didn't go back for more.

Mum was furious when I rocked up at ten, stinking of booze, despite the gum I'd chewed to disguise it. My insides hurt, and not just from all the alcohol.

Michaela kissed Ke.

The thought churned my stomach into knots.

'Where did you get the beer?' Mum asked quietly.

'Michaela took it off Ke's brother.' There was no sense in lying. Mum would see through it, and my head was fuzzy. Thinking was hard.

'How many?'

I drew a deep breath – lying might be best here, or maybe not. 'Six.'

'You drank six cans of lager?' Her eyes opened wide, and this wasn't a good sign.

'No, we shared six cans of lager, and four of cider.' I hiccupped.

She marched me into the kitchen and poured a large glass of water, then handed it to me. 'Drink.'

I made a face. My stomach was full.

She didn't budge. I finally grabbed the glass and took a few sips. My stomach lurched. I made it to the sink just in time and puked violently.

'Better out than in, but you didn't mention the Guinness.'

When I could speak again, I confessed to the two pints of Guinness as well – they'd been handed over by people who should have known better. Mum shook her head as she cleaned me up – and the sink. Once upstairs, in my room, she helped me into my pyjamas, then left me for a moment, returning with a large bowl, which she put beside my bed.

'Mum, is this what you felt like the night I was made?'

She laughed, throwing her head back, and said, 'You have no idea.'

I blinked. What did she mean by that? I was drunk, and I could still see Michaela kissing Ke. Surely Mum must remember more than she had told me. I needed to know.

Thirteen

2025

8 May, 10:15 a.m.

Vlad pinned the pale blue hat in place. Only then was I allowed to look in the mirror. I prayed I wouldn't have a Mia moment from *The Princess Diaries,* looking like a moose rather than elegance itself. Walking to the full-length mirror, I gasped. Who was this creature? I'd been professionally dressed many times for countless award ceremonies, but this transformation was amazing. The person staring back at me looked a bit like my mother, with a hint of Gran. But there was something about my appearance that startled me. Was it my nose, or maybe my mouth? Possibly it was just the makeup Vlad had wielded to bring the light, as he put it.

'Cinderella shall go to the ball,' Gina said.

'Thank you both.' I turned around. 'You have truly worked magic.'

'You can't create a silk purse out of a sow's ear, but we've done our best.' Vlad began packing up his brushes.

'Are you saying I ain't half bad?' I smiled.

'Might be.' Vlad lifted his phone and snapped a few pics. 'But what I really want to know all about is the Prince Charming who has the esteemed honour to dance with you.'

I closed my eyes, trying to think of an answer to give that'd satisfy them, yet keep everything firmly in the past, where it belonged. The last thing I needed was for Gina to connect the dots. Only two people knew the full story, and Tony was gone.

'The longer you take to answer me, the more I can tell there's truly some juicy history you are trying to bury rather than reveal,' Vlad said.

Childlike, I stuck my tongue out at him. He caught it on camera and, of course, that would be the one pic he'd put on socials.

'I've known Ke since school, and I danced my first Children's Dance with him.'

'And?' Gina asked, watching me closely.

'Because both of us were the most unpopular kids in school, we stuck together over the years.'

'Ke Dale, you say.'

I nodded.

'Founder of the coolest surfing lifestyle company.' Gina scrolled on her phone. 'And hot as hell.' She stared at me wide-eyed.

'Let me see.' Vlad leaned over her shoulder to take a closer look. 'Um, he is a fine specimen.'

I couldn't deny that. After a huge growth spurt hit, Ke's fortunes changed. By then he'd already started surfing thanks to Mum. Memories of that summer filtered back to me. It had been that year we'd met Wilf Shaw too, and he'd become a part of our little group. Four kids and four different outcomes. Ke's had been the happiest, until tragedy struck his family. Wilf seemed to be in a good place. Today I'd argue that maybe Micki, the free spirit among us, was the happiest now that she'd ditched the latest man. Me, I was happy – or maybe rather than happy, I was content. I loved my job and had good friends. Those had definitely made for a better life.

Travel was a huge part of my job, which still excited me. But, if I were honest with myself, I was lonely. People could be lonely when in relationships too, but at thirty-eight I was no longer looking to find a life partner. This surprised both Gina and Vlad and my other close cohorts, but after Brett I'd begun to see that having a family wasn't all I'd always thought it was. In a funny old way, the sort of soul mate friendship that Mum and Tony had had was healthier and happier than many a romantic relationship I'd witnessed as I moved through this life. There were obviously marriages I'd seen work, but not so many to think it was something easy.

'Flo, I want to know all about you and this Ke, who you clearly have a history with, even if it's a secret history.' Vlad took my arm and led me to the door. I could hear the rising noise, which meant the Children's Dance was approaching. They'd come through the gate and dance past the house, then out the drive, before continuing through the town.

'Well, back when I was eight was the first time I'd been in this house. It was when Tony's godmother owned it.'

'Fascinating, but that tells us nothing about Ke,' Gina said, tugging at the back of my dress to adjust something I couldn't see.

'He was my partner for the dance,' I said, avoiding her glance as she moved to my side. 'We were the last two left. No one wanted to dance with us.'

'What was wrong with you? Or was it just the usual kid shit of being mean for the hell of it?' she asked.

'Well, I was weird and nerdy, and he was geeky and fat or, as my gran had said, well padded.' Somewhere in my mother's things there was a horrendous photo of us. Maybe not totally awful. Both Ke and I had been grinning like crazy. Our friendship had begun at that point. He no longer had to sit alone at school. I was there for him, and I dragged a reluctant Micki along.

'Charming.' Vlad sniffed.

'But he was good fun, as I found out.' The more time I'd spent with him, the more I'd liked him. He was funny and interested in things I knew little or nothing about, like his passion for the ocean or his pet tortoise. His father had given it to him for his birthday after that Flora Day we watched *The Princess Bride*. He named her Buttercup, and that tortoise went everywhere with him for a while. Despite how long ago it had been, the moment when his eyes met mine had never faded in my memories, even if I'd wanted it to.

'When did his fortunes change?' Gina asked.

Images of him in his teens flashed through my mind. 'It was when he shot up and really began to excel at surfing.' The transformation had seemed to happen overnight, or over a school break. 'Mum and I had gone to London, and when we returned he'd grown, I'd swear, six inches. It was crazy, but he showed me the stretch marks on his legs from it. I found that cool, because I'd thought only girls got stuck with those awful white worm-like marks.'

'Hence the surfing clothing company.' Gina scrolled through her phone, probably on the website for it. She wasn't sporty in any way, so I doubted she'd find the work-like approach to clothing suitable for herself personally, but she might find it useful for a film or the series we were working on now.

'And that environmental charity, Surfers Against Sewage,' she continued.

'Exactly,' I said, remembering how pleased I'd been for him as his success grew, even though I was well out of his life by then. But I'd cheered him on from a distance.

'So, you danced with him for your first dance and...' Gina lifted an eyebrow provocatively.

'Today I'll dance with him for my last dance.' I smiled brightly.

'You know I generally think you're one of the sanest people I know.' Vlad paused. 'Of course, in our world that doesn't take much, but your plan to sell all of this.' He waved his hand in a circle, from the chandelier to the staircase as we made our way down it. 'Frankly, you *are* crazy.'

I turned to him. 'Crazy? No, quite the opposite. It's the only sane thing I can do.' This house was filled with too many memories, and a secret which would consume me if I wasn't careful, as Tony had once warned me.

Fourteen

Flora Day, 2001

Tuesday
Age: 14
Forecast: Sunny intervals

Lismore was quiet.

It was weird to think that people had been coming through the house and gardens forever, and now Lismore was Tony's. Before his parents had kicked him out, his family home had been the big house as you entered Helston. Tony hadn't wanted it and sold it when his father, the last of his family, died from prostate cancer four years ago – it was now a hotel. He'd been drawn to Lismore, he said, because it was in the heart of the town.

Tony was all about heart, but his heart had been broken last year. Angus, his love and partner for fourteen years, had been killed in a terrible bus accident. Tony was broken, lost, a real mess. In fact, I think that was why he left London and bought Lismore from his godmother. He needed Helston and Mum and me to heal. We were devastated too and wanted to help him so much. He loved this town, and it was a constant in his life, a bit like his love of me and Mum.

Mum and I had stayed here last night as it was Tony's first eve of Flora Day in the place. Tony's godmother had moved into a care home. We were almost too excited to sleep. Everything in the house was ready for the festivities, and all we had to do was not mess it up. That wouldn't be hard.

The most exciting part of last night had been Tony letting me pick which bedroom I wanted as mine, excluding his, of course. I'd said Mum should go first, but she just laughed and sipped her champagne. I opted for a room that had a gorgeous view of the garden. The wallpaper was awful, but Tony promised I could help him choose how to redecorate it. It was twice the size of my room at home. Lismore was huge. Mum and I could live in it and never see Tony, but I loved our home too. Mum said she wasn't moving in with anyone, not even her best friend. She said they'd kill each other. Tony had agreed.

They'd once lived in the same house, when Gran had taken Tony in so he could finish school. Tony had spoken about the amount of time Mum used to take in the bathroom, but she said he'd been worse. She'd had to set her alarm half an hour early to beat him to it.

When I finally went to bed last night, I'd left the two of them sitting in the garden talking about all the things they used to get up to. From what I could tell, I was the first one up. I opened my diary and placed it on the desk by the window. Below I saw a gardener fixing rods and ropes around the pond. Sunlight was just appearing from behind the buildings in the distance.

I'd loved last night with Mum and Tony. I guessed this is what a family would feel like. I'd stopped asking Mum about my father because her answers never changed. And I stopped writing lists of possible countries that he might be from and also what jobs he might have had. But my desire to travel hadn't lessened, nor had the desire for a proper family.

Even though there were only three of us, there was something special because we all loved each other. Tony made Mum laugh harder than anyone I knew, even Tricia, who was pretty good at it. It felt like Ke, me, and Michaela. Ke made me laugh, and Micki, as she wanted to be called now, led me into trouble according to Mum. She still hadn't forgotten last year's Flora Day drunkenness. Nor had I.

And *Micki had kissed Ke.*

When I'd asked her why she did it, she'd just laughed and said it was a bit of fun. And why should I care? Since then, neither Ke nor Micki had mentioned it, so I supposed I should just let it go.

'Morning my handsome.' Mrs Brewer called, walking towards Tony, who appeared in his dressing gown in the garden.

Closing my diary, I put it under my pillow, then raced down the stairs to the kitchen. It was six fifteen, and there was no sign of Mum. I put the kettle on and found a loaf of bread and some eggs. If I made breakfast, then Mum could focus on getting ready for the Hal an Tow. Each year more people were taking part. New roles – well, not roles as such but hedges – had been added to make sure everyone who wished to could take part.

Mum was thoughtful like that. She never wanted anyone to feel left out. I think that's why she'd always been so good with Ke. She sensed that he needed to find his place, his thing, and that was when she took him surfing. We'd had a heatwave last weekend, and Tony came with us to the beach. I lay there on the sand with him, watching as Mum led Ke into the waves, Ke clutching his board with an excited grin on his face. It didn't take long for him to pick it up. It was like he'd been born to surf. I couldn't pretend I wasn't jealous. Despite all the lessons, I'd struggled to stand on a board on a regular basis, but Ke was, in Tony's words, like poetry he was so fluid on it.

'That boy is full of potential, but I wonder if he'll be able to see far enough to reach it,' Tony said, more to himself than to me.

'What do you mean?' I asked.

'A bit like your grandmother with me. Sometimes to make something of yourself, you have to be shown it's possible.' He watched where the waves were breaking.

'You don't think Ke sees that in himself?'

Tony smiled slowly. 'Ke is on the brink of becoming. He's shooting up. He has a quick mind, but he needs to know there is more out there for him than working at Woolies, or as a dish pig here in Porthleven.'

'I see,' I said, not sure if I did.

'I wonder.' Tony chuckled. 'You do see a lot Flora, and you want a great deal from the world.'

I stared at him wide-eyed.

'You let little things drop that gives me more information than you think.' He winked.

'You only have to ask me. I don't have any secrets.' That was a blatant lie. I had one big secret. I was in love with Ke, but no one knew. It was as safe as secrets should be. I hadn't even told Michaela. And I never intended to after what she'd done last Flora Day.

'Sadly, we all have secrets and we all keep them. Some for good reason, others for protection, and others for fear.'

'Fear?'

'Yes, if people knew there would be a consequence of some sort.' He picked up a stone from the sand and weighed it in his hand. 'When I was your age, I knew I was gay. It was my secret, but it was very hard to hold that knowledge inside. Because I knew that when it came out it would change everything.'

I watched the expressions moving across his face. 'But you told people. Surely that was the right thing?'

He laughed bitterly. 'It worked out fine in the end and my heart was free but there were big consequences.'

'Your father.'

'And my mother. She sided with him.' He paused, closing his eyes; his pain was clear as he opened them again. His mum had never spoken to him again. She'd died ten years ago. 'It was only my brother who still kept in touch.' He squinted, looking out at a cargo ship in the distance. Probably thinking of his brother, who'd died tragically in a nightclub fire in the United States two years after his mother.

'What they did was wrong.'

'This is true, but I can look back on it now with more understanding than I did at the time. Rejection is always painful, though, and that scale, that public scale, was very painful, because it wasn't only my parents who rejected me but people I'd thought of as friends.'

'Do you wish you'd kept your secret?' I asked, thinking of how it must have felt to be disowned.

'No. I might have revealed it later, or maybe in a better way, but keeping that secret would have destroyed me in the end. Some secrets do that.'

'Do they?' I thought of mine and knew the knowledge of loving Ke would never hurt me.

'Secrets have a way of working their way out of the bonds which hold them. Sometimes they appear and no one pays any attention, but the secret can eat away at the keeper.' He paused. 'Be careful of secrets, so they don't come to own you, change you and ultimately destroy you.'

I didn't reply, and looked out to sea, watching Ke in the water, paddling furiously to catch another wave. His happiness was obvious even from this distance. It wasn't just the wide smile; it was the way he moved, suddenly more at ease with his body. His shoulders were pulled back, and he wasn't trying to be invisible.

Mum padded into the kitchen and kissed my cheek, bringing me out of my thoughts. She picked up a piece of toast. 'How do you feel about secrets?' I asked.

She coughed, spewing out bits of toast. I tapped her on the back. That wasn't the reaction I'd been expecting. Once she'd had a glass of water and some colour came back into her face, she asked, 'What on earth prompted that question?'

'Just thinking about a conversation I had with Tony on the beach at the weekend.'

'And?' She watched me closely.

'Well, he was talking about when he told his parents he was gay.'

Mum began to chew again. Must remember not to ask her questions when she's eating toast. 'Yes, that was a big secret to reveal.'

'Everyone has secrets, don't they?' I put more bread into the toaster.

Mum took another sip of water. 'I suppose they do but most are small, like surprises or gifts.'

'What about people's affairs?' I thought about Tom's mum and the man who put their new carpets in.

'My, you are full of interesting questions today. But in short, since I need to leave soon, sometimes it's best not to say something, and sometimes it's best to say something.'

That made no sense. 'But how do you know?'

She smiled. 'That's a discussion for another day, not Flora Day.' She kissed me and raced out of the kitchen as if St Michael and the devil were on her heels.

The Hal an Tow and the Children's Dance were done. No big problems, which was boring really. Now in normal clothes again, Micki, Ke, and I stood on the terrace at Lismore watching the dancers parade through the garden and take a break.

Suzie Tonks from my class waved from where her family was eating their lunch. I felt like royalty looking down the garden at all these people enjoying the sight of the dancers in their finery.

Tony's friend from Bristol had arrived just ten minutes before. He and Mum were chatting about the time it takes to get here. He wasn't being positive about any of this, and said he wanted to be in Rock. I mean, Rock was gorgeous, but it wasn't for every day. Helston was a more everyday sort of place. All kinds of people lived here. Not just those who came for the summer, but also those who looked after them. Cornwall was funny that way.

Micki began looking about, and I could see we needed to do something. She was never one for sitting still when there were other possibilities on offer. We walked over to where the band were all taking a needed break. A new kid, Wilf, was with them, standing on his own eating a sandwich. He looked wide-eyed and overwhelmed, and I wasn't surprised. No matter how much you were told about Flora Day, you didn't know what it'd be like until you'd done it. And he was in at the deep end, being in the band.

Micki stepped forward. 'There are fairy cakes inside. Do you want one?'

He did a double take. People were still keeping a distance and checking him out as the new kid, but not Micki. She'd already been chatting to him at school and at Ultimate Video. It must have been then she had clearly decided he was one of us.

'Yeah.'

Micki turned to me, and I nodded, going into the house to find the fairy cakes Mum had made yesterday. She hadn't mentioned having any special plans for them, so I guessed it was fine to take some.

They were all laughing as I returned, and I felt cross and left out.

'All for one and one for all,' Micki said as I arrived with the plate.

'Cool,' said Wilf, waiting while Micki and Ke dove in first. I liked him for that. Once I'd offered the plate to him, he carefully selected one – the one with purple flowers on it. I liked him even more for that.

'We are now complete,' Micki said.

I frowned. That made no sense.

'We finally have our D'Artagnan,' she said.

I glanced at her – wasn't that a bit sudden?

'Great film,' he said with a mouth full of fairy cake.

My frown melted into a smile. This must have been why I couldn't rent the film the other day.

'It's the best, except for *The Princess Bride*,' Ke said.

Wilf paused and swallowed. 'What about *Robin Hood: Men in Tights*?'

'Yeah,' I said and bit into a pink-flowered fairy cake. He would fit right in.

Later in the day, the four of us sat on the curb outside The Angel.

'Isn't there usually water in this?' Wilf asked, tapping his big feet in the stone channel running down the side of the street. His large frame didn't quite seem to fit properly. His hands and feet were huge and out of balance with his shoulders, but he was tall. Taller than Ke, he looked a bit cobbled together like Frankenstein's monster with none of his parts quite fitting. But it was the expression in his big brown eyes that was so kind and soft that seemed almost out of place. With a boy of this size, you'd expect toughness, but he was gentle.

'Yeah,' said Micki.

'They redirect the water in the kennels on Flora Day so people don't step in it I guess,' Ke said. 'And there's no tin that needs washing these days.'

I smiled, thinking of the other possible reasons for the kennels that were less appealing, like moving waste through the town and keeping one of the widest streets in Cornwall clean.

'Kennel... Dad calls it a leat.' Wilf tapped the granite lining it.

'Everywhere else but here,' I said. 'Helston's different.'

Wilf nodded. 'Yeah, it is. But I like that.'

'Told you he was the right one to be the fourth Musketeer.' Micki looked at me hard. When we were watching the Evening Dance, I'd only questioned how she made the decision without asking Ke or me first. We were supposed to be all for one and one for all, not one person running the lot.

'So, what are the Musketeer rules?' Wilf looked at each of us in turn.

'Rules?' asked Ke.

'Yeah, aside from the obvious all for one...'

'Oh, we don't have any.' Micki shrugged. 'I mean, who needs rules?'

'Well, "one for all" is one,' Wilf continued.

'Yeah, it makes sense,' said Ke.

'How about no telling anyone else what we get up to?' I suggested.

'Good one,' said Micki. 'And like, we can never get involved with each other.'

Wilf frowned. 'Involved?'

'You know, like get together.' Micki sent me a glance. Was she thinking of the time she'd kissed Ke? I looked at Ke, and Micki saw me doing it. He was looking at his feet. His words came back to me from all those years ago – the night we'd talked about finding true love. The way he'd looked at me. We'd both been so young, but I was still in love with him. Could Micki guess that?

'Yeah, that works,' said Wilf. 'It's a start anyway.'

'It is,' said Micki. 'Shall we head to the funfair? The smell of the burgers is making me hungry.'

'Good plan.' Ke stood up and caught my eye. Was he thinking about the new rule too?

The Children's Dance

A NEW FEATURE

A Children's Dance

Held on Tuesday in glorious weather. There were very large crowds of people early in the town by train, motors and char-a-banc. The early morning dance was held at 7 a.m., with ten couples. The great feature of the day was a children's dance, the first of its kind, which left the Corn Exchange at 10:30. There were 72 couples of boys and girls in white dresses and white shirts with wreaths of flowers on their heads.

The ages of the little folk ranged from three years upwards, most of them being scholars from the local schools.

The Cornishman and *Cornish Telegraph*
Wednesday, 10 May 1922

* * *

HELSTON FLORA DAY

Thousands of people visited Helston – the "quaint old Cornish town" of the famous song – for its Flora Day celebration. Old and young were among those who danced through the gaily-decorated streets and in and out of many houses, including 250 school children dressed in white.

The Daily News and *Westminster Gazette*
Wednesday, 9 May 1928

Fifteen
2025

8 May, 10:25 a.m.

'This... Ke,' Vlad said quietly, looking around at the crowds on the streets. 'He was your first love, wasn't he?'

I could lie, but everyone in Helston probably guessed he had been. 'Yes.'

The sound of the band was followed by the vision of the kids all dressed in white, twirling down the street. I stood back, letting Gina and Vlad get the best view. This was all a novelty to them, and it was a gorgeous sight, from the adorable little ones through to the awkward teens, especially the ones like I'd been, the misfits. Unlike in my day, there were kids in wheelchairs joining in too, and this lifted me. The world was changing for the better, or at least it was in a small way in this faraway part of the world. Helston had evolved from the one I'd known.

But last night while out with Micki, I'd seen that the Beehive was the same as the first time I'd crossed the threshold – throbbing music, sticky floor, sweat, booze and hormones filling the air. It had been many things through the years, including an Irish bar at one point. Yet the mix of people – from the matelots of Culdrose, to the young barely old enough to drink, and those who should really know better, which included Micki and me – were the same. Micki had been up for mischief – nothing changed there either. She was eyeing up anyone fit enough to move. Not that her marriage had stopped her from doing this before the divorce. After all these years, I didn't think it was in her nature. The only faithful bone in her body applied to me alone, and she'd been with me through thick and thin. Which covered a lot of territory. To be fair, it worked both ways, and we'd still had our ups and downs. The only thing that had ever really come between us was Ke.

He was right in my line of sight at this moment and not yet dressed in a top hat and morning suit, but in jeans and a faded blue t-shirt which highlighted his sun-washed hair, surfer's tan and blue eyes. The thirty-eight-year-old man across the road was nothing short of breath-taking. I stared at his lean build, grateful he hadn't noticed me. He was focused on a young girl who was dancing with a boy with two left feet. The girl's blonde hair crowned with cornflowers matched her blue eyes so like her father's. Ke couldn't take his eyes off his daughter, Matilda. Unlike her partner, Matilda eased through the dance naturally, like her father had. Right from our first Flora Day, Ke had been able to dance, despite the terrible attempts at practice in school. But it had come naturally to him, like surfing had.

The transformation of Ke Dale from chubby lost soul to surf god was legendary in Helston, but at this moment he was simply a proud dad. That took my breath away. I could see in his focused gaze that Matilda was his world. He would do anything for her. And on becoming a single parent, he'd taken time away from actively running his business to be there for his daughter. If I hadn't loved him before, I would have with that action alone. Because if I knew anything, I knew what it took to make it in this world, and to make it when you came from a family that didn't quite work in the way the world thought it should.

Even though I'd always pined for my absent father, as a child

I'd wanted for nothing thanks to Mum and Tony. But Ke had wanted for everything, except for the love of his father. Ke's dad was a saint as far as I could tell, while his mother could be a right bitch. It was a horrible thing to say, knowing she was an addict, but the way she'd constantly cut down Ke and his dad at every turn had made me hate her. Yes, she'd had a problem, and there were always two sides to every story. But in my eyes, her side of the story didn't balance the damage she'd wreaked on both of them. His poor father looked twenty years older than his age of sixty-five. But, like Ke, he hadn't let her destroy him. Her two other sons had thrived. Somehow, they made it through unscathed. One joined the Navy and the other took to fishing. Water was the salvation of all three boys in the end.

Now Ke was a local celeb. Hence, they'd decided that putting us together as a couple would be the way to sweeten me up, to make me want to do the right thing for the town with regard to Lismore. Looking at it from the outside, this made perfect sense. We'd danced our first Flora together, and continued to do so, moving on to the Early Morning and Evening Dances, as well as performing in the Hal an Tow together. These things were all true and correct. But it didn't tell the story between those events. It didn't begin to touch on what they were asking me to do and to face, by pairing me with Ke.

It was, in fact, the swiftest way to push me out of Helston again. I was only here to empty the house and continue with the casting work for the series, *Death Comes to Cornwall*. Both things would take a month at most. Then I'd officially put Lismore on the market as soon as probate was sorted. Once it was sold, and my mother's and Tony's things were sorted, I'd be free of Helston, as it would be of me. There'd be no reason for my heart to break every time I saw Ke with Matilda. That wound would close. Micki could come join me where I was going, and find new men to conquer, and I'd find peace. At last.

As the stream of children danced past the house, Gina and Vlad's faces were a picture, but I was afraid they'd spied Ke.

Fortunately, he was trapped on the other side of the road as Matilda entered with her partner.

'Love the frock,' Micki said, arriving at my side.

'Gina and Vlad sorted me out.' I brushed a hand down the blue silk.

'Please tell me you've shagged Adrian?' she begged. He was the lead actor for *Death Comes to Cornwall*, and the local news was full of him.

I rolled my eyes. 'Married men are not on my agenda, and I know just how flaky actors can be.' Brett ran through my mind.

'Do you have to crush my fantasies like that?' she asked.

'I absolutely do.' I smiled to soften my words. I knew actors only too well, which was what made me so damn good at what I did. My mother, without knowing it, had led me straight to this role. Having seen her relinquish her career on account of me, I knew how important a creative outlet was for all actors. It was like the need for air. It was required even if at times it nearly killed them.

'Ke went out on a date the other night,' Micki whispered in my ear as she looked across the road. 'We've all been giving him space, but now he's been single for a while I think I might rekindle what we once had.' She looked at me keenly, as though testing my reaction.

My stomach clenched. I wanted to shout, 'No, he's mine!' But she was stating her claim, just like she had before. This had been our only rule of our friendship separate from the Musketeers. No questions asked.

Friendship was more valuable than any man or anything else, as my mother and my grandmother had taught me. But Micki only applied that rule to me now. Any other man, be it a friend's boyfriend or husband, was fair game to her. We'd argued about that... a lot, but she said if the man in question strayed, he wasn't happy where he was. My counterargument was that all relationships, even friendships, had their moments when things weakened. It was the ebb and flow of things, and never a good idea to take advantage of that. No matter how many times I'd said it, though, Micki had disagreed. After a while, I stopped commenting. It was a waste of time.

'Don't you dare, looking so hot in the perfect dress to flaunt your LA figure, dream of tempting Ke yourself.'

I sent her a look. This was a strange comment as Ke and I hadn't really spoken in years.

She elbowed me as I looked over to Ke, and he glanced back, catching my eye.

Connection.

Years of avoidance, exile and evasion hadn't removed it. But I knew what I was here in Helston to do: get the hell out. And permanently this time. So I'd leave Micki to it with Ke again.

Gina stepped towards me and then looked over at Ke too. This wasn't good. I could see her brain whizzing and making connections. What had I told her all those years ago? It hadn't seemed important then. Now, a distraction was necessary. I needed to leave Helston with my secrets intact. Why hadn't I considered that bringing her here could jeopardise everything?

Sixteen

Flora Day, 2002

Wednesday
Age: 15
Forecast: Sunny

> *This is the year things will change. I might have been Flora Portia Richards, but as of today I'm Flo Richards. It's a bit messed up thinking the day I was conceived is 'my' day. I mean, how did I ever think that was anything but weird? Gross. So, this Flora Day marks a new me. And all I have to do is get through the bloody Children's Dance, ditch the dress, then I'm free to enjoy it all. Micki, Ke, and I plan to disappear for a while and return when most people are well gone, so they don't notice we're loitering around listening to the bands playing and drinking cider. Wilf will be free by then too.*

There was a band who'd be playing tonight at The Blue, and the lead singer was so hot it hurt. Ke just rolled his eyes every time Micki and I started talking about him. But he had enough sense not to say anything. He was finally wising up to the fact he might be able to challenge just one of us on our own, but when we were united, he didn't stand a chance.

In fact, the only one of us who was strong or stupid enough to stand alone was Micki. She sure had the courage of her convictions, as Gran would say. This frequently led to her getting into scrapes, but she didn't care. She was able to pick herself up, dust herself off, and begin again. She wasn't one to lick her wounds. That was me. If I made a mistake, especially a public one, I'd keep a low, if not invisible profile until I was certain the fuss had died down, or another scandal had eclipsed mine.

I wouldn't think about the past today because it was such a beautiful day. We should have headed to the beach for a few hours to soak up the sun while we had it. Basically, what it came down to was that I didn't want to do Flora Day this year. I wasn't a child anymore. I didn't need dancing in frocks and fun fairs to welcome in spring. Spring bloody well arrived when it suited the weather gods, whoever or whatever they were.

At least my dress this year was something remotely modern and not out of two centuries ago. It fitted me nicely and hit the right part of my thighs so they looked longer and thinner than they were. This was a result. The only things that were going to make this dance bearable were Ke and Micki. She was dancing with Tom again. Fortunately, he seemed to have mellowed, and we could trust him to behave, as much as the rest of us would, anyway.

It was almost midnight when Micki pulled me aside and called dibs on Ke. I mentioned our Musketeer rules, and she laughed. This was *our* rule about boys. Whoever called it first had a clear run. And Micki was always calling it. I was mostly unfussed, but this time was different. It was Ke.

'You've already kissed Ke once. What about Wilf, if the Musketeer rules don't matter?'

Micki looked at Wilf. He was playing a lot of rugby now and

had really grown into himself. I said a silent prayer she'd go for Wilf instead. But she shook her head and said, 'No, I want Ke,' her eyes glinting with booze and mischief.

There was nothing more I could do, so I drank sweet white wine, cider, then another cider. Until I'd lost count.

I should have been home two hours ago, but I could barely stand, so I sat slumped on a wall, letting things spin around me.

'I don't feel great,' I announced, or thought I did.

'What?' asked Tom. He was holding a can of Carlsberg. I hadn't had any lager but had done shots, swigged sweet white wine, cider, as well as whatever vile alcohol Tom had had in his hip flask. Micki and I had drunk that before we danced directly in front of the band, eyeing up the hot singer, seeing if he'd notice. I may have lifted my t-shirt at one point, but I'm not sure.

'You can't hold your booze.' Tom peered at me. 'I bet that's because you don't have a dad.'

'Hey, mate, back off.' Ke stood straightish, glaring directly at Tom.

'It's not meant as an insult or anything. It's just that most dads make sure their kids know how to drink.'

I squinted. How did I not know this about fathers? Was this why Gran drank so much?

Micki was swaying as though there were music playing. There wasn't, or at least I thought there wasn't. She lifted her hands in the air, then dropped them to shimmy her shoulders. 'Tom's kissed me but you, Ke,' she paused and I held my breath. What was she going to do? 'You Ke, have not. I've kissed you, but it was one sided.' She swayed up to him. 'I bet you don't have the guts to kiss me properly.'

I couldn't breathe and thought I was about to puke at the same time. A few minutes ago we'd still been laughing about the dance this morning. Tom had tripped over his own feet; he was so tired and hungover. It made a bit of a mockery of the whole thing, but we didn't care. Now Micki was daring Ke to kiss her. Surely, he wouldn't. He couldn't.

Somewhere nearby, someone called out happily. I couldn't sit here and watch this. I couldn't. All I could taste was the sweet white wine Micki had started us on just before the Midday Dance. I hiccupped. We'd managed to dodge any parents and keep the buzz going since then. Now Ke was going to kiss Micki, and I couldn't watch and wouldn't. I was going home, which I should have done ages ago. Mum was going to kill me. I'd promised her I wouldn't do this again.

Ke looked at me, but I couldn't meet his glance. How could he do this? He seemed to wait, then took a step towards Micki. I held my hand over my mouth, hoping I wouldn't puke. Micki looked at me then moved closer.

'Dare you.' She tipped her head up. I found I couldn't look away, as Ke leaned down. Then he kissed her, properly kissed Micki.

She'd won, and I hadn't even realised there was a competition. I jumped off the wall and ran until I fell flat on my face.

Seventeen

2025

8 May, 10:40 a.m.

Once the children had moved on, I wanted to hide from everyone. But that wasn't going to happen. Gina was giving me the eye, and Vlad was too perceptive.

'Beautiful day,' Peter Johns, my solicitor, said, walking towards me in his morning suit, with the top hat in his hands. Half of my brain wondered who he was dancing with this year. Three years ago there'd been a scandal when he hadn't danced with his wife but her best friend. Soon he was sorting out his own divorce.

'It is,' I replied.

'Have you opened the letters?' he asked, then waved to a woman I didn't know across the street.

I narrowed my glance. He'd said he had no idea what was in them, so why was he asking? Could *he* be my father? He and Mum had been friends for long enough. And it had to be someone who was from here. There'd never been any mention of one of her acting friends coming to Helston. They'd only ever made it as far as Truro.

Before I could reply, his phone rang.

'Sorry, must take this.' He turned, and I fled inside the house, presumably hoping to grab a few minutes alone. I tried to think of all the men my mother had said she loved. But would she have told me this? Not if she'd wanted to keep it a secret, which she had, then she'd have played any relationship down. That put Peter in the picture. But who else? Mum knew and got on well with pretty much everyone in Helston. Which would make it harder. A DNA test was needed. It'd be a starting point and could throw up a lot of information. Tomorrow I would order the test and begin a spreadsheet. Knowing that my father wasn't a random stranger only made the dull ache of longing grow again.

Gina and Vlad had wandered into the garden, and Micki was chatting with Ke. The last thing I wanted to do right now was talk to Ke. Once he would have been the first person I turned to after reading my mother's letter to discuss what it actually meant. But I had to put this all out of mind and just get through the Midday Dance. One step at a time.

Ke left Micki. He needed to change his clothes, and before long we'd be coiled in a spiral of dancers in the Guildhall, waiting for twelve and the start of the Midday Dance. Fear kicked my heart into race mode. What the hell would we say to each other? We'd barely exchanged any words in fifteen years. Not that Ke hadn't tried for a while, but I hadn't replied to anything. God knows what he thought of me now. One thing was certain; I didn't want to know.

My thoughts vied between the coming encounter with Ke and Mum's letter. Mum must have told someone who my father was. It was a long time to bury something so deep, and to keep it there. Sadly, I knew how hard it was to do that. Whether I wanted to think about what I'd buried or not, it appeared in the back of my mind at the worst of times. Times when I should have been totally focused on something or someone else. I'd done the right thing, though. That wasn't a question in my mind. Nevertheless, in the small hours I still debated what I'd done. And judged myself.

Especially now that I was thirty-eight and alone. After all these years, that little girl who'd so desperately wanted a family had finally accepted she wasn't meant to have one. I stood here in a film-star gown, ready to dance in an hour, looking nothing like the nerdy girl who rehearsed everything and who'd hoped to bring up a family in Helston. To watch that family dance in the rites of spring, to teach them to swim and surf, and to love all that was magical about this place of granite.

Were Flo and the Flora of old all that different? I was still nerdy and still rehearsed everything. I had places in LA and London. But nothing really tied me to any one location. My limbs were lightly tanned but not the deep brown of a Cornish summer. This was not a bad thing, but I thought of the teenager who'd spent as much time as she could on the beach. Even back then I'd yearned for more. More travel, more learning. Simply more. Micki understood that, even if it wasn't what she herself craved. She wanted at least one sunny holiday per year, and for life to continue here. Ke had wanted to stay too, despite his surfing ambitions. Even if things hadn't happened the way they did, it never would have worked. That was the truth.

Micki caught up with me. 'I have to say you do look fabulous.'

'Thanks.' Looking good didn't help the dread I felt.

She tucked her arm through mine. 'I know it isn't easy on you, being here, with Tony gone and the ghost of your mother hanging over the day.'

I blinked. 'The ghost of my mother?'

'You know, the Hal an Tow, and your conception story.'

'Ah, I take your point.' I smiled sadly.

'She was the best mum, and your gran was an absolute legend.'

This was true. Gran's life must have been hard, seeing Mum's dad in town and his rejection of her. Moral of the story: don't mess with a married man. But of course Micki would laugh at that.

'I've been worried about you.' She paused. 'You flew in and out in a day for Tony's funeral, and I don't think you've taken a breath since.'

I squinted at her, wondering where she was going with this.

'He was like a dad to you and well, with your mum dying so unexpectedly, you've been orphaned.'

'I'm thirty-eight, not ten.'

'That's not the point. I guess I'm not making myself clear. Despite the fact we chat all the time, you never mention how you feel about losing either of them, and I'm damned if I know where you're putting the grief which I know is in there.' She met my glance, and suddenly we were kids again, playing who would blink first.

The silence between us stretched. She wasn't letting go.

'It's not good to hold it all in. It'll find you, and it will be worse.'

'You know this?' I shoved my hands in my pockets.

'Yeah, I do actually, and you know I do.'

'Sorry, yes you do.' She'd lost her goddaughter, Jessica, in a driving incident not too long ago. A newly licensed boy had been at the wheel and driving too fast, and Jessica had been killed instantly. A tragedy the town had been reeling from ever since. I reached out and placed a hand on her arm.

'I've watched my friend Kate pay the price, and I don't want to see you do the same.'

'It's different,' I countered.

'Grief is grief, just as love is love, and you loved Tony.'

I took a deep breath. 'Thank you for the reminder.'

'It wasn't meant as a reminder. It's a wake-up call.'

'Oh dear, what has the divine Flo done now?' Vlad joined us by the window, looking out at the people filing into the garden to find the best spot to watch the Midday Dance as it came through. Flora Day was timeless. The dresses reflected current trends, but a short while ago the faces of the kids had looked just the same as Micki and I had done. Their expressions displayed a mix of boredom, excitement and wickedness. It didn't feel all that long ago that Michaela and Ke had been desperate for the dance to finish so they could get to the fun fair.

'Vlad, allow me to introduce my oldest friend, Micki. Micki, this is the best hair and makeup person in the world.' I put my hand on Vlad's arm, studying him.

'That's some introduction, but seeing how fabulous Flo looks I can see she isn't overstating your talents.' Micki laughed.

'And you must be the one with all her secrets,' he replied.

My stomach hit the floor. I didn't need these two comparing notes. 'Gosh, look at the time, and I haven't found my lily-of-the-valley. Did you see it in the bedroom Vlad?'

He sent me a look before saying, 'Yes, I'll grab it for you.'

'Afraid of what I'll say?' Micki placed her hands on her hips.

'Absolutely,' I lied. I was more afraid of what Vlad might say. He was so damned observant.

'Your secrets are safe with me,' she reassured me with a straight face.

It was my turn to raise an eyebrow.

'I may have shared every secret my sisters or my mother ever told me, but never once did I tell yours.'

'Are you certain?' I asked, softening the question with a smile.

'Ok, fair, let me say never have I knowingly or wilfully done so.' She picked a non-existent thread off my dress.

'Fair,' I said, thinking of all those times when she'd dropped me in it.

At least she didn't know my biggest secret of all.

Eighteen

Flora Day, 2003

Thursday
Age: 16
Forecast: Sunny intervals

> *This year won't be like last year. I won't get drunk and pass out. That was such a mistake. I thought Mum would be really cross but she'd laughed at the state of me. I was ill for days. She simply said it had taught me a lesson I needed to learn for myself. And I have.*

Sweet white wine. I still can't even face the thought of drinking it. How and why we felt it would be a good idea had disappeared with most of my other memories of the night. Except for Micki taunting Ke to kiss her. That one remained imprinted on my mind. And he had. The rest of the evening had been lost after that. At least nothing more, that I knew of, had happened between them since then.

This morning I was in the Hal an Tow with Mum and Ke, then I planned to be with Gran at The Angel. She hadn't been feeling great lately, but wouldn't go to see a doctor, despite Tony, Mum, and me nagging her. The best I could do was to give her a hand and make sure she wasn't shifting kegs or even clearing glasses.

With my hair dried, and my smudged mascara fixed – I needed to remember to do it after I'd done my hair – tired eyes looked at me from the mirror, and I felt hungover, despite not drinking last night. I think maybe I've felt hungover since last year. God knows I drank enough to still feel shit.

This year had been weighed down by that one mistake. No, that's not true. It hadn't helped things, that was all. It might have been that, because I was such a bitch last year and didn't welcome in the spring sincerely, my year hadn't been filled with joy. I'd done well at school but, unlike Micki, I still didn't have a boyfriend. Ke didn't have a girlfriend either, although they were suddenly queueing up. He looked nothing like the boy I'd first danced with. The only thing that remained were his beautiful sad eyes. Those eyes had always got me. He was lost, or his eyes were. Only when they focused on the waves did the sadness go.

The sea transformed him. It was extraordinary. He'd go into the waves broken and emerge whole. He'd also become tanned, blonder and hot as hell. It wasn't fair. He didn't even need glasses any longer. I loved him before he transformed and I wasn't supposed to lust after my best friend. I didn't lust after Wilf or Micki. But Ke. It was hard not to show how I felt. I couldn't act like the other girls around him but part of me wanted to. Even if he wasn't my best friend, I just wouldn't have had the guts.

Micki had guts. Her ease with herself and the world amazed me. She'd been absolutely rat arsed the other weekend and said and done some things I'd never have forgiven myself for, yet she just brushed them off. I questioned her to see if it was true, but she really didn't care. It was in the past, as they said in *Hakuna Matata* in the *Lion King*, and she was leaving it there with all her other mistakes.

I envied that. Despite rehearsing everything in my head, if not in actual life, I always seemed to mess up, and I never let myself forget a single mistake, even if it had been innocent. The smallest thing would emerge from the depths of my brain just as I was trying to fall asleep, tormenting me with my stupidity, carelessness or simple dumb luck. Let's hope that today I'd honour the arrival of spring in the right way, and that it would herald a better year, with fewer fuck-ups.

While the Evening Dance went past, Gran and I quickly wolfed down some pasties. It was my first food since this morning. We hadn't stopped. Gran washed hers down with a pint, but I had water. I was worried about Gran, she seemed different somehow. Her vitality and sass weren't on show anymore. Vulnerable. That was the word.

'Gran, when was your first dance?'

She peered at me over her pint. 'First dance, or first dance on Flora Day, or Furry Day as we called it back then?'

'Both I guess, but I was thinking of Flora actually.'

'It was during the war. Not that Flora Day officially happened then, but the Children's Dance was held. The band was given permission to play one year.'

'Wow, that must have been strange.' I'd seen the pictures in the museum and read enough to know about the war, but I hadn't thought about Flora Day and how that would have been affected.

'Everything was strange to be honest.' Gran laughed bitterly.

'Tell me more about the Floras during the war.'

She stared at me like she was trying to see where this was going. A bit like she used to when I tried to find out if she knew who my father was. 'The Children's Dance kept the tradition going. Dresses mended and handed on to make sure we all looked as bright as we could.' She took a long slow slug of her pint. 'Spirits needed lifting as the war dragged on and we knew so little, in truth.' She paused. 'And Flora was on VE Day. Or maybe I should say it was the other way around.'

I smiled. 'Flora must have been the perfect way to celebrate being alive and free.'

'It's all so clear.' She looked out at the crowds. The sound of the band drifted in. 'The joy was tangible, and as an eleven-year-old I really didn't understand the sadness.'

'I can imagine.' So many people killed – sons, brothers, fathers, lovers and women who each played their role.

'For the Early Morning Dance that year, the women had done their best to make new dresses, and many danced with each other.' She shook her head 'There were still so few men.'

'So few men?'

'Even though the war in Europe had ended they weren't home, and many never came home.' She shook her head slowly. 'So much loss of life.' She laughed sadly. 'I recall my grandmother saying the same thing about the Great War.'

'You never talk much about your mother, or your grandmother.' I'd asked her on many occasions before, but she hadn't indulged me with answers, or she gave me ones that only led to more questions. Mum and Tony hadn't been able to answer the questions either. Why didn't people know anything?

'My grandmother lost her lover to the battlefields of France before they could marry, and my mother never said who knocked her up at fifteen.' She took another slug of her pint. 'My grandmother's mistake was understandable, because of the war, but I just don't know enough of what happened with my mother to know what to feel.' There was bitterness in her voice.

'Gran, didn't you get on with your mother?'

She looked at me. 'My grandmother raised me as the child of her cousin. That's what they told everyone, including me. My mother went away and only came back to Helston at the start of the war.' Gran looked out the window and I wasn't sure what she was looking at.

'When did you find out the truth?'

'When my mother left Helston the day after Flora Day 1945 with the soldier she'd met only the day before.' She paused. 'She emigrated to Australia with him.'

'Oh.' I didn't know what to say.

'My grandmother only told me the truth after that because she was so angry.' She downed the rest of her pint. 'So, the woman I'd known as my cousin was actually my mother and my grandmother's daughter. In one fell swoop I was someone completely different to who I had been.'

This wasn't the story I'd expected. It didn't fit with the single mothers bearing single daughters being something good and something strong. This was broken.

'And your grandmother?'

'She was bitter at many things, but she loved me.' The corners of her mouth turned up in a half smile. Gran herself had been a great mother, Mum had said, and she'd opened her heart and home to Tony too.

'What work did she do?'

'She was the housekeeper at Lismore.' She looked at me. 'It was a big step down for her then as the daughter of a well-to-do merchant. Her life should have been different, but she was built of strong stuff and made it work.'

'Did she ever find love again?'

Gran laughed. 'Love? Love had left her pregnant and unmarried. She became very pragmatic about the romantic side of life and abandoned any dreams of that. I should have done the same.'

The increasing noise outside made any further conversation impossible, and once the dancers had passed, the crowds came back in. My great-grandmother had been a young woman of twenty-six on VE Day. Had she danced with her soldier, swept up in love at first sight? Did they stay together afterwards, once they reached Australia? Too many questions. My thoughts started drifting back to my own father, as they always did. The constant nag of that shadowy figure I could never reach. Was he on the other side of the world right now too? And how would I ever find out who he was?

Lismore, Cross Street, Helston, Cornwall

---

30 October 2003

My Darling Flo,

I'm thrilled you enjoyed your days on the set of Ladies in Lavender. I knew you would. I'd hoped that your mother would be an extra on the film but, as you know, she declined. I am eager to hear your thoughts. Did you meet Judi Dench and Maggie Smith? What did you think?

Is everyone talking of nothing else but the filming in the town? You mentioned that they also filmed in Cadgwith, Prussia Cove, and St Ives. What part did you enjoy seeing most? Has the experience given you an idea of where you want to direct your energies? What appealed to you the most? It makes life much easier if you love what you do. Sometimes it is hard to hold onto this when money or fame or other passing things come into the equation. To sustain you long term, you do need money and you need satisfaction in what you are doing. If you can achieve both it helps.

I found this working in finance. Yet, having said that, as you know I left it behind to pursue other things. I was lucky that my early success and the board positions that came after have allowed me to truly follow my heart and support charities I believe in. Your old uncle Tony is blessed to be doing what he loves. I wish that for you as you consider your future career.

I will be back at Lismore in the middle of November. I am sorry to have missed the filming in the old town. Is there any gossip I should know? Is there anything you want me to buy when I'm in New York next week?

Love,
Tony xxxx

Nineteen

Flora Day, 2004

Saturday
Age: 17
Forecast: Sunny intervals

> *After today, no more white dresses. No more white flats. No more feeling awkward as shit.*

I put the pen down. That summed it up quite well. This was the last year I'd have to dance in the Children's Dance. If Mum hadn't been leading the Midday Dance with Tony this year, Micki, Ke, and I would have been doing the Hal an Tow. But because she wasn't in charge this time, we couldn't talk our way out of the Children's Dance. At least this year's white frock was flattering, which really made a change. Looking through photos last night with Mum, it had been painful to see how bad I'd looked in so many of them. How had she let me out of the house looking like a tubby overstuffed rag doll? Seriously, I'd been such an ugly child.

Although, as glancing through the entries in my stash of diaries showed, I hadn't thought I was that bad every time, just some years. Poor Ke really had been awful in most people's view.

Now he was the hottest boy around. Not that he took any notice of it, and I loved that about him. Ke was Ke. If, on the outside, he'd become a bronzed surf god, he was still the same lost, geeky boy on the inside. No, not lost any longer – he knew what he wanted to do now. Unlike Micki, whose only goal was to find someone with plenty of money to spoil her. Sadly, the local pickings were low on this account, so she'd been looking further afield in Penzance and Truro. This was so boring for me, Ke and Wilf, because the guys she brought back from there were worse than what was on offer here. But there was no telling Micki once she was onto an idea.

So at least this was the last time I'd have to don a white frock and white shoes. The relief was immeasurable. Plus, Ke and I were dancing together again. So many of the girls had tried to lure him away, but he wasn't having it. Which made my stomach flip with happiness. I wasn't kidding myself that he'd ever look at me as anything more than a friend, despite that look all those years ago. But it was weird. I went red sometimes when we practiced together – his breath close to me, holding my hands. But this was Ke. My best friend. The one I'd always had a laugh with, and now I'd suddenly go all awkward at the slightest thing. He didn't seem to notice, though, thank goodness.

Micki was dancing with Tom again, which was quite funny, since he'd been her first partner too. He was marginally nicer now that he was no longer the tallest or the best in sport. Some of the shit had been kicked out of him along the way. Still not my favourite person, but he was OK.

When I came downstairs, Mum was in the kitchen, not sure what to do with herself. She'd been told not to go down to help with the Hal an Tow this morning – she was to enjoy her day. The look on her face said this wasn't happening, though.

'You OK Mum?' I asked, pouring myself some tea.

'You look wonderful.' She smiled, but it wasn't her usual smile, the one that transformed her into the film star she should have been.

'Thanks, and you will too.' I sat opposite her. She was still in her pyjamas. 'What's wrong?' I thought I knew, but I'd discovered last year that it was best to ask and not assume.

'Nothing,' she said as she stood to put the kettle on again.

'Liar.'

She turned and smiled, a real one this time. I relaxed a bit.

'Fair comment,' she said.

'Tell me.'

'The Midday Dance isn't me.' She twisted her hands.

'I know, and everyone else knows that at your core you're the Hal an Tow.' I'd rarely seen her like this: uncertain. No matter what hit, she was usually rock steady and calm, but not now. I understood, though; it had been a tough year for Mum. For us all.

She made a face.

'Unlike you, Tony *is* the Midday Dance.' He'd been in it most years, and after he bought Lismore, it seemed fitting he should always be in it. But this was the first year he'd lead the dance, and he wanted to do it with Mum, for them both to honour Gran.

She had died at New Year. It didn't feel real half the time, and then at others the ache was massive. Walking past The Angel, I kept my eyes focused straight ahead, never looking in because someone else was where she should be and felt like always had been. When your family was as small as mine, the hole left was far bigger. But I could hear Gran's voice now, telling us not to mope about. It was fine; she'd had a good innings. And in a way she'd had, but even just the little bits she told me, it hadn't been an easy life. She would say she'd done the best she could with what she'd been given. And I guess that was true, but it had to hurt like hell that the one man you loved didn't love you enough to acknowledge you or your child.

'He is.' Mum laughed. 'He's good at the razzmatazz, and well, I was once but not anymore.'

'Mum, you're an actor.' I gave her one of my versions of her own stern look.

She rolled her eyes like a kid. 'I haven't been one for... let me see, seventeen years.'

'And why not? I just don't get it.' I stared at her. 'I've told you, begged you, to act again.'

'You have, but my heart isn't in it anymore.' Her shoulders dropped, and I felt my stomach sink too. This wasn't Mum.

'So you've said, but you can act today for Tony.'

She looked down as she spooned coffee into the cafetière. 'Always.'

'Good.' I stood up and gave her a hug. 'You'll have fun. But why aren't you dressed?' I glanced at the kitchen clock. 'It's five to seven.'

'Taking it slowly.'

I studied her. She was forty-eight and more beautiful than when she'd been on stage. I hoped I'd age that well. Gran hadn't, but some of her life choices – such as her love of gin, which was obviously her way of escape – hadn't helped with that. But it was this obsession that'd snatched her from us too quickly, as it turned out. The perfect Christmas we'd had at Lismore had been shattered when she didn't wake on New Year's Day, after a heavy session the night before, celebrating. The memory of hearing Mum's shout to call an ambulance still chilled me to the bone.

Everyone had been talking about Gran this week, lamenting that it wouldn't be Flora Day without her behind the bar at The Angel. It was good to hear her talked about, I guess, but also very sad. It felt like Micki poking at a bruise, as she loved to do. But this hurt so much more, and so much deeper. It was just me and Mum left as the Richards women now.

'Shall we meet at St John's or somewhere else to watch the Hal an Tow?' I asked.

Mum looked at me, looked at me hard. 'I don't think I can.'

'Seriously Mum, as you'd say to me, get a grip of yourself.' I presented her with my rendition of her expression when she was giving me one of those talking to's. 'The town is honouring you and Tony today with the best thing they can offer. You two are the first couple. Think about that. You and your best friend, leading the dance together.'

She gave me a small smile. 'Put like that, I can see your point.'

'And Gran would be pleased as punch, as she'd say.'

Mum laughed, then looked down. 'I miss her,' she whispered.

I hugged her again, the biggest hug I could manage. 'I do too.'

Micki, Ke and I had secured prime spots outside the Guildhall. It felt like it'd never be noon. My stomach was in knots as I knew how Mum would be feeling. Though I doubted anyone else did, except maybe Tony. He was good at sensing things and then getting the rest of it out of you. I'd realised this to my peril. Things that no one should know he'd worked out of me. I glanced at Micki. She didn't need to know what I talked to him about. She thought Mum was my closest confidante, aside from her and Ke, but it was Tony.

He listened.

He didn't judge.

Mum didn't either, but whether she wanted to show it or not, I could always see how she truly felt. Tony had been so harshly judged by his father and society that he never did so himself. As long as you didn't hurt other people, he was cool about it. Unless you hurt yourself – that was always the hard one. But after years of talking to him, I could hear his voice in my head – not lecturing me, just encouraging me to be better, especially to myself.

The clock chimed, and the excitement built. As it struck twelve, the big bass drum sounded, hit by Wilf, and the band started up. Out came the officials, and then there were Mum and Tony. They looked gorgeous. So damned good looking, both of them. Tony's morning suit was perfectly tailored, and Mum had transformed the gown so it suited her. Red was her colour, and it glowed in the midday sun.

When the music changed, Tony dropped Mum's hand and went to spin with Pam Johns, just as Mum did with Peter Johns.

Then, Mum and Tony came back together again, and the smiles on their faces were joyous. A bit like I imagined Ke and I had looked this morning. In the end we'd decided to enjoy the dance of childhood, even though we were no longer children, and had had a ball.

Watching Mum and Tony made me happy. He leaned over to say something to her, and she threw her head back laughing, nearly losing her hat. All was well, and Gran would be smiling from wherever she was, I knew, because two of the people she loved most were enjoying themselves. And that, after all, was what Flora Day was all about: the joy of spring.

We sat cross-legged on the edge of the bowling green, eating sausages covered in onions. The smell had won us over this year, and we couldn't resist any longer. Micki handed each of us a can of cider.

'Here's to no more Children's Dances.' She lifted her can.

'Well, not strictly true for me,' said Wilf.

'Technically...' said Micki, always sure she was right. 'Cause you couldn't dance in it, since you've always been in the band.'

'True,' he agreed.

I glanced at Ke. He was being strangely quiet. Things weren't great with his mum, not that he said, and everything was up in the air for him. Because of this I hadn't mentioned next year and if we'd do the Early and the Evening Dances together. I couldn't imagine dancing with anyone else, nor did I want to. I still had the biggest crush on him, not that I'd ever tell him. But maybe he was ready to move on... I didn't want to even think about this. Without him as my partner, I'm not sure I'd ever dance on Flora Day again.

'So, what's the plan?' Wilf asked.

'Eat the sausages, then hear the band at The Blue.' Ke took a swig of the cider.

'Not what I meant.'

'Oh, I thought the same thing,' said Micki. She drew a deep

breath. 'Do you mean for next year? I suppose I'll see if Tom wants to do the Early and the Evening.'

Wilf chuckled. 'No, not that either. I know I'm a year ahead of you guys, but what's next, what do you want to do with your lives?'

I sent him a look. 'That's a big topic for a Flora Day.'

'Flora is a big day, it can take it.' He smiled. 'I'll start. I want to work with people, possibly sick ones.'

'A doctor?' Ke asked.

'No, don't have the brain for that.' He shrugged his big shoulders. 'But maybe a nurse.'

'Cool,' I said.

'Yeah, I can see that,' said Micki. 'Me, I want an easy life, so I guess I best find an easy job that pays loads. Or a sugar daddy.'

We all laughed.

'Ke?' Wilf prompted.

'Something to do with the sea.' He cast a glance at me. We'd spoken about uni as he'd done well at GCSE but, because of his mum, this year hadn't been too good.

'The Navy?' asked Micki.

He shook his head. 'Definitely not, but something to do with surfing.'

'You're good enough to become world champion.' Wilf raised his tin in Ke's direction.

'Thanks mate.' Ke paused. 'Maybe one day. I don't know how yet, but I do want to do something to help the ocean.'

'That sounds serious.' Micki finished her cider and opened another.

'It is.' Ke's expression was solemn, and I felt a surge of love for him, for his plans to do great things.

'What about you, Flo?' Wilf asked.

'Me?' I paused and looked at them all. 'Well, travel and work in films.'

'Ah, you want to be an actress like your mum,' Wilf said.

'Definitely not an actress.' My insides froze. Be like Mum – a single mum with a small life. No. 'Maybe directing or producing. Whichever one means more travel.' I thought about my days on the set of *Ladies in Lavender*. I'd loved the buzz of all those around me – the crew rushing about, the actors... Of course, exotic locations would be a plus, because the list of possible places my father may have come from was still in my head.

Wilf laughed. 'We are one diverse lot, but it sounds like three of us will be staying put and you'll be on the road.'

'There's so much out there to see,' I said, my tone defensive.

'It wasn't a criticism.' Wilf dropped an arm about my shoulders as we all stood up. 'It was just me noting your goals.'

'Oh,' I said, realising my goal was to not be like Mum, and anything else was a bonus, especially if travel was involved.

Twenty

2025

8 May, 11:00 a.m.

The time that I'd have to face Ke was fast approaching. We'd exchanged very few words since I'd left sixteen years ago, cutting contact so abruptly, so painfully. They'd mostly only been the platitudes we use with acquaintances – *congrats, well done, and so sorry for your loss.* Words batted around continuously, especially on social media, where friendship groups were far wider. And I used these words when inevitably bumping into each other in the crowds on Flora Days, and times when I came back for brief visits. He'd attended my mother's funeral when I could not, finding myself stuck in LA, sobbing alone in frustration and disbelief. He'd been at Tony's too, but the whole town and half of Cornwall had been, so we hadn't spoken to each other then either. Instead, it had been merely a look and a nod of acknowledgement across the room.

Just thinking about the hours ahead of me made my hands shake as I tried to pin the lily-of-the-valley onto the left side of my dress. Gina took it from me and swiftly secured it.

'Are you OK?' she asked, her face showing concern, despite the Botox.

I wasn't, but this wasn't something I could admit. Gina was like a pit bull and knew too much already. 'Just normal nerves at being on display and in front of cameras.' This I knew she'd understand, as she had dressed me for all the award ceremonies.

'OK, so long as that's all. You've been different here.' She paused. 'I know being back in this house and this town brings so many memories, even if they are good ones. It's a big dump of emotional stuff, on top of other things.' She tilted her head to the side, studying me, then tugged slightly at the bodice of the dress. Little did she realise how much it would move again with each twirl in the dance. But that was underestimating her. She'd watched videos, so she knew the requirements.

'I'm guessing that Ke was the father,' she whispered in my ear.

I froze. That lost soul of sixteen years ago, away from home in LA, who'd cried on her new friend's shoulder, and relied on her financial help, was very different from the woman who stood before her now. But it was all still just below the surface. This was exactly what I hadn't wanted.

'He doesn't know?'

'No,' I said, barely audible.

Her glance was solemn as she said, 'Good luck.'

Micki came up to us, tapping her wrist. 'Bout time you made your way to the Guildhall. Would have been easier for Ke to meet you here rather than you both trying to find each other in the fray.'

I couldn't argue with that, but it would have given Ke and me space to talk, and that I didn't want. I wanted to dance. No, actually, I didn't. The truth was, I wanted to take off this dress, put on trackies, and hide with a tub of ice cream. Not possible, though, so the next best option was to arrive at the last moment. Pretend that conversation was impossible with the level of noise, concentrate on the dance, and then disappear into my room and shut the door. And finally be alone. Vlad and Gina were due to leave after they saw the Midday Dance. It was a huge favour from the entire production team that they'd released them for this.

What I wouldn't have given to disappear to North Cornwall, to have only the film crew and actors to contend with. But for me today, after the dance, there'd be interviews with the local paper, and possibly national ones, as Ke and I were the current heralded son and daughter of Helston, bringing fame back to our forgotten borough. Helston had lost its prominence compared to its heyday, when it'd had a castle, Loe Bar wasn't there, and mariners could navigate as far as the boating lake. You mentioned Helston to most people now, and they'd never heard of it. Gone were the days when Flora Day made the national papers. Until perhaps a revival this year because of the timing of the VE Day anniversary and Ke and me being somewhat high-profile people leading the dance.

Gina sent me a look. I didn't need to think about my past. Anything but. Helston and I would be separated soon, and part of me would always remember it fondly. Helston belonged to Helstonians, not the countless tourists who flocked to the chocolate box villages and beaches dotted through the county, or duchy as some would call it. The town was beautiful, but most tourists never stopped long enough to peer down the side streets and opes to spot the architectural gems. The film *Ladies in Lavender* had displayed some of its charm, but most viewers hadn't realised they were looking at the borough town. Yet that year all Helstonians had still held their heads a little higher as they spotted their town on celluloid.

Micki watched me keenly, and I could tell she was trying to read my thoughts. Best to keep them on neutral ground and not on Ke.

'I know this is the last thing you want to do but it's an enormous honour.' Micki straightened my lily-of-the-valley. 'Remember when your mum and Tony led the dance, how thrilled we were?'

I nodded, a huge lump forming. That had been such a day,

but today was different. She wasn't here anymore, nor was Tony. I peered at the ceiling. Now was not the time to cry. It would ruin everything, from the makeup to the dress to the facade I had in place holding it all together. In just over four hours, this would be done. It'd be the first step to freedom and leaving the past behind. I half expected to turn and see Mum and Tony on the staircase, but I didn't believe in ghosts, or fairy tales for that matter. I might help to create them for others to watch, and to hope the experience could change their lives, but that was all. Life was hard, and it was what you made of it with what you were given. I'd been given a loving mother and supportive friends, a good brain, and no fear of hard work and long hours. Gran had truly taught me the latter.

This dance was just another step along my journey, such as it was. It would take strength and all my grandmother's grit to do it, but I would. I forced my mouth into a smile.

'Right, I'd better make my way to the Guildhall.'

Three faces stared at me. They all loved me, and their belief would make this easier.

'We'll be cheering you on,' Vlad snapped another pic. 'Now one of you and Micki.'

'That's not fair.' Micki laughed. 'I haven't had the best in the world making me look like a movie star.'

'You don't need it,' Vlad replied, and I made a face. And of course, that was the picture he took.

Twenty-One

Flora Day, 2005

Saturday
Age: 18
Forecast: Sunny

The day was bright and clear and better than my head. My diary sat on the bedside table. I think I wrote in it before I fell asleep. I was almost afraid to look, but I braved it.

Ke is sooooooo

Well, that summed it up. Best not to think about it at all, especially on just an hour's sleep to get me through today. I had only one responsibility, which was helping Mum make sure everyone was where they were supposed to be, and dressed properly for the Hal an Tow.

I swallowed a yawn and found Mum in the kitchen, brewing coffee. She looked bright and fresh, which didn't seem fair, since she'd knocked back a few drinks last night too. Jamie and Jen, today's Robin Hood and Maid Marion, had got engaged last night, and for a town that was already in party mode it'd upped the ante. I was feeling all of it right now. They couldn't be feeling too bright either. Thankfully, I'd stopped drinking about one in the morning, as had Ke. Micki wasn't having it, but Ke and I had stuck by our cut-off. She'd waved us off at four, as she snogged Kevin Ross.

Whenever she had a new lust, there was no distracting her. Kevin became her obsession after he arrived at Culdrose. Well, she had her prize, and that would be a stinking hangover this morning. I'd have put money on it that Kevin wouldn't be feeling great either. He was attractive but not my idea of boyfriend material. This was the best thing about Micki and me. We never went for the same guys, except Ke, and I'd never told her how I really felt about him. At least her attention seemed to have turned away from him in the last couple of years.

'Go have a shower and be ready in five,' Mum said, handing me a mug.

'Ten?' I pleaded.

'Fine, but be ready.' She smiled, softening her words.

'Of course.' I raced off, hoping the shower would wake me up. Today would be great.

By eight ten, everyone but the newly engaged couple was in place for the Hal an Tow. Green makeup on those who needed it. Foliage securely attached. Everything was ready, except for our Robin Hood and Maid Marion.

I was adjusting the flower crown on one girl when Mum tapped me on the shoulder.

'Doesn't she look great?' I asked.

'Perfect,' Mum said as she pulled me away. 'Ke is putting on a Robin Hood costume and I need you to get this on now.' She pushed a Maid Marian dress towards me.

'What?' I glanced from her to the costume.

'Jen and Jamie are both so hungover from celebrating last night and they can't do it. You and Ke are the right size for what I could find.' She held up the dress.

I swallowed, considering my options. This was something I never wanted to do. People would be staring. I intended to be in the background. 'Mum, you could fit into the dress.'

'I could but it wouldn't look right.' She guided me into a makeshift shelter and helped me change from my jeans and grubby t-shirt into the frock. Her last action before hugging me was to place a crown of flowers on my head. 'It will all be over before you know it.'

Being in the spotlight would be horrific enough, but being there with Ke would make it worse. Jamie and Jen had been doing it for a couple of years, then they'd fallen in love. Would everyone be able to tell how I really felt about Ke? Would *he*? The thought made me want to curl up and hide. Ke was my friend, along with Micki, and Wilf being the fourth Musketeer. Some people may think falling in love with your bestie was a good idea, but friends were more important than romantic love. Just look at Mum and Tony. He'd always been there for her and always would be. She was there for him too, of course. You didn't mess with best friends. And I didn't want to ruin what Ke and I had, and then there was Micki's claim.

I walked out, and the first thing I saw was Ke. His smile nearly stopped my heart. Mum had an easy job not falling in love with Tony. He was gay, and there was never any question of romance between them. But Ke was straight and so hot it hurt. It wasn't fair.

Once I reached his side, he took my hand.

Connection.

We'd get through this together. I smiled back up at him.

The first performance at St John's Bridge went pretty smoothly, except I nearly keeled over when we kneeled before Friar Tuck and he asked, 'will it be you two next?'. Ke's hand steadied me just in time.

Slowly but surely the magic of the beat of the drums and the scream of the whistles seduced me. Something about the whole spectacle was like a spell, as we sang and we danced. By the time we reached the last stop at the Guildhall, I was completely relaxed and enjoying myself. Or maybe it was better to say I'd forgotten myself. I flirted with Ke, and he with me. I must still have been drunk. But I wasn't, nor was he.

The raucous calls from the crowds didn't make me cringe and, in fact, seemed to make me braver. Or maybe it was my true self who danced freely for those joyous moments. I let the jolly rumble play within me. It was May; the sun was shining and anything was possible, including falling in love with your best friend.

I practically fell out the door of The Beehive onto the street. Ke wasn't far behind me, laughing at my stagger. Micki, Kevin and Wilf followed. The way down to The Blue was steeper than I remembered, and Ke helped me to my feet when I mis-stepped. I paused outside The Angel, trying to picture it as it had been in the past, hosting balls for the gentry. A sharp pang for Gran hit me. Tonight it was filled with drunk people like me.

I turned to Ke and opened my arms to dance. Not the way we'd just been doing in The Beehive but as they'd done it of old. He laughed.

'Flo, you're so drunk you can barely stand and you want to waltz?' He placed a hand around my waist and took mine with the other.

'Yes.' I hiccupped.

'Any song in mind?' Ke asked.

'You pick,' I slurred. That didn't sound good. No more cider for me. I couldn't get any drunker anyway. I'd never been this pissed before. Or maybe once.

'Maybe I just count it out.'

I nodded rather than speak. It was safer.

'One, two, three... one, two, three.' And we began with the gentle whisper of his voice in my ear.

'You two practicing the wedding waltz already?' Mum's friend Peter Johns called from the other side of the street. 'Took Jen and Jamie a few years before the fertility nonsense of the day worked on them.'

My heart beat faster. *Marry Ke, Marry Ke, Marry Ke, Marry Ke,* it said. *Kiss him, kiss him.*

'Get lost,' shouted Micki. 'Leave the love birds alone.' She came up to us and took my hand from Ke's shoulder. 'Boys, head to The Blue and get the drinks before the town crier starts announcing wedding bans in the morning.'

'On it,' said Wilf, strolling with Kevin and Ke the rest of the way down the street.

Micki linked arms with me. 'You're drunk and you've forgotten that Ke is mine,' she whispered, as she held me upright.

I shook my head. Ke was hers?

'Three years ago, I made my claim.'

I blinked. We'd been so drunk that night. It was when he'd first shot up and no longer looked like the serious, chubby boy of the past. His spots were disappearing, and his shoulders, his shoulders were a thing of beauty.

'Kev?' I slurred, remembering I was meant to be heading to uni in September, while she and Ke would be here.

'He's good for now but Ke is the end goal.' She drew a deep breath and grinned.

'But he's your *friend,*' I sputtered.

'Yours too.' She stopped outside the pub. 'Just remember, I called it and he's mine.'

Twenty-Two

Flora Day, 2006

Saturday
Age: 19
Forecast: Sunny

I had the booze sweats. My hand had shaken earlier as I wrote in my diary.

I feel shit.

That was all I'd written. Not a lot, but accurate. Drinking Rattler until the sun rose had seemed like a good plan at the time. But right now, it didn't. We were pressed into the Guildhall like sardines. Ke sent me a sheepish smile. He couldn't feel any better than I did, but he looked amazing. While I was ghostly white, having been locked in the library all term at uni in Manchester, he was a bronze god of the sea. His hair was bleached white in places, and there was a small smattering of freckles across his nose. I still wouldn't tell a soul I fancied him like mad and had done so for years. We were best friends and, as I reminded myself again, one didn't mess with a good thing. Friends were everything, as I'd learned myself, let alone from what my mother had always taught me. And of course, we were the Musketeers and Micki herself which was a bit annoying if I was honest..

This day was a bonus. Flora Day had been moved to the Saturday, like last year. I shouldn't have been here because I should have been cramming for exams. I'd arrived at nine last night and gone straight into the fray, needing to catch up with everyone who was already well drunk. Micki had thrust a Jäger-bomb at me, and that'd kicked things off. It'd seemed like a good idea at the time, but these things always do. I'd needed the courage too. Having been away from everyone, I felt more of an outsider than I ever had, except with Wilf, Ke and Micki. With them, it was like I'd never been gone. Micki's latest boyfriend was another story. He wasn't local and was rude about everything in town. I just couldn't understand what she saw in him. I suppose I should have been grateful she hadn't made a move on Ke.

Yet.

But it was possible, and with me being away it somehow seemed more likely. This new guy didn't like that she'd be dancing with Tom for Flora Day, despite the fact Tom was married now, with a kid on the way. It'd all happened so quickly, but sometimes these things do. He seemed happy about it, which was good.

It was weird to be back after months lost in the history of the First World War and in Film Studies. The latter I'd added in once I'd arrived and found out it was possible. So, now I was doing a combined honours degree. When I asked Tony and Mum if this was crazy, they had encouraged me to follow my passions and both subjects were. What I would do with them was a question for later we'd all agreed at Christmas.

Christmas and New Year didn't feel that long ago, but each time I returned I saw it differently. The very granite stones that held the place together seemed colder and less welcoming. Which was totally crazy, and maybe more of a reflection of my hangover that was gaining strength. The air in the Guildhall was thick with the smell of stale booze, and bodies not quite as fresh as they should have been for the task in front of us: dancing the longest of the day's dances.

The crowd around me stilled. Ke took my hand and gave it a squeeze. My heart stopped. The big bass drum sounded, and it all began. This was my first Early Morning Dance. At my side, my dancing partner, was the hottest guy I knew, and he'd refused to dance with anyone else but me. It would break tradition, he'd said, and Flora Day was all about tradition.

Once we moved outside, the air was fresh and cool, which was a huge relief. The press of people and the closeness of Ke had my thoughts spinning. The crowds cheering us on were lighter than they would be for the Evening Dance at five o'clock. As we danced past, people spilled out of The Bell and The Rodney with their early morning pints in their hands. It was the eager and the mad up at this hour, especially if they'd been enjoying last night's entertainment. Most of Helston had, from the young to those old enough to know better. But it was those of us in between who hit it the hardest. This was our moment. Flora Day was ours, and of course it would always be mine.

Stealing a glance at Ke, I found it hard to believe he was the same boy I'd first danced these streets with – both of us in ill-fitting clothes. We'd bonded, but I hadn't realised just how important he'd become to me. I only wished I didn't fancy him so much now.

We danced up Meneage Street, and it already felt endless. Ke turned to me with a half-smile. 'We should have called it a night sooner.'

I laughed. 'Yeah, when it was still night.'

'I could murder a pint.' He grinned.

'Of water?' I asked as we swapped partners and then, after a spin, came back together.

'Not a bad idea first, then the beer.'

Mum was outside Lismore as we danced down Cross Street.

We were only halfway. Tony walked to her side and draped an arm across her shoulders. They waved as we danced on.

By the time we made it back to the Guildhall, I felt like I'd run a marathon. But I didn't want to let go of Ke's hand. He was mine for the whole of the dance, and that was something that kept me going. And we would do it all again at five.

'The Blue?' asked Micki, leading us down the street through the growing throngs of people.

'Was that an actual question?' Ke asked.

'No,' she called over her shoulder to me and Ke. We walked side by side at a slower pace. Every so often his hand brushed against mine, and all normal thought left me.

It was near midnight, and I was happily pissed. Everything in the world was good. The Evening Dance hadn't been as hard as the morning. That could have been because I'd had a few pints during the day, which had taken the edge off the hangover.

Now I was leaning against the Monument, looking up at the sky. The plough was clearly visible, and the North Star seemed especially bright. Ke walked up to me and handed me another beer. 'Hiding out here?'

'Maybe.' My ears were still ringing from the noise inside. He stood beside me, then leaned his shoulder against mine. He was warm and smelled of cigarettes and beer. Familiar scents, yet there was something different about them. Exciting. Forbidding even.

'What're you thinking about?' he asked.

I closed my eyes. 'Too much.'

'What does that mean?' His breath tickled my neck, and I shivered.

'Exams, this summer, next year, the future.'

'Yeah, too much.' He laughed softly.

I opened my eyes and looked into his. 'What do you want to do?' He couldn't be happy with his assortment of odd jobs, although they allowed him the flexibility he needed to surf. But doing some gardening, washing dishes and waxing boards were not stimulating work, or I didn't think so. Ke was clever. He should have gone to uni, but he'd ended up pulling out of half his A level exams when his mother had a relapse and overdosed. He'd insisted on staying with his dad to help nurse and watch her. I couldn't imagine the emotional strain he must have been under, but he didn't like to talk about it, so I didn't push it. My heart ached at his wasted potential, though.

'Now?' He moved his hip next to mine.

It was hard to think. 'No, not now.' I wanted to be in his arms, but I wasn't going to say that. 'In the future.'

'Oh, that.' He paused. 'It hasn't changed. I want to campaign to protect the ocean, to surf and to be happy.'

'All of those things would make you happy?' They all seemed attainable, unlike any list I'd put together.

'Oh, and win the world surfing championships.' He laughed.

I smiled. He was good enough, but I had a feeling that getting sponsorship to pay for it would be harder than winning.

'You?' he asked as we watched another couple walk around the bowling green. It still blew my mind that there'd been a castle here, in this spot, in the 1100s.

'I love the sea too, but this question of happiness... that's interesting.' No matter how I tried to think of something else, Ke was all I saw, all I thought about, all I wanted.

'What would make you happy?' His voice was so low it was almost a whisper.

You, I wanted to say loud and clear, but instead said, 'Travel, I want to see the world.' Which was also true.

'The surf championships take place all over...' His voice trailed off. Now that was a dream I could imagine. Ke and me in far-flung places beside the sea. I lifted my eyes to the sky, wanting to make a wish, or even say a prayer.

He looked up too. 'Can't see the Milky Way tonight.'

'No, too much light pollution, and noise too.' Helston was

partying almost as hard as it had the night before. Tomorrow would be a slow start for most of us, except for the poor clean-up team.

Ke nudged me and pointed to a shooting star. 'Make a wish.'

I held my breath. What I wished for was completely crazy – it was Ke. I hungered for him so much. But it would never happen. We wanted different things. He planned to stay in Cornwall mostly, after he won the surf championships, and I wanted the world. Well, to see all of it at a minimum. There was so much out there beyond this place. It called to me, but not to him. I knew this all too well. We'd spent hours talking about it.

'Did you make a wish?' he asked, looking down into my eyes. He was asking more, or I thought he was.

I nodded, unable to form words when he was this close. It'd be so easy to kiss him, and I leaned closer. 'Did you?'

'I did.' His breath tickled my mouth, and then his lips touched mine. We both stilled, waiting. Everything hung in the balance.

Everything.

All my yearnings stirred, and I raised my hands and rested them on his chest. His heart raced like mine. I was home, just like all those years ago when he'd taken my small hand in his. I'd been home and safe then. Yet safe was the last thing I felt right now. Reckless, more like.

'Got to take a piss and there's no bloody privacy. Go get a room Ke,' his brother Pawl shouted, disrupting the moment.

Ke took my hand in his and led me back onto the street. I would have followed him anywhere. We both hesitated in front of The Blue.

'There you two are!' Micki slurred. 'Wilf's just bought another round.'

'Bloody D'Artagnan,' Ke whispered and sent me a look. I didn't want another drink. I wanted Ke.

'Come on.' Micki walked up to us and wedged herself between us. She wrapped her arms around our waists and led us back to the pub. 'The Musketeers to the rescue.'

Ke and I looked over her head and said in unison, 'All for one and one for all.'

''Xactly.' Micki pushed us through the door. I didn't want to be in The Blue. Something had happened, changed.

It was the magic of Flora Day. But tomorrow I would go back to uni, and Ke would be here.

The Midday Dance

GAY SCENES

In and out the dancers went, through the houses and the gardens, until, at about half past twelve, they danced on to the lawn of Lismore, Dr. Michael's house, and the band stopped, the dancers broke up for a rest. As they sucked lemons provided for them in a scene reminiscent of a half-time in an impossibly decorous football match, the garden became a scene of a fashion parade with women from 'all over' anxious to see what the other dancers were wearing.

The Cornishman, 11 May 1950

* * *

THE LEGEND

A "Fiery Dragon" (possibly a large meteorite) is reputed to have appeared over Helston many centuries ago and a large stone dropped on what is now known as the "Angel Yard". The people of Helston, after believing the town was to be destroyed, celebrated their escape by dancing through the streets and each other's houses. More than hundred years ago, this large rock was used for building and a part was incorporated into outside wall of The Angel Hotel.

Twenty-Three

2025

8 May, 11:20 a.m.

Leaving Lismore, I walked down Cross Street towards the Guildhall, wanting to be away from people, but of course there was no escape from them. The cold east wind raised goosebumps on my bare arms and I shivered as I tucked my hands into the pockets of the gown's full skirt. Crowds spilled out of The Red Lion, clutching pints. Beautifully attired couples mixed with people dressed casually, not as though they were heading onto the set of *My Fair Lady*. Like Eliza Doolittle, I was a fraud. Everyone expected me to be delighted with my legacy, Lismore, and inheriting enough money to keep it. But I wasn't. It was a burden that should tie me here. Why had Tony done it? He could have left it in trust to the town or donated it to a charity.

Currently, Lismore's garden was full of happy people sharing picnics and fizz. The sun was out, and despite the cold wind, summer was in the air. We'd survived another winter. The feeling of survival was powerful. In order for me to not only survive but thrive, I needed to leave this all behind me.

It would be over soon. There was no obligation for me to do more than the dance, then pose for a few pictures and do some quick interviews. Then I could hide and lick my wounds, which were opening up again with every step closer to meeting Ke. All I wanted was peace, but looking around at the crowds milling about, that'd be impossible. It was noisy – that was Flora Day. Last night the town had been noisier. Live music had played in a few venues, with happily drunk people spilling out into the streets, only to stagger home in the early hours.

Now, for the big event. Was I ready? No. Did I have a choice? Not really. I caught sight of Tricia. She waved cheerily as she disappeared into a house. Our conversation from last night came back to me again. To be honest, I was still too shellshocked by everything, especially now standing here in a gown, to think about it too closely, but I realised what bothered me most was that Tricia knew, or had known all this time, that Mum had lied to me. She'd sworn repeatedly that she didn't know who my father was, but did she? For all I knew, I might be looking at him right now. The list of candidates ran through my head again.

Peter Johns, Mum's solicitor.

Sam Hicks, the head teacher.

Martin Stevens, the mechanic.

The Butcher

The Baker

The Candlestick Maker

I stopped. This wasn't helping my state of mind, and just made my thoughts circle more. They'd now turned to the fact that Micki had taken Vlad and Gina in hand, and they were due to watch the dance with her. What would they say to each other? Vlad was like a ferret. When he wanted info, he'd keep digging. Then there was Gina, who was piecing things together.

I needed to be at the Guildhall in ten minutes, by half-past eleven. Could I hold my head up and get through today without breaking down or killing someone? Each hour I'd been here, I'd had to face at least one trial or another, and today's final test was dancing with Ke. It would be the hardest. But I was good at exams, and if I thought of the dance as this, then everything would be fine. After all, this was a public event.

Several people waved to me, and I automatically waved back. They all knew me, and I should have known them. Every man I saw, I scrutinised. Was my father my old headmaster? He'd been good friends with Mum over the years, but I didn't look anything like him. Genes were funny things, though. Wasn't there a saying that children frequently looked like their fathers? That was probably just an old tale to quell the doubt people had often had over paternity. I wanted to scream, 'Mum, why did you have to say anything at all?!' Maybe she'd thought she'd live long enough that telling me about my father wouldn't be a big deal. But it always would be. She knew that really. And Gran knew it too. Who your father was was a huge part of your identity. Over the years I'd learned to live with the gaping hole, telling myself it wasn't important. I'd made it in life without him, and without knowing who he was. Now it sat at the front of my mind, battering my every thought. Who the hell *was* he?

Stop.

Stop now.

No more spiralling.

Focus.

Game face on.

Beautifully dressed couples were laughing as they entered the Guildhall. No sign of Ke. My shoulders dropped a bit. Should I wait here in the crowds and avoid the small talk in there with everyone? It would all be about Lismore and my plans. And I wouldn't be able to deflect their questions with questions of my own. I no longer knew who'd done what in the town. Mum and Tony had been that source of knowledge. Micki kept me abreast of the most salacious stuff, but that wasn't a good start for opening a light conversation. 'Oh, I heard that your husband had an affair with so and so.' No, definitely not something to be discussed today of all days.

Somehow, I had to reach within me to find all my previous love for this day and hold it at the front of my mind. I needed to focus on my early years, when it had been all candy floss, fun fairs and first kisses, then try to freeze time there. If I managed that, this would be easy. It was only later that things had turned into a tragedy. Could I have done anything differently? Absolutely. I knew this in my heart and soul. But I just needed to remind myself that I'd done what I thought was right at the time. The way I'd treated Ke was the bit I'd done badly. Really badly, in fact. I'd been cowardly. This was what kept me awake at night, and what I was afraid of now as I saw him standing alone by the door. I couldn't do this.

Unable to move back or forward, I stood like a statue. Ke glanced at his watch. Nothing in his stance gave anything away. Once, I could have read his thoughts, but now, it was all guesswork. He couldn't be looking forward to this either. My behaviour had been terrible, and even if the years had eased things, I'd hurt him badly. I was a shit. Not that I hadn't had my reasons. I loved him but, in the end, I'd made the choice without him. I'd had three choices, and none of them had been good. Had I picked the easiest? It had seemed to be the only viable one if I loved him. The other option would have meant following the fate of the Richards women. And I didn't believe in fate.

Now, sixteen years later, that pain moved inside me, disturbing all the other loss. I couldn't go through with today. Surely I could beg off sick or blame work? There had to be something I could do.

Ke glanced up and looked my way. There was no place to hide, dressed as I was in a gown and wearing a hat. I could bow my head and pretend I hadn't seen him, but he deserved better than that. I nodded to him and put one foot in front of the other. Weaving my way through the crowd, I tried to think of what, if anything, I could say. Maybe silence was the only answer.

Ke held out a hand as I reached the steps and he smiled vaguely, as though greeting a distant acquaintance. I hesitated. This was a man I'd known most of my life, and we were acting like all those years before hadn't happened. It was wrong, but at the same time, it was the only way to get through this.

Thankfully, we were both wearing gloves, so there was no real contact. Which was a weird thought. Why did I need protecting? He was the one *I'd* hurt. He had never been anything but wonderful to me, even after I ghosted him. I took his hand, holding my breath. Nothing. I relaxed a bit. Unlike the past, when even a touch through a gloved hand could set my heart racing. But, to be honest, my heart was already at full speed.

We entered the Guildhall together without saying a word. This was good, but I hated it too. He dropped my hand and flexed his, probably in disgust. It was clear he was not the one who'd put my name forward for this dance. Again, I wondered who had. Was someone standing on the side laughing as we squirmed?

Inside the hall, it was raucous with people calling out to friends and complimenting appearances. The chatter died down as we worked our way through the crowd to the front of the spiral. I wasn't sure this was a good thing. I was more used to the good-natured banter than this almost reverent silence. Was I the cause? Was Lismore the reason?

Names started to be called out as though it were the attendance register at school. And, to be honest, it did feel a bit like that, with the added complication of people in their finest. Aside from the odd wedding or a day at Ascot, most men never donned a morning suit. The women were beautifully dressed too, in full-length gowns like me, but with hats fit for a wedding. I tilted my head down, so no one would be able to see my face, and I couldn't see their scrutiny. They all knew what I looked like but this, of course, was different. I was no longer just a daughter of Helston but the owner of Lismore.

Surely Flora Day could happen in the future without the house being involved? The festivities had taken place long before it was built. Yes, the tradition of going through the houses and shops was fun, but it wasn't an absolute must. It was good to have a break partway through the dance, as it required some endurance, but another place could easily be found for this. Maybe there wasn't a garden as lovely, or in a place so central, but traditions change and evolve over time. Or perhaps any new owner would be only too happy to continue the tradition it held.

Ke and I reached the front, where the mayor greeted us both.

'This is wonderful.' He beamed.

I smiled in reply. Anything I said would be used against me once I put Lismore on the market. But Ke didn't speak either. Clearly, we were both of the same mind.

'I realise you both haven't had a chance to practice, but once learned, a bit like riding a bike, the steps are never forgotten.' He laughed. 'Ke, you know Bill Penny and Helen Trelawney, and Flora, I'm sure you remember them?'

I nodded, still having no ability to speak, just to smile woodenly.

'This will be fun,' said Helen. She shimmied her shoulders, making her dress sparkle.

'Such an honour,' said Bill, nodding at me.

Ke cleared his throat. Was he thinking of when we were eight and it had all been new? Or of the year he'd danced with his wife? Or of our last dance, sixteen years ago? Hopefully, he wasn't thinking of that. There were so many better memories. Had the events following that day been different, maybe I would have looked back on things through a golden haze, remembering the irresistible cocktail of love, hormones and cider. But it was best to push that to the back of my mind.

'Don't look so concerned,' the mayor said, laughing.

Ke swallowed, his discomfort palpable. There was nothing I could do or say that would make this easier for either of us. In fact, it would probably make it worse. Just focusing on the dance and reaching the end was all I could do. What I wouldn't have given to know who put us here.

The mayor stepped onto the platform and called everyone to attention. 'It's almost twelve.' He paused. 'We will begin the dance today at twelve o' two, after the two minutes silence in remembrance of VE Day, eighty years ago today, and all those who gave their lives for our freedom.'

Silence was good. I could do that.

A hush descended, and the cry of a child outside was the only noise. With the first strike of twelve, heads dropped. Two minutes to remember. I thought of Gran and her mother, both who'd danced on this day eighty years ago. Flora Day and VE Day combined. Happiness and loss but, most importantly, survival. I said a silent prayer of thanks.

The big bass drum sounded. Ke looked at me. Those sad eyes reminded me of the lost boy of the past. They held a hint of confusion, questioning.

It hurt.

The questions he was asking I still couldn't answer.

His expression changed, and a mask fell.

I desperately wanted to explain, but words wouldn't form.

Movement reached us. First out were the officials. Ke held out his hand, and I placed mine in his. The band played on and in moments we were dancing out of the Guildhall, with the sun shining brightly.

Step, step, step, hop, step.

Step, step, step, hop, step.

People waved, and I spied Micki – she was grinning like a loon. As we headed towards Meneage Street, the music ran through me. My heart missed a beat. *I can't do this.*

One misstep, and then my feet found the old pattern again. Ke didn't falter. His hand held mine steady. We could do this, I prayed. The music changed, and Ke dropped my hand as Bill came towards me. We spun around. I tried not to listen to the jolly shouts, to see the phones held aloft, or the proper cameras of the television teams and newspapers. A drone buzzed overhead. It was all so different from the last time.

In seconds I was back to Ke and we spun around. It was almost easy to forget the now and to step back into the past. But other than the smile Ke put on for the watching crowds, his face was blank. As was mine. We both held our masks firmly in place.

Lismore, Cross Street, Helston, Cornwall

---

1 April 2007,

My dearest girl,

This is not an April Fool but a letter full of concern. When we spoke last night, you were low and homesick and feeling you were missing out by being away. We have all felt this and it is normal but not nice. I know you are knee deep in research for an essay and beginning to prepare for your upcoming exams. All of this is pulling on your energy reserves. Be gentle with yourself. Remember to spend time outside. The library is your friend, but so is the big sky above you as you walk there. Take a longer walk. Spend longer over a pint with friends in the pub. Let them know you are down. Don't hide it away and pretend. You will have been there for them so let them be there for you.

Remind yourself of your goals. You have so much you want to achieve and I know you will do it. Think of the travel you long for. Place these things at the forefront of your mind and then allow yourself to reach for them. Stretch yourself. Helston will always be a part of you and there for you. Think of Gran saying those words to you as she did to me. Take Helston with you and the world will be a better place for it.

I love you and I believe the world is yours. Reach out and grab it and I wait to watch you fly.

Love,
Tony xxxx

Twenty-Four

Flora Day, 2007

Tuesday
Age: 20
Forecast: Cloudy

I'd had to stay late to meet with my professor so I didn't get home until nearly eleven. It took a while to locate Micki, and then I spoke briefly to Ke, who was working the bar at The Bell. He had tomorrow off because we were doing the Early Morning and the Evening dances again. In fact, he was due here any minute. I quickly picked up my pen and wrote:

> *Another Flora Day. Another dance with Ke. I wish I could stop thinking about him.*
> *Not likely.*

Closing the diary, I looked in the mirror. I'd chosen something totally out of character for me – a cherry-red dress. But it worked, and I felt like a different person. A bit like how I'd felt when I'd started insisting everyone call me Flo instead of Flora. It had marked a change in me, and this dress was definitely marking something. I looked pretty. That wasn't a word I would have used about myself before. Micki was pretty; in fact, she was beautiful, with blonde hair and deep, brown eyes. She always drew everyone's attention. But that wasn't me. My hair was dark brown, my eyes were green, and I usually always chose clothes I was sure would fit me but never draw attention. Until this dress, which said *look at me.* Part of me was terrified, while the other part was so damn excited.

Mum had already left and was doing her thing with the Hal an Tow. I glugged the last of my coffee, then brushed my teeth, wondering if this dress was the right thing after all. Wasn't it best to stay in the background?

'Flo?' Ke called as he walked through the back door.

'Morning,' I said, trying to quell my nerves as I came into the kitchen to greet him.

He whistled. 'You look amazing.'

'Really?' I held my breath. He wouldn't lie, would he?

'Yes.' He picked up my hand and twirled me around. 'Cinderella shall go to the ball.' My heart started racing, and it wasn't from the exertion. *Connection.* I shouldn't feel this way; it wasn't workable. But I did. I was due to be in London on an internship all summer while Ke would be here surfing. And I had another year of uni, while he'd be climbing the surfing ranks. It wasn't possible for us to be together. I was learning that the heart doesn't listen to sense, though.

Ke was still holding my hand, and we stood staring at each other. His eyes didn't leave mine, and we leaned closer. *He's going to kiss me.*

Kiss me, I willed silently, leaning more. *Kiss me.*

We'd kissed on New Year's Eve. We'd been drunk and surrounded by people. Micki had then quietly reminded me, again, that Ke was hers. I hadn't taken her seriously – she was so deep in with another new boyfriend, Rob. I still hadn't told her how I really felt about Ke but once she knew, it would clear this obstacle in my head. Or at least I hoped it would. Friendship was everything. He was just as much a friend as Micki was to me, but what we had was different.

I held my breath, waiting, wanting, needing.

We both jumped as my phone rang.

Mum's number flashed on the screen. Ke dropped my hand and took a step away.

'Hey, Mum.' I sounded breathless.

'Forgot my flower wreath in my room. Can you drop it here?' she asked.

'Yeah.'

'Thanks, love.'

I put my phone down. 'Need to grab something for Mum.'

'Sure.' Ke shoved his hands in his pockets. He didn't look too comfortable, but I wasn't either. This, whatever this was, was hanging between us and needed resolving.

At uni I'd tried falling for other guys – I really had – but none clicked. Some were great on an intellectual level, and others were fit, but none were Ke. If I couldn't persuade Micki to release her 'hold' on him, this could become tricky. It wasn't as if she'd ever made a play for Ke properly, apart from the little Flora Day kisses. And he certainly hadn't for her, even after the kissing incidents had occurred. In fact, there hadn't been anyone else for Ke that I knew of. Well, no one serious. He'd snogged Kate once when we were all at a party. It had been the first time he'd tried weed, and he swore off it after that. He'd said if he thought beer goggles were bad, weed ones were dire. He'd been so embarrassed afterwards, and she'd followed him around like the love-struck girl in Harry Potter. Micki never let him forget it.

I hadn't been able to forget it for other reasons. I'd wanted to be Kate so badly it hurt. There was no place to put how I felt. I couldn't talk to Micki, Mum, and certainly not to Ke. The next day I'd spoken to Tony, though. He'd listened without saying a word. I hadn't been asking for advice, but I needed to get this want, this desire, outside of myself. The only thing Tony had said was that best friends were worth doing everything for. This was certainly true. I put Micki and Ke above everyone, including myself. This kept me sane, thinking of others first.

Clutching Mum's wreath, I set off with Ke. It didn't take us long, and Mum was grateful. But I couldn't stop wondering if Ke would have kissed me if she hadn't called. Maybe I should kiss him now. But what if that wasn't what he'd been planning? I might just have had a bug in my hair or something that he'd been gazing at.

The number of people taking part in the morning and evening dances had grown so much over the years. In the past, the participants had been fed breakfast after their morning exertions, but there were now far too many for the organisers to do that. Ke and I moved into our place in the middle of the pack. All around us, there were yawns and banter in abundance. I was glad I didn't have a hangover, unlike Micki and Tom, who made up our foursome.

At seven, the big drum sounded, and I fought the urge to cry. There was something about the beginning that always got me. We were all ready to dance the four miles. This was a straight run through the town, encompassing it all but not going through gardens, houses or shops. That would happen later. Endurance was required for now but with Ke at my side and well-wishers lining the streets, my feet and my heart were light.

The Evening Dance had finished, and I'd lost Micki and Ke in the crush of people. I roamed the streets, popping my head into various pubs. The phone signal was worse than usual. It was probably the incoming weather. The day had been dry, if cool. The wind had picked up, and it didn't feel like the spring we'd been welcoming. I shivered and thought about heading home. I really wanted nothing more to drink, so there was no point in just joining any old group of people. That was what Micki would have done, but it wasn't me. I envied her ease in doing things like that. Ke was more like me, watching events from the outside.

I left The Red and headed home feeling a bit like the bluebells hanging limply off the doorways. This morning, things had looked fresh, but now the decorations were more tired than the dancers. By the time everyone was up tomorrow, the finery adorning the buildings and houses would be gone, and the countdown to next year's Flora would begin.

Tony came out of The Rodney and waved.

'What's up?' he asked as he neared me. 'Not feeling it this year?' He placed an arm across my shoulders.

'Thinking of calling it a night.' I sighed.

He stopped walking and turned to me. 'It's not yet nine. The night is young and it's Flora Day, your day.'

I grunted. 'No one to play with.'

He raised his eyebrows. 'The town is full of people.'

I crossed my arms.

'But,' he whispered. 'You only need one to play with, and he's in The Rodney.'

I kissed his cheek. 'Thank you.'

He handed me his house keys. 'Can you grab Ke and check I locked the house?'

I stared at him.

'I was distracted and think I did, but I'm not sure and I can't be bothered to check.'

'OK. Will do.'

'Have fun,' he said as he set off down the street. I felt like I'd been played, but I wasn't complaining.

The air was sweet with the scent of lilacs. Ke used his phone as a torch as we wandered around the outside of Lismore, checking all the doors. We came to a standstill in the silence of the garden. You'd never have known you were in the centre of a town that was partying hard.

'This place,' Ke said, close beside me, 'is so special.'

I looked about, remembering past dances.

'Our first dance and my first visit here.' He paused. 'It all still feels so exciting.'

'Exciting?' I didn't see that, but a calm oasis.

'Yes, exciting. You pass the front of the house and it looks impressive, but then there are these tall walls around it and they show you nothing.' He waved a hand. 'All this hidden from view, it's pure magic.'

'I get that.' I breathed deeply. Spring. It was here despite the north wind making me shiver. There was something so intoxicating when everything was bursting forth – bluebells covered the woodland floors, primroses tucked in nooks and crannies, and leaves unfurled as the sunlight lingered a little longer every day. It was all promise of warmer and finer days to come. People said we were full of promise too, or they had done when we were younger. There was potential in us. I saw it as longing.

'It's mad that Tony lives here all alone.' Ke slowly turned around.

'Yeah, I know. I suggested that Mum should move in. It's so big they wouldn't even see each other.'

Ke laughed and turned to me as the distant sound of music drifted on the air. It was a slow, mellow tune I knew but couldn't place. He held out his arms, and I slipped into them. Resting my head on his chest, I listened to his heartbeat as we swayed together. Nothing had ever felt so good. The vying emotions of peace and need ran through me. We couldn't do this, but we couldn't not. Both of us wanted it.

'Ke?' I whispered.

'Hmm,' he said into my hair.

I had to think clearly. If we crossed this line, then nothing, absolutely nothing, would ever be the same. It would risk the Musketeers. My friendship with Micki too. There would be no light balance between us, no playfulness, as the dynamics would change. This I told myself firmly as I nestled closer to him. He wanted me. I wanted him. It shouldn't be complicated.

Ke's hand slipped down my spine. All coherent thought

faded. Surely we could be lovers *and* friends? Some people managed it.

'Hello?' a woman's voice called. Ke's hand dropped, and we stepped apart like naughty kids.

'Hi,' Ke said.

'There you are.' Mrs Wearne walked down the hill towards us. 'I left my bag in the house.'

I walked with her to the door and waited there for her. Meanwhile Micki rocked up with Wilf. Interruptions, so many of them, beginning with Mum's call earlier. The magic was broken, and I knew tonight wasn't going to go as I'd hoped and dreamed.

Twenty-Five
Flora Day, 2008

Thursday
Age: 21
Forecast: Overcast

Everything was hanging in the air at the moment. Papers and exams loomed in front of me, the application to do my masters in Film Studies, and the endless waiting for replies on internships. In fact, I shouldn't have come home, but Mum said the break would do me good. This morning I'd written in my diary this question:

> *Will I or won't I get the internship with my dream production company?*

Now I held the envelope in my hand. It had been delivered to the wrong address annoyingly, but Mrs Wearne had just handed it to me. This was my future. My hands shook as I opened it. Why had I even checked now, in the middle of Flora Day? I closed my eyes. Did I land the internship at Landmark Productions? It was my number one choice, making exactly the type of films I loved and believed in. But did I want to know now, this minute? If I didn't get it, it would ruin the day.

Micki walked into the garden at the back of The Red carrying three pints. It was the break before the Midday Dance started up again, its second part. Ke and I were dancing again at five, so we couldn't get too pissed now. Doing the Early Morning and Evening Dances had seemed like a good idea when we signed up for them again but, at this point, less so. Ke was currently chatting to someone I didn't know on the other side of the garden.

With the pints on the table, Micki sent me a funny look. 'What's up? You have a pained expression on your face, like you need to poo but can't make up your mind.'

'Charming.' I took a sip of beer, letting its coolness calm my insides. I handed the letter to Micki. She sent me a sideways glance.

'There's a response on the internship,' I said.

'And?'

'I haven't read it yet.' I didn't want to, even though I was dying to know.

'Fool.' I watched her face as she scanned the paper, but she was good at poker for this reason.

'Well?'

'I thought you didn't want to know yet.' She handed Ke his pint as he returned to the table.

'Bitch,' I said, not meaning it.

She stuck her tongue out at me.

'Ladies,' Ke said, looking between us. Micki handed the letter to him, and he glanced down at it.

'She doesn't want to know whether she got it or not. But, of course, she opened the letter anyway, then couldn't read it.'

Ke laughed, covering the weird expression on his face. 'Fair.'

'What's fair?' I asked, grabbing the letter back.

'Today is Flora Day and you don't need to know right now,' Ke said, picking up his pint.

Micki sent him a funny look. Did that imply I hadn't got it, and he didn't want me to be upset for the rest of the day?

I gripped the paper, debating what the hell was going on here.

'You know you want to.' Micki grinned.

'But does she? Isn't ignorance bliss?' Ke cracked his knuckles.

'Go on and read it Flo. Put yourself out of your self-imposed misery, so we can enjoy Flora without you being in your head the whole time.'

'Are you going to do what Micki says?' Ke asked, looking at me keenly.

Micki sent me a taunting look. My hand shook as I held the letter.

'Open or not, that is your choice.' Micki stared hard at me. It was my choice but I was terrified too.

My mouth was dry. Fear of failure and fear if I didn't get it, it would indeed ruin the day.

'Well?' Ke tilted his head, waiting. Did he want me to open it or not? I couldn't tell.

'This is beyond boring now.' Micki stood. 'Don't open it then and let's do something, anything but sit here and watch you be afraid of what might be in the letter.' She huffed. 'I thought you had more guts but maybe Ke's right. Don't open it and be ignorant.' She sent Ke a funny look.

They were winding me up, but something else was at play too. Rather than dive into it, I shoved the letter back into the envelope, and into my pocket. A couple more hours couldn't hurt. Later, when I had a moment of privacy, I'd read it, and maybe then figure out what was going on. Right now, I just needed to move these two on from whatever was playing between them.

Never had I enjoyed the Evening Dance so much. A happy buzz enveloped me, and it made the inning and outing of shops even more fun. The old tradition worked its magic as the dance and music seeped their way through my skin, to my blood, where the rhythm played. It was only once we'd reached Lismore, and were having a drink, that I had a moment to myself without Ke – he'd gone to help a dancer who had slipped into the pond. I pulled the letter out of my pocket and opened it.

Shit. They'd offered me the internship, but had required my response by today! It was now five forty-five. I typed their number into my phone as fast as my fingers could manage. There was no answer, so I left a rushed, slightly breathless message on the contact's answerphone, saying yes, I very much wanted to accept their offer. I could only hope I was in time. As I hung up and put the phone back in my pocket, I looked up to see Ke walking towards me, damp but not too bad. What had he been playing at, saying I shouldn't read the letter today? Did he not want me to get this, potentially my perfect job?

Before I could ask, the band struck up, time to move on, and he grabbed my hand, leading me off to finish the dance. All the joy I'd been feeling withered and died with each step. Ke kept sending me questioning looks, but during the dance wasn't the time to chat. And with the way I was feeling, as though my best friends had deliberately sabotaged my chances at my dream career, I wasn't sure I ever wanted to speak to him again.

Micki was quite drunk when I caught up with her. She had wine eye. I'm not sure when she'd switched from beer to wine, but it had taken its toll. I needed to get some sense out of her, though. Immediately after the dance, Ke had been called off to help with a collapsed tent, and I hadn't seen him since. I didn't want to either.

'Micki, why didn't you tell me I needed to reply today to the production company?'

She blinked. 'I did.'

'No, you didn't. You and Ke had some weird banter about it going on.' It was taking all my strength not to scream.

'Well, you've clearly read it now.'

I ground my teeth. 'Probably too late.'

She shrugged. 'You won't be such a wuss next time then.'

I looked at her hard.

'Or you won't listen to Ke over me.' She slurred her words a bit, but she was right. I'd paid more attention to his words than hers. What did that say about me?

Micki looked up from her glass. 'You did call them back today, right?'

I nodded.

'They didn't say it had to be by a certain time, just today.'

'True.'

'Then forget about it for tonight and get pissed.' She waved her arm around, knocking over her nearly-empty glass. She grinned. 'You can start by buying both of us a drink.'

It was almost midnight when I bumped into Ke as I was heading, or slightly staggering, home. I'd just dropped Micki at her parents' having pried her out of the arms of Tom, who was in a worse shape than Micki. He'd been hopeful it was his lucky night, but wasn't Micki going to sleep with the boy who'd pushed me into the dirt and was now married with a child on my watch.

'Hey,' Ke grinned. He didn't have wine eye, which I no doubt had, but he was pissed.

I bit back what I wanted to say and remained silent.

'You OK?' He stepped closer. He smelled of stale beer and cigarettes. Not that he smoked, but he'd clearly been with someone who did.

'Yeah,' I lied. I was still seething, and no one had called me back in response to my acceptance message. Checking my phone every five minutes had done nothing but kill my battery. Each time I'd looked, I'd cursed Ke. Maybe not fairly, but as the night went on, the more certain I became that if I'd lost this chance, he was to blame.

'I may be drunk but even I can tell you're far from OK.' He leaned against a wall.

'Hmm.'

'That's not an answer. How about...'

I cut in, saying, 'Neither of us need another drink.'

'A cup of tea.' He half-smiled at me. How could I stay angry with him when he looked at me like that?

'I guess.'

'Yours or mine?' he asked.

I thought of Mum, who was no doubt enjoying the sleep of the virtuous, or Ke's makeshift place in Mrs Long's garden shed. He did her garden in exchange for the space. When his mother's continued drug use had grown worse, and she'd even started to become violent at times, his dad had told the boys it would be best for them to live elsewhere if they could. My heart went out to them all, and I'd wanted to offer my friend more support, but Ke still avoided the subject if I ever brought it up – he didn't want to talk about her.

'Yours.'

'Good choice, although doesn't your mum have saffron buns?'

I laughed. 'She does but we might wake her.'

'Or we could detour via yours and very quietly get them.'

'OK.' We began the walk up the street to Mum's and I had to ask him. It wouldn't stay inside. 'Why did you tell me not to read the letter until tomorrow, when you knew they needed a reply today?'

He stopped walking and looked down. I waited, not patiently, but I did. When he finally looked up, he said, 'Honestly, it was a confused strategy.'

I raised an eyebrow.

'You know how I hate it when you leave?'

'Do you?' I frowned.

'Well, here you are, about to do it again and...'

'And what?' I crossed my arms, not wanting to be angry, wanting to understand.

'Well, I was trying two strategies to make my conflicting desires work.'

'You're not selling it.' My arms remained crossed firmly against my chest.

'No, and I guess I did a shit job of it earlier.'

I nodded.

'I figured if I said not to open it, you would.' He shrugged in an endearing way, and I hated him for it.

'I'm not a child, you don't have to use reverse psychology on me.'

'No, and I kinda also hoped you would think like that and not open it until it was too late, then have to spend the summer here…' He looked at his feet. 'Here with me.' A shiver of anticipation ran through me. Did he want me as I wanted him?

'I see.' And I did. How could I want to kiss him and to hit him at the same time?

'Do you forgive me?' He looked me straight in the eyes, and I could see he was sorry. Truly sorry.

'I didn't mean to play games. I want you to succeed.' He took my hand in his. 'I really do. And I know there's no steady job in film here, even with the German crews arriving every summer to film the Rosamund Pilcher books.' He drew a breath. 'Have you thought of studying German?'

I laughed. 'Nein.'

'You forgive me?' He stepped closer.

Was he going to kiss me? I wanted that, but it would complicate things. If I were lucky, I'd be away for the summer. Now was not the time to start something.

'Yes.' I gave him a hug and then pulled back. 'But I might not if I find out I've lost the internship.'

'Fair.' His stomach growled. 'Saffron buns?'

'Yes.'

He threw an arm across my shoulder, and all the mixed-up emotions of the day settled. If I didn't get the London internship, I could brush up on my non-existent German. And we were friends again. Just friends.

Twenty-Six

2025

8 May, 12:15 p.m.

We had just come out the front door of Boots and I was ready for it to all finish, but the dance was no way near ending, it had only just started. The band played on, and Ke and I moved through the steps with Bill and Helen like old pros. Which I suppose we were. But the last time Ke had done this dance was with his wife. Each step had to be painful for him. He didn't want to be doing this any more than I did, and he had a better reason not to want to.

In order not to think about Ke, I focused on what I knew of the history of Flora Day, or any May Day celebration. They all heralded the arrival of spring after the hard winter. It was pagan, it was joyful and it was about rebirth or fertility. That it all still happened was a bit mad. Our lives were so different now to the people who'd first danced, welcoming the arrival of May with its warmth and abundance. What would a person from five hundred or more years ago have made of the ritualised processional dance happening now? Would they have seen themselves in it? Would they have thought they might find their partner for life as they twirled through the borough town? Shit, that wasn't what I wanted to be thinking about as Ke held my hand. The gloves we both wore were not the protection I'd thought they would be.

The music changed and we twirled through the next store, and down the aisle past the furniture. The beat changed again and Ke took my hand. Tears hovered close to the surface. *Focus.* Not on Ke and the touch of his hand, but on something else. Helston.

If only the story between Ke and I had been a simple one. If I'd only kept to the rules: never fall in love with your best friend. Or maybe if I had never come back. There were too many 'if only's and today I had no choice but to face the now and all its ugly repercussions. Ke's face told me all of that. He certainly hadn't deserved what I'd done to him.

We danced down Church Street, with the kennels happily burbling having been redirected here away from Coinagehall Street for the day. Watching the water, I nearly missed my footing and Ke grabbed my arm. His look was stern and I pulled back, but the music altered and we changed partners. The quiet beauty of Cross Street was disturbed with the throng of people watching our progress to Lismore.

Lismore.

The very reason I was here. Tricia, in honour of Mum and Tony, was waiting to lead the dancers into the garden. The band entered first and stood in the drive, playing us all in. Wilf grinned at me and Ke, and for a brief moment it was like old times. It was like my final dance sixteen years ago. Ke and I and the magic of the day. But moments like that in life were fleeting. No one could be, and possibly should be, that happy for any length of time. It wasn't good for you, as life would inevitably take it away, and all that remained would be hollow memories.

A stab of sadness suddenly hit me that I hadn't been here last year to see Tony do this for the final time, and I felt even sadder that Mum wasn't here now to see Tricia in her finery, as well as me. What would she have said, or what would Gran have said? Actually, Gran was easy to guess: 'It's about bloody time the

Richards women took their rightful place.' I smiled. Mum might have thought the same, but she'd been much more careful with her words. Was that because of the secrets she'd been carrying? The weight of it must have been exhausting, with me constantly on about wanting a father, and not any father but my own. I thought I'd made my peace with the unknowing, but I now realised it had been more about burying it. I scanned the crowds gathered in the sunshine, wondering, always wondering, was my father here.

We finally stopped dancing and suddenly I was face to face with Ke, the moment I'd been dreading. I still didn't know what to say to him.

'Why did you come?' he asked, in a voice so quiet no one around us could have heard. I met his angry glance. I understood it.

'I...' I paused. What could I say? This part I hadn't rehearsed. How could I? 'Tony.'

'Blaming a dead man.'

'No.' I was handed a glass of fizz and Micki came rushing towards us.

'Just look at the two of you together again after all this time.' She beamed like this was a good thing. Why was she acting so oblivious to what she must know was unbelievably awkward for us? She'd asked about the rift between Ke and I often enough in the past. Of course I'd never explained what really happened, but still she should understand this wasn't easy.

I took a big sip while Ke sent her daggers. This wasn't a way to get into his good books. But then Micki had never been known to do anything other than say what was on her mind.

'Later I thought it would be great if the four Musketeers had a drink together.'

Ke shook his head. 'Sorry, I've got Matilda.'

'I thought of that and asked my niece if she could watch her for a bit.'

Ke looked like thunder.

'I knew it would be OK, as she already babysits for you.' She smiled sweetly back at him. What was her game?

He sighed and then took a sip of the fizz too.

Glancing around, I looked for someone else to chat to, anyone at all, but there was no escape. Ke's eyes focussed at anything but me. Even though I understood, this didn't make it feel like anything other than a kick in the gut. One I deserved.

Things couldn't have been more awkward. Ke stood resolutely beside me as person after person came up and either directly, like Barbara Williams, or indirectly, like David Trengelly, asked me what my plans were for the house.

'Flora, you're so lucky to have had such a legacy from Tony. The Clemens family were an odd bunch and plagued with such rotten luck.' Barbara fanned herself. 'To lose one son, the one who could have produced an heir, and then to lose the other to the same disease as old man Clemens.' She tut-tutted the way she always had whenever Micki and I had walked past her after dying our hair pink the summer we were seventeen. Currently Micki was 'strawberry blonde'. It was more orange than strawberry, though I wasn't going to point that out to her. My hair was lightly highlighted these days, thanks to Vlad, who ruthlessly told me that my natural dark hair was aging and that didn't fly in LA.

'So, Flora, what are your plans?'

Best to answer the question. 'On Monday I return to the set of *Death Comes to Cornwall,* and by Friday I'll be on a plane to New York.' I gave her my best sweet smile, as if I didn't know this wasn't what she'd been asking.

'That's fascinating,' she said, and before she could launch on, I continued.

'I'm excited about the series, and I'm now working on casting a new film, which is why I'm off to New York. Have you seen the announcement for *Lethal Intent*, the latest Tom Cruise blockbuster?'

She pulled her head back as if I'd hit her, which made me want to laugh. The corner of Ke's mouth lifted in the way I'd always found wildly sexy in the distant past. This hadn't changed. Ke was far more handsome than he'd ever been, even with a ridiculous top hat on. His blond hair contained silver now, and the lines around his eyes and mouth added to the appeal. His face showed the life he'd lived outside, on the water, as well as the emotions he'd lived through, particularly in recent years.

Finally, Barbara Williams wandered away with no answer to satisfy her and, as she had no interest in crime thrillers, no real gossip to share around.

'So, what *is* your plan?' Ke asked.

I cast him a sideways glance. What should I tell him?

'I know you'll have one, as you never do anything without planning it.'

You.

I didn't plan you.

Us.

It happened and *then* we planned.

But he knew that.

'Nothing at present. Probate first.' This of course was true. Best not to lie, especially to Ke.

He looked up at the house. I couldn't read his mind, and I wished I could. Though I doubted even if I could, that I would like what I'd see there.

Twenty-Seven

Flora Day, 2009

Friday
Age: 22
Forecast: Sunny

This morning in my diary I'd written my dreams for the future.

A job in the film industry.
Ke.

Part of me knew these were mutually exclusive, but this was the dream, so I could have both. One I'd approach with open drive, and the other I'd keep a secret. Ke had just won the English National Surfing Championships days ago at Watergate Bay, home ground. The latter part was key for him. He'd hated leaving Cornwall to pursue his dreams, and was considering abandoning the goal of the world championship.

Cornwall.

Helston.

Home.

These things didn't drive me, though – or maybe they did differently. Mum and Gran's lives had been limited to this place because of each having a child. There was Gran's whole Richards women fated thing. The world could have belonged to Mum, but she'd given it up for me. This still bothered me, along with not knowing who my father was. Maybe that was what was pulling me out of Helston. But I knew that my grounding here would allow me to fly. And I couldn't wait.

Sitting at The Blue on Flora Day with people partying around me, I felt something was different. Maybe it was me. My education was done and thanks to Tony, I was off to LA to shadow an acquaintance of his for a few months. The world was finally going my way. Everything inside me fizzed. That could also have been the booze, or Ke. He was being so attentive, and we were having such fun. Wilf was dancing with his new girlfriend, Deana. They were adorable, if you could call a man as big as Wilf adorable. He was totally into her, and we all liked her, so hopefully she felt the same about him. I'm not sure if I could cope with someone breaking his heart. Micki was glued to her latest boyfriend's side and had decided she wouldn't dance this year, because he was from London and didn't get all the Flora Day stuff. But, looking at him now, he seemed to be enjoying himself.

I'd had enough of the noise and longed for a bit of peace.

'Fresh air?' Ke asked. How did he know what I was thinking?

'Yes,' I answered, trying to catch Micki's eye before we left. Waving madly didn't work, so I detoured to her side. My words, even shouted above the music, didn't seem to reach her but her boyfriend nodded. Ke grabbed my hand as we wove our way through the crowds. It was quieter once we were out on the street, and I felt lightheaded. What I wanted was the sound of the sea, not the buzz of a crowd. But both of us were too drunk to drive to the beach.

The night was balmy, and the streets were full of people. It was a Friday night, and it was Flora. The party would be going strong through tomorrow.

'I don't know about you but I've had enough of the crowds.'

Ke continued to hold my hand. It still felt like coming home after all these years, except now it tingled with something more.

'Me too. Last night, this morning, all day.'

Yup.' Our steps took us along Church Street, and we wound our way towards Lismore. Tony and Mum had last been seen in The Red, with Tony holding court. We bypassed the house and went straight into the garden. Evidence of the festivities had already been cleared. Only the portaloos at the far side of the garden were visible.

Two years ago, we'd stood here on the brink of something but had been interrupted, or maybe saved, by Micki and Wilf's arrival. I hesitated now. Had things changed? No, nothing had. Ke was still my best friend. We hadn't crossed the invisible line. It didn't mean I didn't think about crossing it every single day, though. In my head, we'd been lovers, lifetime partners, soulmates forever. Nothing could separate us.

Now, standing here, I didn't know what to think or do. Ke was so close I could feel the heat of his body. In fact, all I really wanted to think about was the feel of him. I moved the fingers on my left hand, reaching out to his. And they wrapped around mine. There was an urgency to it. Hunger. Was he thinking the same thing I was?

I leaned towards him. He *was* thinking the same thing. But maybe we weren't thinking at all. I pushed that idea out of my head as I tiptoed forward and placed my mouth against his. He stilled. I stopped breathing. The distant sound of the Black Eyed Peas's 'Boom Boom Pow' played somewhere nearby. My heart raced to the music's beat.

The kiss deepened, and we moved in unison. My hands travelled across his back and under his shirt. The feel of him. Warm. Solid. His hand moved from my back to my waist. I gasped when his fingers trailed across my ribs and higher.

He breathed my name against my mouth.

'Yes,' I whispered again and again. This is what I wanted. Had always wanted. I pulled his shirt off, and mine followed. The feel of skin against skin was too much to bear. I tugged at his jeans.

'Flo, you sure?'

'Yes, you?'

'Yes.' He groaned and kicked his jeans aside, lowered me to the ground, before he helped me out of mine. The grass was cool against my skin. I gasped but soon forgot everything as we slowly discovered each other totally.

'I love you,' Ke whispered.

I laughed, and the tall clock in the hallway chimed eleven p.m.

'That's funny, is it?' He propped himself on an elbow and stared at me. The sheets on the bed were a mess. We'd moved into the house an hour ago, when light rain began to fall.

'I know, because you almost told me years ago.' I traced his mouth with my finger. 'And I've been waiting years to hear you say those words.'

'It hasn't changed.' He nuzzled my neck, and shivers ran across my bare skin.

Did I dare tell him how I felt? It had been my secret for so long I wasn't sure I could say the words. 'I love you too,' I finally whispered.

He stilled.

Silence spread between us. Should I have said anything? And what should I do now?

'Ke?' I asked in a barely audible voice, doubting everything. Had I ruined things by saying it back?

Light from the hallway suddenly streamed in under the door, and it hit me that everything had changed.

Everything.

Tony had arrived back home, humming the tune of the Hal an Tow to himself. We didn't dare move. Tony wouldn't mind our being here, or would he? I didn't want to know. An icy gust blew through the window. Goosebumps covered my skin, and our confessions of love hung between us.

The church clock chimed the half hour. I waited to turn into a pumpkin, but nothing happened. Ke then leaned over and kissed me deeply, and I responded with all my being. His silence had started to eat at me, but lying here with him, skin to skin, was all I wanted to do. For years I'd tried to imagine what it would be like to do what we'd just done not once, not twice, but three times. The last being the best.

'Are you OK?' he whispered, touching the goosebumps covering my stomach.

'Chilly but never better.'

'Me too.' He dropped light kisses across my shoulder, sending warmth through me. 'I've wanted to be here for so long.'

I pushed myself up onto my elbows. 'What, naked in a bedroom in Lismore?'

He chuckled. 'Definitely.'

'I'll let Tony know.' Tony's bedroom was down the hall. This was the room I'd always used whenever I stayed. It had been cheeky of me to bring Ke in here, but somehow it had felt right at the time. That could have been the Jägerbombs we'd done earlier, though.

'I know where the key is now too,' he whispered into my collarbone.

'True, Tony will have to be on the lookout for tanned surfers invading his space.'

'Don't think he'd complain.' He laughed and so did I. I closed my eyes, enjoying the moment. Ke's silence after my declaration of love hadn't meant anything. It was just me. And after all, he'd been first. This wasn't planned, and I was way out of my depth. But he was strong enough to swim for both of us. I traced the line of his biceps.

'What are your plans for tomorrow?' he asked.

'You mean today?'

'Not quite. It's not yet midnight, when we return to our former state of pumpkin and mouse.' He kissed me.

'Pumpkin and mouse. Don't you mean prince and servant.'

'Well, if you say so.'

We both laughed.

'Seriously, tomorrow, I want to see you. Then I need to go back to Manchester, to finish up my exams and graduate.' I paused, looking down. 'Then I'm off to LA.'

'Do you have to go? Stay instead.' He looked at me with eyes full of sadness, then kissed me. It was hard to think. But he knew what this chance meant to me. We'd talked about it enough. 'Sorry, that wasn't fair.' He leaned away from me, and cool air filled the space.

'No, it's not.' I pulled him back against me.

'I miss you when you're gone,' he whispered.

'I miss you too... But I'll only be gone for a couple of months.' The last words were more for my benefit than his.

'And then what?' he asked, propping himself up on his elbow.

'I'll look for a proper job,' I said, stating the obvious.

'Which means London, or at best Bristol.' He sat up, wrapping his arms around his legs. I shivered without his body beside me.

'You could join me.' I pulled the sheet up to my chin before I sat up.

He laughed bitterly. 'Not much surfing around either of those places.'

'Definitely not.' I drew a breath. Ke loved Helston, and I did too, but there were no opportunities for me here.

He turned to me. 'This isn't something we can solve now.' He smiled. 'But we *will* solve it.'

'Yes,' I whispered, wondering how but believing with my whole heart that we could sort this.

The clock struck the final stroke of midnight.

Twenty-Eight

Flora Day, 2010

Saturday
Age: 23
Forecast: Overcast

I had no excuse not to go home for Flora Day that I could say. How many times had I looked through last year's diary, trying to make sense of everything? Too many. If I didn't show my face, questions would be asked, making any return at a later date harder, if not impossible. But since last year, my world had altered beyond recognition. On the good side, I was now working in LA as an assistant to Laura Donald, who was a top casting director. I'd finally found exactly what I wanted to do, and the job took me all over the world.

I'd met her at a party soon after I'd arrived in LA for the internship Tony had set up for me. My off-the-cuff comment about who I would have cast in a role should have landed me in trouble. Instead, it resulted in an invitation to meet and talk further. When my internship had completed in October, I'd then begun working for her. At the start, I mostly made coffee and ran errands, but slowly, as I learned more, Laura began to ask for my thoughts on strategy and decisions. And now she not only asked for my thoughts, but felt they were worthy of sharing and acting on. I'd been given a promotion to senior assistant and a raise. Life was good. I loved what I was doing, even if some days it was still all about making the coffee.

And that was what I had to focus on. No one needed to know what had happened. It had been exactly three months after Flora Day when I'd realised that my lack of period and upset stomach were more than nerves. I was pregnant, just like my mother had been after having sex on Flora Day. Even though my encounter had been protected by condoms, it appeared we'd pushed the boat out too far by making love too many times, and something had slipped in, so to speak.

No one at home knew.

That was important.

I hadn't been able to eat, sleep or think clearly. All that had gone through my head was that I was pregnant with Ke's child.

I loved him.

He loved me.

We'd made plans.

This should have been wonderful, but all I saw was my world crumbling before it had started. I saw Gran behind the bar at The Angel until she died. I saw Mum giving up her career. I saw Ke. He was the problem. Not in a bad way, but in a way that I couldn't get around. I wanted this baby. This child had been made with love, but it would mean the end of everything I'd dreamed of for myself.

I'd longed for his loving hand to hold mine as I decided what to do. I would not be like my mother or my grandmother and have a child alone. Not that I would have been alone, with Ke being the father. But that was also the problem. As he'd said that night, we wanted the same things – a whole functioning family. And I wanted that, but not this way. Not by accident. And definitely not at twenty-two.

I barely knew myself yet. If I had a child now, I wouldn't have the chance to find out what I really wanted to do, wanted from life. Ke didn't have a full-time job; he was chasing waves to make it to the big time. He wouldn't be able to continue his surfing dreams either. The child would have become a source of resentment. So, I'd made the choice for both of us.

All this didn't stop the awareness in the still of the night that I'd chosen me and my needs without even talking to Ke about it. I'd tried. I'd called two or three times before the appointment, but he didn't pick up. So I'd gone ahead with it, kind of relieved. And I'd denied him a say, let alone a choice. When he'd eventually called back, it was done, and I just couldn't talk to him.

How could I face him now, knowing this? My decision had been the right one; I was certain of that. But I didn't trust him or myself. Talking about it then would have been terrible, but now it'd be even worse. I'd been ghosting him since then, and how this must have seemed to him I could only imagine. He hadn't stopped trying to message, though. Finally, today I would have to see him and, if I was truly unlucky, speak to him.

The thought of getting absolutely plastered crossed my mind. But if I got that drunk, I wouldn't be able to avoid letting slip what had happened. Even if I said nothing to Ke, I would to Micki. And once Micki found out, she'd feel betrayed too because I hadn't turned to her. It was all a mess. Thank God for Gina, who'd quickly become my closest friend in LA. She'd loaned me the money for the appointment, picked me up from the clinic, and stayed with me until she was certain I was OK. She'd been the angel I needed. After the tears had stopped, she had listened. No judgement, no questions, only warmth and empathy.

I should have stayed in LA for Flora Day like I had for Christmas, enticing Mum and Tony to join me. And because I kept them so busy it was easier to hide my pain. Not coming now would have been better, but then there was Mum. She'd never missed a Flora Day, even when she was touring. Her delight when I'd walked through the door just after six this morning had been worth the sleepless night on the train, and the questions from

Tony as he'd collected me from Truro. Would I be able to put on enough of an act for him and Mum too?

'Oh Flo, this is the best surprise ever,' she'd said as she wrapped her arms around me. I hadn't told her I planned to come, in case I ended up bailing at the last minute. Then, the lying had begun. I'd feigned tiredness so I wouldn't have to assist with the Hal an Tow. A strategy was going to be needed for today, and for that I needed strong coffee and maybe a dose of Gran's wiliness. Her cunning at deflecting and avoiding issues she didn't want to deal with was one of my strongest memories of her. Especially when I poked around in both mine and Mum's paternity.

She hadn't been forthcoming on her own, or her mother's, either. I'd only been able to find the details of my great- great-grandmother's paternity because a father had been listed on the birth certificate. But the rest of us Richards women merely had 'unknown' marked in that box on ours. My heart went out to Gran's mother, who'd become a mother at fifteen. But why had she abandoned Gran and gone to Australia with that soldier? This must have been why Gran turned it into a story, saying it was fated. That twist probably made it all easier to digest. Or had it?

Tony had kissed my cheek, asking in a whisper if I was OK, before he headed back to Lismore to prepare for the day ahead. Now that Mum had left, I sat in my room. The posters were gone, but the faint shadow marks remained as a testament to the child I had been. I'd thought my childhood ended at fifteen or sixteen at the latest, but it had really ended when I'd made adult choices. And today would require more. I wouldn't drink – that should ensure I wouldn't say a word to anyone.

By the time the Evening Dance arrived, I was exhausted. Staying at the back of crowds and making every conversation light had proved harder than I expected. Thus far I'd kept Ke on the other side of the street or pub. But it wasn't proving easy. I'd bumped into Wilf and, thanks to the press of the crowd, I'd been able to avoid any proper conversation. Micki was even harder, as she sensed something was up and tracked me down, despite every evasive move I'd made.

'I get that now you have the big job in LA, we aren't your priority, and I'm big enough to take it. But Ke isn't. He's been a bear since you left last year.'

I raised both eyebrows in my attempt at surprise. 'You do understand that it takes everything to break into film.'

'I do, and so does he, but he says you aren't even replying to his messages at all.'

The truth was I'd stopped even reading them because he knew when I did. This act had taken more self-control than I'd known I had. And yet I'd found comfort in the fact that he still kept trying. That was bloody cruel. I'd become so selfish.

'Haven't I?' I whipped away a fly that didn't exist.

'Something's happened between you two, and I'll get to the bottom of it.' She finished her pint.

'Shall I get you another? I'm just going to get myself one.'

Her gaze narrowed on my empty glass. It looked like a gin and tonic but had actually been soda water and a lemon.

'Isn't it my round?' she asked.

'No, definitely not.' I grinned and escaped to the bar, hoping she had enough booze in her to forget our conversation, or that I could find a legitimate excuse to disappear. Having had almost no sleep on the train wasn't going to cut it. Most people in this town hadn't been to bed before four in the morning and they were still standing.

By the time I'd returned from the bar, Micki was deep in conversation with someone I didn't know which allowed me to slip away after delivering her drink. I swiftly finished the soda water and left the pub, planning on heading home. I'd dodged the bullet of meeting Ke. It should have looked innocent enough to anyone watching from a distance.

Who was I trying to fool? I stopped on the pavement. At every Flora Day since I'd been eight, we'd been inseparable. Even when I was helping Gran, he'd pop in to shift kegs and clear glasses with me. That I hadn't said a word to him was more than strange, and it was heart-breaking. Both mine and no doubt his. Or maybe he was over it. Maybe my silence had killed any love he'd ever felt for me. I deserved that.

With my head down so I didn't have to meet anyone's glance, I walked slowly home. Mum might not be there yet, which would be brilliant, letting me off the hook of conversation with her too. I hoped she was with Tony, and they were having a laugh about something that had happened this year. Something usually went wrong every year. Thankfully, nothing dire.

I exhaled as I reached the front door without having encountered a soul I knew well. Sanctuary was mine and tomorrow, after breakfast with Mum, I'd be back on a train to London, staying there for a week for a job I could put my whole heart and soul into. And I needed to do that, so I wouldn't have time to think of the what-ifs.

Once inside, I closed the door and headed straight to the kitchen. Toast, tea, and then bed were my plans. The air in the kitchen was stuffy, so I opened the door to the patio garden, expecting a blast of scented air. Instead, I found Ke.

My breath hitched, and I felt my hands go shaky. He sat with arms across his chest. 'I figured if I waited long enough, you'd come home.'

It crossed my mind to close the door on him. Instead, I pulled a second mug out of the cupboard and put another slice of bread under the grill. His comment didn't require a reply. But I needed to find something to say that wasn't hurtful, and which would make him leave. Could I tell him the truth? I took a quick glance at him, trying to summon the nerve to say the words aloud, but my mouth was dry. Having him this close was a nightmare. It reminded me of what we'd had last year, including the silly dream of a future together. How could I have been so naïve as to believe we'd make it work?

Ke loomed in the doorway. 'Still not going to speak to me?'

I flipped the bread over. There was so much I wanted to say. *I love you* was one of them, but that wouldn't help. It would lead to more questions, with answers that hurt so much that even when I was rehearsing alone, I couldn't utter them.

The silence thickened as I poured the boiling water onto the teabags and pulled out Mum's small jar of sugar. He was the only person who visited her who still took sugar. Mum and I had given it up for one Lent – and our waistlines – years ago. But Ke was still surfing and needed the calories. In fact, glancing at him, I saw he'd lost weight. There was a hollowness about his face as well, despite the tan. Had I done that?

'All year I've tried to figure out what I did wrong.' He leaned against the counter with his arms still across his chest.

I buttered the toast and shouted 'nothing!' in my head.

'And after months, I still haven't figured it out.' There was so much pain in his expression I could barely breathe as I handed him his mug, and put his toast on a plate.

When I still didn't answer, he continued, 'I've speculated. I've done that loads.' He blew on the surface of his tea. 'But no matter which direction I've pushed the thoughts in my head, nothing's felt right.'

I added a bit more milk to my tea, needing to tell him he'd done nothing wrong; it was all me. This might be the answer.

'So, I'm hoping a year after I had the best night of my life, and the best morning waking up with the woman I've loved forever beside me, that she can tell me what the hell is going on.' He ran his fingers through his sun-bleached hair, revealing the darker tones of blond beneath. 'The only answer I've come up with is that I'm just not good enough for you. Not educated enough. That in California you've found some intellectual guy who can do what I can't.'

My head shot up. He was destroying himself. Somehow, I had to stop this. I put my mug down and stood squarely in front of him. Drawing on all the reserves in me, I said, 'Ke, it has nothing to do with you, but everything to do with me. I haven't met anyone else.'

He started to speak, but I put my hand up.

'It's me, not you. You have to believe that. We live on different continents now, and I don't have room for anything else in my life. It's better this way.' I held in a sob, turned abruptly and walked away from him, going up to my room and closing the door before he could stop me. I couldn't stay any longer, or say any more – just looking at him and his pain, all I wanted was to stay and fix it. But I couldn't. I couldn't fix my own either.

I heard the taps run in the sink and, a few moments later, the garden door, before finally the front door closed. He was gone, and part of me died tonight.

Twenty-Nine
2025

8 May: 12:45 p.m.

Despite the sun shining brightly, I shivered at the east wind blowing through the garden. As if on cue, the phone in my pocket vibrated.

> You looked amazing. So good, it could have been your wedding day. In fact, if I don't get a report that you've shagged Ke Dale, I'll disown you. He's too hot for his own good but perfect for your uses. Vxoxoxo

I angled the screen to make sure no one else could read it. The phone vibrated in my hand again, and a picture appeared. I blinked. There was a woman with a big smile on her face, looking at the handsome man beside her. My brain acknowledged it was me and Ke, but rejected what the picture showed. This wasn't what had been going on in my head. I must have Mum's acting gene, or maybe some of the talent of all the actors I'd worked with had rubbed off on me.

I studied it again, this time looking at Ke's face, partially in shadow from his hat. He too smiled, but it didn't light his face like a true one. He wasn't the actor I was, but then he hadn't needed to be.

Shag him. Promise me.

If Vlad only knew the truth. I stopped my thoughts there. Only two people knew one part of the story, and two people knew the other. Three different perspectives. Three different camera angles, actors' interpretations or, as the late Queen had said, 'recollections may vary'.

Ke was now chatting to someone I didn't know. It was an animated conversation. This might be my opportunity to wander away and... to get lost on purpose. But something held me in place – I couldn't help wondering what Ke's view now was on what had happened all those years ago. One thing was clear: I was the bad guy, the antagonist who'd held all the cards.

Tony, may he rest in peace, would have told a different story. Knowing him, it would have been laced with Shakespeare, and it would have been a tragedy of Romeo and Juliet proportions. But no one would have taken the poison, because he, as the priest, would have never presented us with this choice. He'd have twisted the tragic romance into a comedy.

My take was still that I had acted the only way I could at that age. Apart from the cowardly way I'd treated Ke.

Anyway, it was history and I needed to leave it alone. Being back here, and dancing with Ke, made that so difficult, though. Glancing around the crowds of dancers and spectators I looked for the camera angles. How would this all play out? Would the heroine find her father? Would she reconcile with her one true love? Or would someone die, actually or metaphorically? I needed a script, and I didn't have one. Sadly, I'd discovered life was like that, especially when it swept you up and threw everything at you like a vindictive god. If my mind mixed any more genres or metaphors, it might explode. The past was the past. I could only work on the now, as the future was unknown, no matter how much I wanted to prepare for it.

My phone pinged.

Have you shagged him yet?

I had to laugh. Vlad was the eternal optimist. He'd say that things would work out, even if all the markers predicted death. He always looked on the bright side.

What was the bright side of this?

'It's so good to see you two old friends back together again.'

I jumped. This wasn't the bright side. One glance at Ke and it was clear he looked distinctly uncomfortable as our old primary school teacher walked up to us. She hadn't changed. I remembered how I'd thought she was old when she taught us, but she'd probably been what my age is now.

'I always thought you two would become a couple.' She smiled, glancing between us.

My skin began to itch. Ke ran his finger around his collar. It was then that I realised Ke was wearing Tony's morning suit. They were the same height, but their builds were different. It had been made by someone on Saville Row, as Tony had told me, delighting in all the details. It must have been tailored again to fit Ke as well as I could see it did. My eyes tracked the line of his shoulders, down to the way the seams highlighted his trim waist. I stopped there. Never had I ever thought about tailoring in this way before.

Instead, I thought about Tony's closeness to Ke. This had never surprised me, and yet it did now. They were so different. Tony had had culture dripping out of every pore, while Ke had saltwater doing the same. Where had their relationship found connection? Not in Tony's love of Shakespeare. Caring about my mother was one area; a love of Helston and Cornwall was another. *Me*, my brain shouted, but that must have divided them as well. Ke didn't know what I'd told Tony, and he never would, yet here he was at my side wearing Tony's suit. This just highlighted my lack of knowledge, and I didn't know how I felt about that, or anything else. One part of me was pleased that Tony would have passed it on to him... possibly last year after he knew he wouldn't be needing it again. The other part of me still couldn't believe Tony was gone, even though the fact that I was here confirmed it. This was the reality, even if I didn't want it to be.

'How good to see you, Miss Potts.' Ke said.

She laughed like a girl. 'Always a charmer,' she lied. Ke hadn't been a charmer; he'd been too afraid to talk much at all in school when he was younger. I glanced between them as they spoke about what was happening in the town, and about Matilda. She was eight, which was the same age Ke and I had been when we first danced – the beginning of our friendship. But I'd killed it by crossing the line and allowing that friendship to move into passion. He had too.

She focused on me. 'Now, I hear you're working with that dishy movie star.'

I snapped back to the now. *Which dishy movie star?* was my first thought, but then I smiled. Adrian, of course. 'Yes, he's a delight.'

She fanned her face. 'Lucky you.'

'Indeed.' I smiled, hoping our time in this limbo of chatting to people who all wanted to know my plans, wanted to see Ke and I together, and all thought they knew the future, would be over. I'd lived in purgatory, as dear lapsed Catholic Gina would have called it, for so long that I deserved some form of heaven. I'd atoned for my sins, surely. You couldn't remake the past. This I knew for certain, because my dreams were still filled with a future that didn't happen.

Lismore, Cross Street, Helston, Cornwall

---

15 April 2011

My dearest Flo,

Thank you for your last letter. I'm so pleased the Richard Curtis film will be partially filmed in Cornwall. Porthpean House is wonderful and I am always jealous of their camellia collection. I wish you were on set. It would be lovely to see more of you. And, of course, I will keep this news under my hat.

Our dinner in London two weeks ago will have to sustain me, as will your letters. I do wish you were dating more. I know your life is full with work, but no man nor woman lives by work alone. It's easy to fall into this, though, when we feel broken. I know because after Angus died, I nearly did the same. It seemed easier to hide away in work than to face life. It was your mum who kicked me up the backside and reminded me I was still alive, and as such I should live.

I am not kicking your backside but gently pointing out that you are young. Work will be in your life a long time, but as the old adage says: work to live, not live to work. I know you love your job, but you need to find the way to love your life again. I have every faith you will do it.

Enjoy LA for me and please come for Flora Day or at least consider it.

Love,

Tony xxxx

Thirty

Flora Day, 2011

Saturday
Age: 24
Forecast: Light rain showers

These days, I was mostly in LA, and I'd hoped that would be the case for this year's Flora. But I couldn't use it as an excuse. Brad Pitt had been papped at the Savoy having cocktails with some of his film crew, and I'd been one of those there, clearly visible in the pictures, so I couldn't say I wasn't in the country. Mum always liked to flick through the celebrity gossip mags. I couldn't do that to her. She and Tony had flown to LA for Christmas and New Year, so I could hardly justify not coming home when I was only a few hundred miles away. But I'd wanted to. I'd even rehearsed reasons in my head that all sounded like pumped-up, inflated-ego type excuses: Pitt was such a big star I had to be on hand for the first day's filming. In fact, nothing could have been further from the truth – it was only occasionally that I'd be on set, to be my boss Laura's eyes and ears once filming had actually begun.

No, I had no excuse. So, I'd arrived about nine o'clock last night and pleaded exhaustion as the reason I wasn't hitting the town when Micki arrived to drag me out. I won in the end and spent the night scrolling social media and reading dire scripts. Well, they might not have been dire, but nothing was going to please me being here. It was fraught. After the confrontation with Ke last year, I couldn't have hated myself more. He was hurting, and I'd simply made it worse. Not that I hadn't tried to take the blame, but he wasn't buying it. I'd torn myself apart all night, debating again whether I should tell him the truth. He deserved the truth, of course he did, but would it help make him feel better? Would it allow us both to move on and, perhaps in time, mend our broken friendship?

The thought of saying the words out loud made me want to curl up and hide. And I just couldn't see them causing him anything but sharper, deeper pain. For his own sake, it was better I just disappeared from his life. So, I eventually decided that this year my goal would be not to see him at all. With good timing, it'd be possible. He was dancing in the Early Morning and Evening Dances with Micki, which left me clear to lend Mum a hand with the Hal an Tow. I'd simply catch sight of the two of them without having to engage. Then I'd be helping Tony at Lismore.

With all the venues in town, it would be easy for me to appear in a few later on so people knew I'd been around, but to steer clear of old favourites, where I knew Micki and Ke would likely be. Micki had been strangely quiet when she came to Mum's house last night, not pushing me as much as she normally would have to go out with her. Something was up. She was due to visit me in London next weekend, so I'd get the lowdown then. And my lack of time with her today wouldn't seem so cutting. It'd all work out, and another Flora Day would pass. My diary simply said:

Make it through Flora Day in one piece.

Listening to the church bells, I ventured downstairs. When I declined the toast Mum offered, but went for black coffee, she sent me a look. My stomach couldn't take food.

'You've lost weight,' she commented. It wasn't something

she'd ever mentioned before. Of course, I'd never weighed less than I did now, but it wasn't because of a conscious act of dieting. It was a byproduct of a busy life, and something inside that stopped me from eating much. I didn't want to dwell on it.

'Just too busy to eat most days.'

She sent me another look that said more than words. 'Right, if you're not going to eat, we might as well head off.'

Strangely, our walk to the Epworth Hall was in silence. As though Mum was cross with me. I doubted it was the weight loss, but her silence spoke of something.

'Do you want to tell me what's up?' I asked.

She turned to me, her expression sharp. 'I'm not you and I don't interfere in your life or your decisions – you are an adult. But I do wonder what's happened between you and Ke.'

I swallowed. How could I answer that? This was my mother, not Ke, not Micki. Time had passed, and I was doing everything I could to bury my pain, my mistakes and my fear. The Richards women were all supposedly destined to be single mothers. I didn't want that. I never had. But I also hadn't wanted to tie a man to me because it was the right thing to do. I loved Ke too much to do that to him. Ke was a free spirit. We couldn't have survived with him doing odd jobs, and me... Well, good question there. What was I qualified for in this town, with a degree in History and a Masters in Film Studies? One German television series didn't put a roof over your head, buy food and clothes and keep you warm.

'Nothing really, just going our different ways at the moment.'

She didn't say a word, but her look told me she knew I was lying. She was never a mother to push information out of me, though. 'Well, I'm incredibly proud of him. This year he sat his A level equivalents in biology, chemistry and physics and is off to Plymouth to study Marine Biology in September.'

I stopped in my tracks. The urge to jump for joy and cry happy tears for Ke threatened to overwhelm me.

She watched me closely. 'It's obvious you still love him.'

I blinked.

'I'm not blind.'

I drew a deep breath. If she'd seen it, who else had?

'It hurts me to see him so down, and you so silent. The only Musketeer with any joy is Wilf.' She paced. People were already securing a spot to view the Early Morning Dance. Something like pain stirred within me. I had done the right thing. It was the only thing I could have done. If I hadn't, I would have been letting Tony down too. He'd helped with my uni fees, and he'd pulled strings and called in favours to secure me the internships. I also would have been letting myself down, and I wasn't willing, like Mum, to throw it all in and come home. Looking at her right now, though, despite her mouth still set in a line of displeasure, I could see she was content in her life.

Once I'd finished organising with Mum, I nipped out to catch the early dancers. Summer frocks twirled in the early morning light. Cheers from the crowd and laughter from the dancers filled the air. My blood pounded to the beat of the music.

I then spotted, bringing up the rear, Micki and Ke. Micki was laughing, looking up at Ke as they moved through the steps, their hands clasped. Ke, who'd only ever been my dancing partner, smiled. Something inside me ripped apart. All the promise and all the pain surfaced, and it took everything in me not to turn and run, run as far away from here as I could. Instead, I fixed a smile on my face, secured my sunglasses pretentiously on my nose, and waved to them both. Micki's flirty grin told me something I didn't want to know. She was currently without a man, and her look said Ke would do just fine, just fine indeed. Ke's glance met mine briefly.

Hurt.

Anger.

Sadness.

I wanted to throw up. This was my fault.

Once the dancers had passed, I escaped to a good place to

watch the Hal an Tow by the bowling green. As the whistles and cheers heralded their arrival, I tried to focus on anything but the gleam I'd seen in Micki's eye, and emotions in Ke's. Well, she had called it after all, all those years ago. Her time had now come. Her chance with Ke. She'd waited long enough, and her patience would give her what she'd wanted all along.

Bitter was the taste in my mouth, and bitter was how I felt. After the joyous Hal an Tow moved on, I made my way to Lismore, passing the children all lined up ready for their moment. I couldn't help but smile at their antics, and their sudden jump to attention as the big drum sounded. If I could have gone back in time, where would I have gone, and what exactly would I have changed two years ago? Would I not have made love to Ke? Would I have cancelled the internship, as Ke had wanted me to do? Or would I simply have savoured the moment longer, now knowing that was all it was going to be and there wouldn't be a future for us?

Turning from the happy kids, I dashed into the safety of Lismore. It was chaotically busy there, but I found Tony calmly standing in the walled garden, smoking a cigarette. He offered it to me. 'You look like you need this more than me.'

'Maybe I do, but as I don't smoke it might cause more upset than help.'

He arched an eyebrow and sat on an old bench, patting the space beside him. Gratefully, I sank down and closed my eyes. The last thing Tony needed at this moment was the complete disintegration of the woman beside him. It was best not to say a word – I feared once I began, the whole sorry tale would spill out.

He glanced at his watch. 'It's a little early but you look like you need a drink, and as they say the sun is past the yardarm somewhere.'

I laughed. 'No, alcohol won't help in this minute either, but I might take you up on it later.'

He studied me closely. 'It's a date. Meet me back here at the house at nine p.m.' He took a drag of his cigarette. 'The place will be quiet then, and you and I can have a proper catch up.'

'Should we invite your mother?' he asked.

Mum.

I shook my head. After what she'd said recently about Ke and me, I couldn't talk to her. In fact, by nine o'clock tonight I should be fully back in control of my emotions. I too could playact if necessary, and today had already called on these skills I'd learned while playing dress-up.

We sat for a while in silence until the noise of the band brought us both to our feet. 'Time to watch the urchins,' he said, stubbing out his cigarette.

I nodded, though not intending to watch them.

'If there's one thing I know, it's when someone needs a hug, and you do.' He wrapped me in a swift, fierce bear hug, then dashed out to watch the Children's Dance pass by.

I stuck to my plan and basically bought a soft drink at every pub, chatting to people and showing willing. Mum was helping at The Angel, as they were down two people due to stomach flu. She was full of apologies about our planned time together later in the evening, but I told her not to worry; we'd catch up in the morning before I left. To be honest, when I'd agreed to meet Tony, I'd forgotten about my plans with Mum. What was wrong with me?

It was eight thirty by the time I slipped into the garden of The Bell, and the sight there stopped me in my tracks. Micki and Ke were caught up in a passionate embrace. If it had been any two other people, I would have made some light, funny comment, but in that moment my heart twisted and cracked open. Losing all control, I sobbed and ran as if the devil himself were chasing me.

Tony was just heading in the front door of Lismore when I came barrelling his way.

'Are the dogs of hell after you?' he asked with a gleam of humour in his eyes. This faded swiftly when he saw my face. He ushered me in the door, closed it behind us, and then wrapped me in his arms. The tears came in a way I hadn't let them since I'd had the abortion. I cried until there was nothing left but a hollowed-out shell. Tony handed me his hankie and led me to the kitchen. As I began to shake, he found an old cardigan he used for gardening and wrapped me in it.

With a flick of a switch, Baroque music filled the room. I sat in the chair by the range, and Tony filled the kettle, then opened a packet of digestives and a bottle of champagne. 'First hydration and some sugar. Then some booze and cheese, and only then, if you wish, you can tell me what's happened.'

After he'd plied me with tea and biscuits, he went to change his shirt, which I'd soaked with my tears.

By the time he'd returned, he looked ready for whatever I might throw at him, and I found I could talk about it. In fact, I needed to. The pressure of keeping this secret to myself alone was proving too much. And Tony understood the destructiveness of secrets, as he'd told me years ago.

'Thanks,' I said, when he put a glass of fizz beside me. On the table, he placed a platter of cheeses, then a basket of bread and crackers.

'Now if you're warm enough, come and join me here.' He sat at the table.

As I stood, my legs still wobbled a bit – I hadn't run that sort of dash in years. I refused to put it down to what I'd just seen. What had I expected from Ke? If it hadn't been Micki, it would have been some other woman, and for all I knew there may well have been hundreds already. No, not hundreds, but possibly tens. It wasn't my right to know, and I had to be OK with that.

I sat across from Tony at the table.

'Do you want to talk about what brought you to this state tonight, or about the root source?' he asked, slicing through a piece of Yarg cheese.

I laughed bitterly. 'How do you know it didn't just start

tonight or today?' I recalled my earlier distress, which in light of what I'd just seen seemed inconsequential.

'These things always have a beginning, and rarely is that on the same day of an outburst, if it has touched deep feelings.'

I sighed.

'See, I'm right.'

I picked up the glass and took a sip. Dutch courage might help. Where should I start?

'Shall I help?' he asked.

I stared at him.

'Right, how long have you been in love with Ke?'

Had he and Mum been comparing notes?

'It was obvious when the two of you were shagging in your room here.'

He *had* known. Part of me died of embarrassment.

'Of course I knew, but I was never one to spoil young love's fun, so I pretended I didn't.'

'Thanks, I think.' Would it have helped if I'd realised more people than Ke and I had known we'd been together? No, it wouldn't have.

'You haven't answered.' He sliced another piece of cheese.

There was nothing to do but answer truthfully. 'Since I was eight, if I'm honest.'

'And why aren't you with him now?' he asked.

I took another sip of fizz. 'Because... because we want different things.'

'Like love, friendship and family.'

I made a face. It wasn't that simple, and he knew it.

'What went wrong?'

I closed my eyes, telling myself to just say it. But once it was out, it was no longer my secret to bear.

He leaned forward and placed his arms on the table. 'Flora Portia Richards spit it out. I can see that whatever it is, it's killing you.'

'I think it might already have done.'

'Nope, because if you were dead, you wouldn't have cried like you just did. There's still life left in your twenty-four-year-old body.'

'I'm the embodiment of the walking dead,' I countered.

'Not buying the zombie business.' He tapped his fingers.

'Fair.' I nibbled a piece of cheese.

'It's clearly a big thing, and not some little tiff that should have blown over.' He paused. 'I've known you your whole life. You don't give up, you are loyal, kind, and loving. It had to have been significant for you to cut him off as you have.'

Drawing a huge breath, I debated what to say. 'Can you keep a secret?'

'Ah.' He looked me directly in the eyes. 'Secrets are hard, as I've mentioned before. But knowing you, you're doing it for someone else.'

'Not so sure about that.' I finished my glass, and Tony topped it up. 'When I set off for LA, Ke and I had something of a plan to move our relationship forward and make it public.'

Tony nodded encouragingly.

'When the stint in LA was over, I would hunt for a job in Bristol, and he'd come and join me.'

'Sounds good.'

'It might have worked, who knows.' I twisted the stem of the glass in my fingers. 'But it might not have.'

'You both would have given it a chance, though.' He took a sip.

'True.' I couldn't deny that. We had both wanted it badly.

'But you didn't come back and move to Bristol.' He studied me as if the answers were written on my face.

'No, I couldn't.' I laid my hands flat, looking at how pale they were compared to the old oak tabletop.

'I'm sure you're right.' He topped up our glasses. 'But I feel like I'm missing a step.'

'Three months after that Flora Day I discovered I was pregnant.' I swallowed and closed my eyes. Tony was smart enough to fill in the gaps, to finish the rest of the story.

'And you did absolutely the right thing.' When I opened my eyes again, his were filled with sympathy and understanding.

'Thank you.' Even though I was sure it had been the right thing, it was good to hear someone else say it too.

'And I'm certain Ke agreed.'

I shook my head. 'He doesn't know.'

Tony stared at me, unblinking. I'd shocked him. Saying the words aloud now, I could see why. Ke was my best friend, the love of my life, and I hadn't told him about the pregnancy.

Tony twisted the stem of the champagne glass. 'OK.'

'It's not, though, is it?' This was what ripped me apart.

'That's not for me to say. You were a young woman alone and away from home. I haven't walked in those shoes.'

'Be thankful for that,' I said with more force than I'd intended.

'I am.' He reached across the table and took my hand in his.

I sighed. 'I mean, you saw what Mum gave up because of me.'

'Flo, this isn't about your mother and her choices, it's about yours. And I know this was absolutely the right one for you, just as I know the one your mother made at thirty was absolutely the right one for her.'

I watched the bubbles rising to the top of my glass and popping, then disappearing, just like my dreams of a life with Ke.

'There you two are,' Mum said, walking through the kitchen door. 'Neither of you answered your phones.'

I sent Tony a look, and he nodded. My secret was safe with him.

Thirty-One

2025

8 May, 1:30 p.m.

Clouds crept across the sky, obscuring the sunshine, as we stood behind the stewards ready to dance out of Lismore garden, and down Cross Street to Penhellis – once another grand family mansion and now a care home. These architectural gems tucked behind the businesses fronting Meneage and Coinagehall Streets were a further testament to Helston's wealthy past. On this May day, they were bright and cheery, adorned with greenery and flowers, completely the opposite of what I felt inside. A heaviness I couldn't explain filled me. Was it because I no longer knew the man standing at my side? This wasn't a bad thing. We were different people now, both filled with grief.

Relief should have been my overwhelming emotion, knowing that my connection to Helston would soon be, if not totally severed, then stretched so thin as to be transparent. Meaning I wouldn't have to think about it anymore. Micki would be my last remaining link to this place, along with administering the scholarship Tony had set up in my mother's name. That, however, would only take me as far as Falmouth. My split from here would soon be final.

Ke turned to me and held out his hand. 'Ready?'

No.

My hand shook in his as the band started and we took our first step away from the house and garden.

'Yes,' I said, attempting a smile.

Liar. I wasn't ready for any of this. After all these years of accepting I'd never know who my father was, that tormenting question had been pushed right to the forefront of my mind once more. What to do with Lismore also vied with the paternity question. Instead, I should have been somehow enjoying the one dance I'd never done on Flora Day. The big one. The one that, in the past, only the great and the good could take part in, and which I would never have made the grade for as a fatherless woman, even if I was now a woman of substance. But that, like many other prohibitions such as no divorced people, had changed.

Mum dancing with Tony had been a joyous sight I'd never forget – a moment of happiness to cling onto. Gran had never danced it, nor had her mother, but her mother's mother had. She'd held some respectability in the town before the First World War.

Thankfully now, entry into the Midday Dance was by ballot which reminds me who entered us. At least now you didn't need to be a member of the gentry to trip the light fantastic through the town. Progress had been made in the world, while there was still far to go. A bit like with this dance, which was way too long.

The music changed, Ke handed me over to Bill, and we twirled through the doorway of Penhellis, then I was back with Ke as the care home residents watched us head through the hall and out through the garden. There more residents sat in the May sunshine where it was warm, protected from the bitter east wind by the building. Bunting celebrating the eightieth VE Day celebration hung above their heads. So many of them would remember that day, as Gran had. She'd been ten, and her world had changed in ways she'd never seen coming. A bit like my mother's letter and the legacy from Tony had changed everything for me in an instant.

It was entertaining to look at the crowds as we made our way towards the bowling green. Some appeared fresh, embracing the festival, while others were happily tipsy. There was no set group age-wise watching the dance. I enjoyed hearing the various foreign languages being spoken, which were rarely heard when I'd been young, and in this age of Instagram many people were taking selfies with the dancers behind them. Both Ke and I smiled and waved to familiar faces, or in my case, unfamiliar ones. It was clear how far my life had moved on from this place. This, of course, was a good thing. And I wouldn't miss it in the future. It would fade into the past, perhaps just eliciting the occasional pang when key dates came around.

That thought settled in the pit of my stomach, along with the glasses of prosecco I'd had at Lismore during the break. This was not a happy mix. But I was now a stranger here, and that was freeing. A boyfriend I'd once brought here for these celebrations came to mind. One I'd been seriously falling for in a way I hadn't with anyone else except Ke. He'd found it hard to reconcile the woman I was with the one he'd seen on that Flora Day. Looking at Helston through his blinkered vision had been brutal and frustrating. He'd expected whitewashed houses and flower boxes, not the faded glory of a once eminent town and the strange pagan ritual of the Hal an Tow. How could I have made it work with him?

But today, as the sun came out again, Helston glowed. Wisteria tumbled over walls, bunting hung across twisting lanes and alleys. It was magical for one day of the year. He had seen it at its best and still rejected it. Rejection always stung, and I'd done just that to Ke, without the decency of a proper explanation. One minute he'd been receiving emails and texts from me, then silence. Total silence.

A glance at Ke's face as he waved at people in the crowds

showed me it was controlled with a fixed, easy smile. Mine probably matched his as I let the music roll over me. The sounds of the various instruments taking the lead at times, from the depth of the euphoniums to the beat of the drums. As the band reached the corner of the green, I watched the young children play their part and my heart filled watching Wilf with a young drummer. The community in the band represented so much about this town, with the older mentoring the young in the joy of the music and the traditions.

Today was all about tradition and pride in Helston. A town built on hard work, and existing now almost in its own bubble. It was less recognised outside of Cornwall than Porthleven, the town it had been cobbled together for governance. Porthleven's waterside location made it more attractive to visitors, who fed the coffers of its communities to keep them going over the long winter months.

Each step of the dance brought me closer to the end of this day, and to the meet up, for old times' sake, which Micki had planned. It was the last thing I wanted to do. Once we'd been all for one and one for all, but I'd made my life far, far away and didn't belong anymore. This dance through the town had brought all the old times back closer than they'd been in years, including things best left forgotten. With each step, hop, or twirl, the weight of things held tightly inside became even heavier, along with the knowledge of my mother's deception. She'd felt it was best that I never knew the identity of my father. Why?

Crowds lined Coinagehall Street, jostling each other for the best spot. The end was in sight: the Guildhall. Once we made it there, I'd be through, and this farce of Ke and I dancing together would be over. Someone must have found this setup amusing, or it was vengeance for some sin I'd committed. If it'd been hard for me, it had to have been worse for Ke.

Standing in front of The Blue was Matilda, still in her white dress from earlier, waving wildly to her father. She rushed up to him, and he took her hand briefly.

'You dance so well, Daddy, I love you,' she called as the music changed and Ke dropped my hand to dance with Helen. I couldn't take my eyes off his daughter. Her face was glowing with adoration. And she had her mother's warm smile and freckles. My heart died a bit more. Soon it would be unable to beat. That was why I needed to close these chapters of my life. It was for my sanity and my soul. It was also for Ke and his daughter.

Ke twirled me around as we came back together, and the beat changed. This man had been my best friend, my lover and my biggest regret. He belonged in Helston, and any time I spent here hurt him as much as it killed me.

'How are you holding up?' Ke asked.

'Just.' I smiled. 'You?'

'Could murder a pint.'

'Not long.' Each beat of the music brought us closer to never having to see each other again. I swallowed back tears. Farewells were always tough, and this one would be final.

My phone vibrated. No doubt it was Vlad telling me they were stuck in traffic and wondering again if I'd shagged Ke yet. Out of the corner of my eye, I watched Ke. He was relaxed in his own skin as we followed the ancient steps, and he waved to friends in the crowd. In my head, I replied to what I thought Vlad's text had said. *No, Vlad, I haven't shagged him, but I did years ago.* And with Ke's hand holding mine, it felt all too close to the surface. How could I still be in love with him, after all this time?

But I was and had to accept I probably always would be. Maybe having loved this deeply once was all I'd experience. It would be the memory that comforted me through the years. But in this moment, there was no solace in that thought.

First loves.

Only love.

Micki waved wildly at us. Her grin was infectious. She didn't let things like this trouble her, and I envied that. I'd give anything to stop reliving all my mistakes again and again. It was bad enough that I rehearsed things in my head endlessly, and then to live through the reruns continuously. Each time taking away a bit more of me.

Micki had told me to let the past go. Move on. That was what selling Lismore was about. Yes, Mum and Tony's ashes were interred in Helston, and Gran was buried here. But nothing else tied me to it. I would prove Gran wrong. You *could* take the girl out of Helston, and this time Helston would stay out of the girl.

The music shifted, and automatically I swapped to Bill with a smile on my face, going through the steps. *Be present.* This was the last time I'd do this. It was a big honour. Gran, Mum and Tony would have been proud. I smiled as Ke returned to me, and he smiled back. There was a question in his look, but I just leaned into being present for now. I, Flora Richards, was here in Helston on Flora Day with Ke Dale, and we were leading the Midday Dance. Once this would have been impossible, but someone had made it happen, and I would enjoy the last moments of it.

Thirty-Two

Flora Day, 2012

Tuesday
Age: 25
Forecast: Sunny

Mum had sprained her ankle and been mildly concussed after slipping while collecting greenery yesterday, so I'd wangled a couple of days away from work in London to come down and make sure she didn't do too much on Flora Day. Tony was worried about her. For the day itself, we'd insisted she use crutches, because it involved so much standing. She'd tried to argue, but with Tony, Micki, and I standing strong against her, she'd had no choice.

After picking us up early in her car, Micki was a total star, dropping us as close to the Hal an Tow preparations as she could by talking her way through the barriers to Epworth Hall. I then ran around doing Mum's bidding, while Micki became her voice to ensure everyone was clear on their parts in the procession. Hell, they should all have known them without thinking by now, except for the few new people who'd found their way into the Hal an Tow.

Micki then led them all to their waiting positions. Mum

managed to hobble to St John's Bridge with me by her side, and we caught sight of the Early Morning Dance. The crowds were already in fine spirits, everyone calling out to her. I tried not to think of Ke, who I'd seen in the arms of Tina as the dancers moved past us. He hadn't even glanced at me. He and Micki had been a short-lived thing last year. It had ended as soon as he'd gone to Plymouth for university. Micki hadn't said too much about it – it was as if she'd figured out from my reluctance to talk about Ke, let alone explain why he and I had fallen out, that I didn't want to hear. At least she'd finally stopped asking me why Ke and I weren't really talking anymore. She'd been more interested in me, and who I was meeting through work.

One of the films I'd been a casting assistant on had won a BAFTA for best British film, and Micki had quizzed me about that. The event, the glam, the parties, etc. She'd told me she needed to live the high life through me. I'd laughed. Yes, there were the big moments, but mostly it was meetings, reading scripts and keeping egos massaged. The latter being the biggest part of the job most days, and that wasn't always with the actors but their agents.

The best bit of my job, aside from the travel, was seeing the actors my boss, Laura, and I had championed nailing their roles, even if films failed to deliver in any other way. It was better when the total package worked, but those I knew were rare. Laura had a string of them, and that was my goal once I moved up. It was matchmaking, but without the breakups and divorces as the result. Well, mostly. There had been one case in which we'd cast a household name, yet once on the set they hadn't had the right touch for the part. The director had raged after finding out their visions didn't match. It had turned into a public lesson of when casting goes wrong.

The joy was that I'd found my skill. I realised I understood actors, and I loved film, from the first idea to the finished product. Reading scripts was a highlight for me, as I played the story in my head, trying out actors long before they, or anyone, knew the role even existed. It was such a creative role and was almost alchemical when it worked well.

Whistles, horns and drums sounded, and the Hal an Tow began. Mum tensed. I stroked her arm. She was the director of it all, although she'd never call herself that. But she orchestrated this show every year, adding on bits, adapting, and making sure it was as inclusive as possible. That was important to her, and I loved her for it. I also loved the way she'd let Micki step up and help. It couldn't have been easy, but there was a genuine change visible in Micki. I'm not sure anyone had really ever thought she could pull herself together, let alone help to marshal two hundred people to perform for Flora.

The song finished, and the troupe moved on noisily to the bowling green to perform. But there was no way Mum could follow. She wasn't moving fast enough on her crutches. It was best for us to get her up to the Guildhall for the final performance, and there she'd have a good view for the Children's Dance. We'd all agreed she could then stay and enjoy the start of the Midday Dance, but after that it'd be time for her to sit down, foot raised.

Once we'd watched all this, I longed for some help to get Mum away from the crush of people by the Guildhall. She was flagging, and the crutches kept slipping. But there was no way I could support her myself alone. Tony was dancing, and Micki had disappeared into the crowd. I searched for a familiar face to help but was out of luck. Easing Mum back away from the edge of the road, I propped her against the wall of the Guildhall. It'd be too difficult to manoeuvre her through the press of crowds filling the street, behind the dancers, to get her home. Lismore would be easier to head for at this point.

'Mum, do you see anyone who could give us a hand?'

She shook her head, then her face lit up, and she waved. Relief swept over me. It was clear she'd spied someone. I turned, and my heart fell. Ke was making his way towards us. The past year had not made him any less attractive. His glance met mine, and neither of us flinched until I could take it no longer. I looked down.

'Ke.' Mum smiled.

'Need a hand?' he asked.

'Yes, despite my best intentions, I'm done in and can't manage these crutches home.'

'No problem.' He looked around, people in every direction. 'There's only one thing for it.' He scooped her up and made his way through the crowds, who parted as if he were Moses and they the Red Sea. I scrambled in their wake, clutching Mum's crutches to my chest like a shield that could protect me. The question was, what from – Ke? He'd never hurt me so it must be from myself.

By the time we'd reached home, I'd pulled myself together. After I'd opened the door and he'd put Mum on the sofa with cushions lifting her leg, I was ready to be normal with Ke, whatever that meant.

'Tea?' I asked, knowing that was exactly what Mum needed.

'Not for me thanks,' he said, not looking at me but leaning over to adjust the pillows under Mum's foot.

'Enjoy the pub,' Mum said, as he stood straight to leave.

'Will do.' He smiled at her, and the crack in my heart widened.

'Have a couple for me,' she said.

'Consider it done.' He turned, and the smile left his face. 'Flo.'

'Thanks for your help,' I said.

'Anything for Maria,' he replied.

I nodded, not sure what to say, if anything at all. 'Congrats on uni.' Awkward.

His glance narrowed. 'Yeah, it's good.'

He bent to kiss Mum's cheek, then left without another word. I focused on making the tea and not thinking about what I'd done to him, to us, while trying to ignore Mum's look, which I could feel boring into my back.

Lismore, Cross Street, Helston, Cornwall

---

10 October 2012

My dearest Flora,

I know you are broken, but you will heal. Try not to heal perfectly, though. Think of your grandmother's bowl mended with copper. It is far more beautiful and rich now than before it shattered. Humans are the same. Our strength and our beauty comes from the events that have shaped us. The tougher these are, the more we can shine.

You have always been hard on yourself. I have watched this from your early attempts to walk, to drive a car, to pass your exams and to excel at life. This is possibly because you feel you need to make it up to your mother for the sacrifices she's made. You want to show her it was worthwhile. I could tell you this is unnecessary, but I know you wouldn't listen. Those of us who have had a few things thrown against us become stronger, and hopefully more human, if we can find our way beyond the pain. The first step is to forgive yourself.

You did what was right. You know this and I do too. What I can't work out is why you can't forgive yourself. If it's because of Ke, I know you had his best interests at heart as well. So work hard to forgive, so you can move forward. If you don't, it will become a tragedy of Shakespearean proportions, with you holding onto this 'false' guilt, not living fully. Remember my darling girl, we only have one life, be it short or long, so live it well.

Enough of the lecture. Know you are loved, no matter what.

Love you always,
Tony xxxx

Thirty-Three
Flora Day, 2013

Wednesday
Age: 26
Forecast: Light rain showers

It had been quite a week. I'd been Micki's maid of honour, which was always going to be problematic from the start. First, I didn't think she was marrying for the right reasons, and on top of that, Ke had been an usher. Thankfully, not the best man. I think I would have had to bow out if that'd been the case, and that would have been tricky. Micki still didn't get what was up with Ke and me, and I wasn't about to break my silence and explain. Instead, it all went into my diary, as I had to put the emotions somewhere, and somewhere safe. Yesterday's entry leapt off the page at me.

Ke
Micki
Me
Pain.

Acknowledging how much this all hurt didn't take the pain away, but it helped me to understand it. A best friend's wedding, no matter how happy you were for them, always raised the questions: *why not me? What's wrong with me?* But I knew the answers. Inside, I was still an open wound, and I couldn't ask for help, or even say why I was a bit off, as Mum had commented. Hopefully, it was only Mum who'd noticed. Of course, Tony knew why, but however understanding he was, however much he told me to be kind to myself, I still couldn't seem to lift myself out of this.

Micki had been a stunning bride. With my help, she'd tracked down a second-hand dress that was exactly what she'd wanted. I'd also sourced the bridesmaid dresses, which technically could be reused, but who were we fooling? It was a rare soul who actually reused wedding garb, unless you were a man. Our dresses were lavender – not my favourite shade, but the gowns were elegant and suited the diverse group of women Micki had pulled together. Even though the wedding had been last Saturday, they weren't due to go on honeymoon until tomorrow. Micki would not miss Flora Day, not even for her honeymoon. She was crazy, but so were most of the people in Helston. Flora Day was sacred.

Her wedding had rocked me in so many ways I hadn't anticipated. Seeing Micki's father's chest puffed out, full of pride, as he walked her down the aisle set me off. Crying at your best friend's wedding wasn't unusual, but I wasn't crying for Micki; I was crying for myself. Because this was something I'd never have. A proud father by my side. Obviously I'd known that, and had thought about it many times, but it actually hit me that day, and it hit hard. Fathers were, of course, for more than just this moment, but watching the two of them laugh and smile brought it all home. Again. Some things you think you've left behind in childhood, but no, they're just lying in wait, picking their moment to cause the most problems. Thankfully, Micki had thought my tears were for her. As her father handed me his handkerchief, I'd cried even more.

The other thing had been not coming with a plus one. Micki had said I should bring a hot actor, but I knew mixing work with pleasure was always a mistake. Just as mixing romance with a friend had proved a disaster, or more correctly a life-changing fuck-up. So, I didn't know if I was actually relieved or devastated when I saw Ke had brought someone. Truthfully, I was both. My stomach had churned when I caught sight of him walking into the room, his arm encircling the waist of a gorgeous woman at his side, both of them moving together with ease. Claire was another student on his course, according to Micki. As Wilf, seemingly oblivious, introduced her to me, I couldn't help but respond to her warm, open smile. She was lovely, from her soft brown hair and the splash of freckles across her nose. She suited him. And that was the biggest kick in the gut. It hurt like hell, but somehow it was less painful than when I'd seen him and Micki together. Perhaps the shock of that had hardened me for all his future girlfriends.

Throughout all the wedding events, I'd had to work hard on being happy for Micki, and for Ke. I'd made choices, and I was well on my way to having the career I'd always dreamed of. My days were filled with meeting actors, agents, directors and scriptwriters, and my nights were spent at the theatre, and in comedy clubs, whether I was in London, New York or LA. Laura was fabulous, guiding and encouraging me, and every day I learned something new about human nature, and how to manage people and their expectations. That was, except for my own.

No, I wasn't good at managing myself. Not that this was visible to those around me. To all and sundry, I appeared to have a perfect life. Thanks to Tony helping me, I owned a small flat in Hackney, which I loved. It was my haven. Most of my days were then spent in the new office in Soho, scouting for talent and simply being Laura's eyes and ears in the UK. This was a big step and showed Laura's faith in me. The thrill never got old any time an actor I put forward to Laura for a specific role came though. It was such a high.

Of course, there were also the lows, when we weren't selected by a producer or a director because we hadn't matched their vision. It was always such a let-down, having invested so much time and energy in diving deep into the script, and working through actors who we felt would bring something special – if not magical – to the role. My favourite part of my job was when I could bring a new talent to the table. Nurturing young actors at the start of their careers was the best feeling.

This morning I'd been awake since five, answering emails and keeping on top of things, even though this was technically a holiday and I'd been here since Friday. But, truthfully, I couldn't wait for my train journey back to London tomorrow, to get back to work, where I had some sense of control over my life. Here, things were being thrown at me left, right and centre. Such as the brunch on the beach on Sunday, the day following the wedding. I'd known about this, but somehow I'd missed out on the fact that it would just be the wedding party.

During the wedding reception itself, it had been easy for me to avoid Ke and his girlfriend in a crowd of nearly two hundred people, but with only twenty, it had been tricky. At one point, Ke and I had found ourselves in the queue for the barbecue, and there'd been no way I could walk away without it looking odd. At least his girlfriend had gone back to Plymouth before the brunch. Ke and I stood there, not speaking, although it was all I wanted to do. I longed to know how he was doing, and whether he was enjoying his course. What were his plans when he finished next year? But neither of us said a word, and the longer the silence, the harder it became to break it. I almost blurted out everything as we stood there – anything to halt the widening gap between us. But I didn't. I held it all in, feeling sick in the process. It had been a relief when we both got our burgers and could go our separate ways.

Today I was helping Mum with the Hal an Tow, then I'd be free to do as I pleased, which would include a good catch up with Tony. He'd only been at the wedding briefly because a dear friend had had a fall. Tomorrow I'd also be wishing Micki farewell and bon voyage for her honeymoon.

. . .

Tony and I sat on a bench in the garden of The Bell. The rain had passed, and the sun was trying to make a proper appearance.

'Well, Flora are you happy with your day?' Tony lit a cigarette.

'As Flora's go, the weather could have been better, but it was great to see Micki dance the Midday, and as a married woman.'

'Yes, that bit was interesting.'

I took a large swig of my lager. I wouldn't be dragged into saying anything about her choice of husband, especially. He was local, but that was the only thing in his favour. Micki would say he was handsome. And I could agree that, on the surface, this was true. But his eyes were cold, and he never listened to her. In fact, most times he cut her dead in conversations. I'd raised it with her and had barged in a few times when I probably shouldn't have. He didn't like me.

'Are you OK?' Tony asked.

I frowned.

'You wept in the ceremony as though you'd lost your mother.'

So much for no one noticing because they'd been looking at how beautiful the bride was.

'Want to talk about it?' He nudged me.

'Not really.'

'So you'll leave me to speculate that... you feel abandoned by your best friend?'

'Seriously?'

'Thought not.' He took a drag of his cigarette while I looked at my empty glass. 'Do you want me to continue, or will you just tell me?'

I looked from my glass to him.

'After you enlighten me, I'll get us both another drink.'

I looked out towards the church tower. 'It was seeing her father walk her down the aisle. And knowing I'd never have that.'

Tony stilled.

'That's all.' My voice cracked.

'That's easy then – you've got me for any wedding day of yours, and well, I'm fabulous.' He stood, taking my empty glass.

'You *are* fabulous, and if the day ever comes, I couldn't think of anyone I'd want more to lead me up the aisle.' Except my real father, I added silently.

'I should hope not.' He kissed my cheek and disappeared. I sank back against the picnic table. There was no need to think, let alone stress, about such things anyway. I was currently living a celibate life, and the likelihood of my getting married was as doubtful as it could be.

Micki rocked up to me at eleven pm. I was drunk, and she was rat-arsed.

'Wasn't it the best?' She grinned and then steadied herself.

'Saturday?' I asked.

She fixed her gaze on me. 'Saturday? No, Flora Day. It's Christmas, birthday and wedding all wrapped up in one.'

I laughed, for what else could I say? Flora Day *was* great, and for once had been more enjoyable for me than I expected nowadays. But the woman had just had the most beautiful wedding a few days ago. Today it'd rained, and Saturday had been sunny. But as her new husband, Carl, walked back towards us, carrying drinks for us all, it wasn't the time to challenge her.

Once he'd delivered them, he wandered off to chat to his mates. Micki threw her arm around me.

'You are the best, even if you bawled your eyes out at my wedding.'

'Sorry about that.' I looked down.

She took a sip of her cider. 'Everyone thought it was sweet you were so happy for me.' She tilted her head. 'But it wasn't that, was it?'

I didn't reply.

'You can't lie, which I like a lot. No, I reckon it was two things. My dad, and Ke's girlfriend.'

I opened my mouth.

'I know you've had the hots for him for like, forever. Seriously who wouldn't? I mean, I sure did, but it didn't last. And now, because you guys aren't really talking anymore, for whatever reason you still won't tell me, it makes you sad.'

Across the room I spied Ke chatting to Wilf. He looked up and our eyes met for a moment, a moment too long. I jerked my gaze away.

'Anyway, neither of us can have him now,' Micki said, then promptly passed out.

Thirty-Four

2025

8 May, 3:00 p.m.

It was done. The dance was over. I'd survived.

The crowds cheered. Ke and I were swiftly hauled off for photos to be taken, as though it was our wedding day. I grimaced. That wasn't a helpful thought. Once that had been all I wanted, and it still hurt if I was honest. In fact, all of today had been an exercise in pain of one level or another, from the sharpness of a paper cut to the deep low ache that hits your every move.

'Right, just here in front of the Guildhall.' The photographer positioned us, then stepped back. 'Could you two step a bit closer together.' He smiled. 'You know each other, right? Or if you didn't, you do after today.' He laughed to himself as Ke and I moved nearer. The photographer waved his hand, indicating closer still. We shuffled and stood hip to hip, then Ke slipped his arm around my back, resting his hand on my waist. A sharp stab of longing shot through me at his touch. His fingers had sat there before, caressing my skin. Memories.

The phone in my pocket pinged a few times – we must have been standing in a spot with decent signal. Although I didn't look at the messages, I knew it would still be Vlad saying 'Shag him!!!' and I felt my face flush.

'Now, look at each other and not me,' instructed the photographer.

I swallowed and turned to Ke. What was he thinking, feeling? Were his memories as close to the surface as mine? Our eyes met and everything stopped, the crowds, the noise, the wind. Everything, including my heart. In that moment, I saw his pain. And not just the pain I'd caused him, but more... from his mother's behaviour and eventual death, from the loss of Claire. Then it was gone, his expression guarded.

'Perfect. Just a few more, with big smiles.'

How could I smile after what I'd just seen? Ke turned to the camera and smiled like a pro, which I suppose he was. He was the face of his company. Photoshoot after photoshoot had featured him. Could I do that? Mum could. She'd lit up a room with her smile, and that's what I thought about now, projecting it to the camera.

'Great.'

'There you are.' The mayor walked towards us. 'This reporter just wants to ask you a few questions.'

My heart sank.

'Shall we head into the Guildhall so you can talk more easily?'

That wasn't a question. Ke led the way. His shoulders looked like a brick wall laid straight and strong. They were the wall protecting him. He was no longer the boy without friends. Now he was at the heart of this community. I was the outsider, and I wouldn't breach his protective barriers.

'I'll go get you both a drink,' the mayor said as he left.

'So, the mayor has told me the two of you first danced together at the age of eight. Is that right?'

We didn't look at each other but said in unison, 'Yes.'

'How sweet.' She fiddled with her phone to make sure it was recording.

'Were you two ever more than a dancing couple?' she asked,

and I immediately guessed she worked for the *Mail,* or was planning on pitching this to them.

'No,' we both said together.

Her perfectly arched eyebrows went to new heights. She didn't believe us, that much was clear.

'Interesting.' She glanced at us. We both stood ramrod straight, a good two feet apart. 'You're both the golden children of Helston, having gone on to achieve much in your careers.'

'I'd hardly put our achievements alongside the likes Henry Trengrouse, who created the safety rocket,' I said.

'Nor have we reached the sporting heights of Bob Fitzsimmons,' Ke added.

'I take your point.' She smiled. 'But you have won surfing championships and founded a global company, and you've worked with many of the top names in film, on Oscar and BAFTA-winning movies.'

We nodded.

'Ke, you still live here in Helston, while you Flo are based in...'

'I divide my time between London and LA.'

'Not Helston?' Her eyebrows couldn't climb any higher.

'No.' I crossed my arms.

'But I heard you've just inherited Lismore from your godfather.'

'I have.' I didn't like the direction this was going. More questions about what my plans were for the house.

'So now you'll be adding Helston to your list, surely?'

Had someone put her up to this? If so, who? Was it the same one who'd decided that Ke and I should lead the Midday Dance?

'Indeed,' I replied evasively.

'And Ke, you stepped back from your very active position at your company to spend more time parenting your daughter.'

Even though he was standing a distance from me, his tension reached me.

'I'm so sorry about your wife.' Her tone didn't carry the words sincerely. There was nothing sorry about her.

'Thank you, but my daughter and my wife have nothing to do with today, and with Flo and I dancing together.' Ke snapped out the words.

I knew my role now.

'We first danced together at eight years old, as we said, and like so many people in Helston, the dancing partner you have as a child usually continues to be your Flora Day partner throughout your life. There are marvellous tales of people returning from all over the world to partner with their old friends.'

She looked at me as though I were insane.

'My best friend Micki danced her first Midday Dance with Tom, who'd partnered her first dance at the age of seven. In her words, Flora Day is like Christmas, your birthday and your wedding all rolled into one.'

'Your wedding?' she asked pointedly.

'As I've never married, I can't comment on that, but according to many residents it is.'

'Is it that way for you?' she asked Ke.

'I got married on the eighth of May.'

A memory pierced me, Tony's sympathetic hand on mine, then fled just as quickly.

'How romantic. That way Flora Day could never overshadow the anniversary.' She smiled. 'Now let me just check a few details. Flo, your mother was Maria Richards the actress, and your father?'

I tensed and Ke reached out, touching my arm.

'Unknown.'

She arched again, just one of those impossible brows. 'I see.'

She didn't at all, and I could tell what this article would become already. Taking the barest facts and spinning a tale of dramatic lies.

'Sir Anthony Clemens, knighted for his services to charity and Cornwall, was your godfather.'

'Yes, Tony was.'

'And he was an angel investor in your business too, Ke. Practically the only one.'

'Yes.' His mouth drew tight, and if the mayor didn't arrive with a drink in a minute, I could tell Ke would walk out.

'So, he was a fairy godmother, or father as it were, to both of you.'

'He was a friend to many in this town, and out of it,' Ke said.

'I don't see what this has to do with Flora Day either,' I said, in my most killingly professional voice.

She smiled. 'It adds colour.'

'Flora Day is the welcoming of spring and summer, and a celebration of making it through another winter. I'd suggest you focus on that, and not my godfather's, Ke's, or my personal life.' I issued the warning. 'It's so easy to get facts wrong, especially when children, or people who are no longer here to speak for themselves, are involved. Misunderstandings ensue, and that can become very messy.' I smiled sweetly, then turned to Ke. 'Now, I think you owe me a pint or two.'

'I do indeed.' He took my arm, and we headed out the door of the Guildhall, into the raging party on the street outside the Red.

Ke turned to me. 'Thank you.'

'She'll still spin whatever untruths she can, based on hearsay, but it will be a bit less salacious. Sadly I can't stop her.'

'But you tried, and I appreciate that.'

The mayor spotted us and called down, asking why we were leaving so soon. We smiled back, waved, and walked off into the crowd.

Thirty-Five

Flora Day, 2014

Thursday
Age: 27
Forecast: Overcast

They'd been filming the new series of *Poldark* last month, and I'd been on hand for most of it to gain greater insight into the exploding market in long-form storytelling. It was threatening to eclipse the film market, with bigger and bigger names being pulled into it. It demanded a lot from the casts and not just time. Laura wanted my take on it.

The big upside was being able to see so much of Mum, Tony, and Micki, and, despite my protestations, they'd enticed me to stay through the long weekend, as well as for Flora Day. But unlike previous visits, I'd holidayed in Cornwall more like a tourist. The food scene in Porthleven had really taken off, and I enjoyed the buzz. What I loved most was that the seaside town had still kept its Cornish heart. Not that St Ives and Padstow hadn't, but they'd been on the tourist route for a long time, so locals had been pushed aside. The money tourists brought in was vital, but it was a finely balanced thing. I hoped that wasn't the future for Porthleven, because it still felt real and Cornish. Hopefully, it would remain discovered just enough but not too much – the elusive fine balance again.

Having moaned in my head about tourists over the bank holiday, I'd loved visiting the Tate St Ives and having my chips stolen by a seagull. I, of all people, should have known better. I'd warned the cast of *Poldark* enough about the perils of the pesky gulls, but forgot about them myself when I closed my eyes to enjoy the heat of the sun. The weather had been glorious, which didn't always work in our favour for the filming. Mizzle added atmosphere, and sun-baked fields created a whole different mood. My role in casting the series had been minimal, but I made myself useful to the location scouts. And it was good to showcase different places in the part of the county I was from.

The crew had gone off to finish filming further north, while I'd dashed about with Mum exploring Cornwall in a way I hadn't done since I was a child. From the Eden Project to the Lost Gardens of Heligan, we walked, talked and relaxed. I treated us to a two-night stay at Tresanton in St Mawes, and it was such fun to spoil her. The weather had been so good that as we sat on the terrace; it felt more like the Mediterranean.

This year one film I'd worked on had won at Cannes, and it was such a thrill to have been even a small part of it. My boss, Laura, had been encouraging me to step forward more, to take on a bigger role in casting. At first I'd found it terrifying, but as each project worked, I'd started growing in confidence, and in my instincts. I now actually felt like I was beginning to hit my stride. It was a good place to be.

This morning I'd written just that in my diary. I'd also written that a small part of me still hungered for Ke. I really thought by now it would have gone, but it seemed it was still a constant. Maybe I had to accept that my need for him would always hold a place in my head and my heart. The self-help books all said that first loves did just that. Looking at it logically helped me to prepare for today.

Now I was standing by the Epworth Hall, because Mum had

roped me into being part of the Hal an Tow, as a wave for St Piran. How could I have said no? I couldn't, but I still wished I hadn't agreed. Because Ke was St Piran and Claire, his girlfriend, was a dancing girl. The last thing I wanted to do was spend the next hour and a half in their company, but I couldn't back out now.

Two days ago, Mum had casually dropped into the conversation the news that Ke had received a first for his degree. Of course I was so happy for him, and as we all gathered it seemed as good a time as any to say so.

'Hey Ke, congrats,' I ventured, with a subdued smile.

'Yeah, thanks,' he replied, a small frown of confusion on his face, his eyes questioning. Claire smiled easily at me, tucked closely into his side. I was relieved as hell when Mum then called out for everyone to begin to make their way to St John's, but in silence. Saved from having to say anything else, I hustled along, edging as far away from both Ke and Claire as I could.

By the time we reached Meneage Street and were performing in the tight space in front of Boots, I'd managed to smile and say a few polite words to Claire. What did she know about Ke and me? It was always awkward meeting someone's ex, but I wasn't officially Ke's ex. For all Claire knew, I was just an old friend who'd moved away. I couldn't read anything in her behaviour about what she did or didn't know. She was warm and friendly, and this drove me mad. I wanted her to know that Ke had loved me first, and for far longer than he had her. I also wanted her to know what I'd done, so she'd realise the chance she had with him now was only because of me. But in that way of thinking lies madness, as they say. Instead, I swallowed all the anger and frustration and smiled my way through the performance.

As soon as I'd shed my costume and helped Mum to gather the rest, I was straight into The Blue to meet Micki. Never had I needed a drink so much. But as I strode into the pub, eager to find my friend, I stopped. Already standing there with Micki were Ke and Claire. This wasn't going to work. Before they could notice me, I fled back to Mum's to lick my wounds and plan how not to come to Flora again. It wasn't good for me. I was behaving like a toddler, and I hated that about myself. I needed to move on, as Tony kept telling me. It was time for me to start dating properly too, and to get Ke Dale out of my head, once and for all.

Thirty-Six

Flora Day, 2015

Friday
Age: 28
Forecast: Light rain

The colour of this year's diary was grey. When it had arrived with a long letter from Tony, it had reminded me of Cornish skies. Every day of late had been bright and beautiful, but not today. The sky was flat grey.

> *I wish it was sunny. I've invited Nick for Flora Day and I want him to see Helston at its best. It's important. He's important.*

Putting the pen down, I paced my old room before heading downstairs. I was in Cornwall again for the next *Poldark* series, so there'd been no excuse to avoid Flora Day. The mania that had erupted over the first season of *Poldark* had been astounding, and I was pleased to have been involved in it. After all, I was Cornish. Mum had been an extra in the filming of the original series decades ago, which led to her career taking off. She'd spoken fondly of that baking summer in 1976 and being stuck in period dress over at Botallack.

Her photos from that time showed a different world. Snapshots with a distinctly 1970s tint. Would we look back on our photos from today in the same way? Now everything was captured on our phones, except for the occasional resurgence of Polaroid cameras, and single-use film ones popular at weddings. Nothing said love better than a disposable camera filled with drunken shots of your friends making fools of themselves.

God, I'd become a cynic. Maybe I'd been to too many weddings of late, matched with divorces shortly after. Mum was right to say friendship was the most important thing. It was stronger than romantic love, and less fickle. Well, once you were an adult, that was. The friendships of childhood could change with the wind, from love to hate in a second.

How I'd hated Micki after she'd taunted Ke into kissing her, but a few days later, once I didn't feel hungover anymore, I'd quickly got over it. And we'd had so many more ups and downs over Ke since then. But, somehow, we'd got over those too. That was the joy of friendship, and it helped you to discover who you were, and what was important to you. It was friends who were key to this. They pushed you and pulled you until you were formed. At twenty-eight, I was feeling pretty fully formed now. I loved my job. I had great friends, and of late I had a new partner. Nick was a literary agent, and we'd met when his client was working on the script of their book.

On our first date at the Groucho Club, I'd laughed more than I had in a long time. He'd regaled me with one of his client's antics when they hadn't been shortlisted for the Booker, and I'd followed with tales of a certain client's particularly uncompromising requirements on set. Before I knew it, it was after one in the morning, and we were standing on Dean Street looking for taxis. Somehow we ended up in one together, although my place was in Hackney and his was in South Kensington. We went to his. Despite the walk of shame, wearing the same clothes the next day into the office, I hadn't felt so happy in years. Someone finally got me, and I could relax and be myself. He'd become so much a part of life, we'd started talking about living arrangements.

Nick had arrived in Helston twenty minutes ago and just freshened up at Mum's. Now that he was ready, we walked down Meneage Street to watch the Morning Dance.

'I didn't know things like this still existed,' he said, not taking his eyes off the dancers.

'Surely you've seen Morris dancers.' I searched his face, trying to figure out what he was thinking. Sadly, I was none the wiser. He was good at keeping his internal thoughts to himself, which was most often a requisite of his job. But what I'd found smooth and charming before now felt unsettling.

'Of course, but this is on a different scale altogether.'

I smiled. Yes, it was the heart of Helston on display for all to see. All those old news clippings in the museum that I'd catalogued one year were a testament to how well-known Flora Day had once been. Gone were the days when visitors came by train and charabanc. Now one of the supermarkets turned over its car park for the day, and the rugby club bolstered its coffers by offering parking. Spectators were mostly those from around Cornwall, who came to experience the spectacle and the joy of the day.

I tucked my arm into Nick's.

'Is that man drinking a pint?' He glanced at his watch.

'He is. The pubs open at six in the morning on Flora.'

He whistled. 'Long day.'

'It can be, and pacing is required to make it through.' Times when I hadn't been good at that were best left in the back of my mind. Flora Day had much to atone for in the past, and I was certain it had been that way for many people. The merry month of May was played out large on its eighth day in this part of Cornwall.

'What's next?' he asked with a hint of boredom in his voice.

'The Hal an Tow,' I said, leading him through the town, hoping I'd been imagining it. He was all eyes, and I began to see

Helston from his perspective. It was worn around the edges, but the beauty of the architecture was still there.

'This town feels like a place that time forgot,' he said as we strolled down an ope to St John's. 'Ope is not a word I've seen before,' he said.

'It's an alley anywhere else.'

He nodded. 'Odd, like the kennels you pointed out earlier.'

His tone had a critical edge, and part of me wanted to defend my hometown, to explain every bit of its esteemed history, but the other part of me didn't feel I could.

'Just wait until you see this.' I found us a spot high enough that he could peer down onto what was to come. At eight thirty sharp, the distant sound of the drums and whistles pierced the air. Nick turned to me in amazement as the greenery-clad people arrived, with colourful dancers and actors creating their circle, then the show started. As the song began, the tingling started up in my toes, and the words sprung out of me as the ancient antics were performed.

'Aunt Mary Moses?' Nick raised an eyebrow. 'Really?'

I was about to explain, but there was nothing I could say. The Hal an Tow made no sense, but it made all the sense in the world. It was tradition, pulling on the rejoicing that summer was here and life would go on. Yes, it looked crazy to someone who had never seen and didn't appreciate the folklore and history behind it. Now was not the time to rationalise it, so I didn't try.

We followed the crowds up to the Monument and watched the whole thing again. Maybe seeing it more than once, and the way in which the crowds embraced it all, would help. But as it drew to its completion, he turned to me, saying, 'So this is who you are.'

I stilled. Was this me? It was certainly a part of me. Not a part he'd seen before. His version of me was chic, insightful, and ambitious. A city girl who moved between London, New York and LA. This part was more pagan and instinctive. Earthy and free-spirited. And, in that moment, I saw what a powerful combination it could be. Just as Gran had always said – you could take the boy or girl out of Helston, but you couldn't take the Helston out of him or her.

'When you said you were from Cornwall, I pictured sandy beaches, buckets, spades and maybe even a Rosamunde Pilcher family saga, but not this, definitely not this.' His voice was even but there was judgement in it. I felt it.

'There's much more to Cornwall than pretty views.' I tried not to bristle. Sandy beaches and, since the new *Poldark* series had dropped, stunning cliffs and vistas were what people wanted. Tourism may have been key to the economy, but people forgot the rest, namely the granite spine that ran down Cornwall. Its industry had shaped the Duchy, and had once given it power. Now it was holidaymakers, pasties, ice cream, farms and fishing.

'I can see that now.' He smiled, and I softened. He wasn't to know. It was up to me to show him my world here, and that was scary. It had been safer to keep this part of me hidden, and not to have to explain my history. It didn't always make sense to me, let alone to someone who came from such a different background. Nick's posh West London upbringing had been all grand art galleries and cosmopolitan theatre.

I was falling hard for him, though. So, logically, I knew he needed to see this side of me. I had to let him into my world, all of it.

'Provincial towns have their charms.'

I bristled at the word and his patronising tone.

'The architecture here, all grey stone, is a bit bleak.' He looked the building up and down.

'Solid.'

'Like you,' he said.

I bit back my reply. It wasn't grey stone but granite, and it ran in our blood. It was who we were, as Gran would also have said.

Mum dashed up to us as they finished the performance in front of the Guildhall.

'Well, Nick, what did you think?' she asked.

He paused, and I watched his glance dart around to the charity shops, the tattoo parlours and the betting shops, all festooned with flowers and greenery. 'I can safely say I've never seen anything like it.'

Mum's lips pursed before she switched gears and smiled. It didn't reach her eyes. 'See you both later in The Blue?' She glanced at me. 'I think Nick needs to sample Spingo Extra Special. It might all make sense to him then.' She disappeared with her greenery fluttering as if a thunderstorm was imminent.

I'd thought introducing Nick to Flora Day could be a good start to opening myself up to him further but it was now looking like he might not make it to the end of the day. And I could feel the bruised part of my heart that'd tentatively begun to unfold closing up to hide again.

Thirty-Seven

Flora Day, 2016

Saturday
Age: 29
Forecast: Light rain showers

Because of work, I'd only been able to drive down this morning, which meant that I'd missed the Early Morning Dance, the Hal an Tow, and the Children's. Quite why I was here, I wasn't certain. Somehow three people had convinced me I must come, that it'd be good for me, and finally that they longed to see me. Namely Micki, Tony and Mum.

Before I'd left, I'd written in my diary:

Survive. Surely this should become easier...

But after last year's fiasco with Nick, I wasn't holding out hope. I parked the car at the rugby club because there was no way to reach Mum's house with the streets closed. Lugging my overnight bag through the town, I looked – let alone felt – like an outsider. The crowds were five deep on the pavements, and it was quarter to twelve. The excitement was palpable. I jostled my way through, and with each step asked myself again, why was I here? Mum was waiting for me at Lismore.

The crowds were thinner on Church Street, but it'd be a while before the dancers reached here. I didn't know which shops they'd be going through this year. Last year, a highly offended Pam Smith had informed me that several shops had refused entry to the dancers. One had gone out of business now. Everyone knew it wasn't connected, but there were so many superstitions attached to Flora Day.

The gates of Lismore were hung with flowers, and the entrances draped in laurel and bluebells. I took a sniff. Golden days when life had been defined by asking the fairies permission to pick bluebells seemed so far back in time it could have been someone else's childhood, not mine. My life was fated to be different. I wouldn't be a single mum to a single daughter. I'd broken the chain of the Richards women. Maybe I'd offended the fairies. Of course I had. I had thrown away love.

Walking through the house, I noted the new artwork Tony had acquired, and that his favourite Gainsborough portrait had moved. I peered into his study and saw it hanging opposite his reading chair. This made me happy, but I couldn't say why. Maybe because Tony had always said it reminded him of me.

Coming out through the conservatory, I was struck by the crowds on the sloping lawn and more flowers than usual, as well as a marquee that didn't normally feature in the day's proceedings. Was Tony having a party?

'Hello, Flo.' Mrs Wearne beamed. 'Glad you made it.'

'Me too.' I lied with a big smile. With each step I took, a sense of unease arrived. Something wasn't right, and I couldn't pinpoint what it was. 'Tony?'

'In the garden, love.'

'Thanks.' I scanned the crowds. Would he be hiding out in the vegetable garden having a cigarette again? He'd decided not to dance this year, as his knee was giving him problems after a fierce tennis match against an old rival. As he said, the bad knee was his own bloody fault. His letter had had me crying with laughter from his report of the defeat he'd suffered.

Diving back into the house, I walked slowly, coming out through the side door and into the walled vegetable garden. Tony was sitting in a puddle of sun, with his eyes closed and a cigarette in his hand.

Quietly, so as not to disturb his peace, I came and stood in front of him, blocking the sunshine. His eyes flew open, and a big smile covered his face.

He jumped to his feet. 'Flo, you came!' He wrapped me in a big hug, and the tension I'd been carrying disappeared. He held out a cigarette, and I shook my head.

'My darling you might need something.'

I squinted at him.

'I didn't want to say anything over the phone, or even in a letter.'

'Are you OK?' I took his hand in mine. I couldn't bear anything to be wrong with him.

'Fit as a fiddle, or as much as one can be having had too much fun last night.' He rubbed his forehead. 'And of course, my knee.'

'What's up?' If it were something big, then surely Mum or Micki would have said something. They definitely would have if someone had been ill or had died. But they'd both been filled with the joys of spring.

'No one has died,' he said, taking a seat and patting the space beside him.

Now I was really worried. 'Then why do you look like your father's ghost has appeared?'

'Hmm, what a horrific thought.' He shivered.

'Indeed.'

'You know that Ke and Claire are engaged.' He took a drag of his cigarette.

This news had come at Christmas from Mum, who was over the moon for the adorable couple. She'd been guarded at first, testing how I'd take it, but with my insistent repetition of 'It's fine,

I'm happy for him', her enthusiasm had burst through. She hadn't been able to see my flinches as she commented on what a lovely girl Claire was, and how happy they looked. She didn't know how much it hurt me. But how could she, since I hadn't told her anything? And I'd become a master at disguising it.

'Well, tomorrow they are marrying.'

'Oh,' I said. Tomorrow was the eighth of May. Flora Day. My day. Of course, the Flora Day celebrations were happening today because the celebrations for it were never held on a Sunday.

'And the reception will be here,' he said flatly.

'Here, Helston?' I asked.

'Here, Lismore.'

'I see.' Dear God, anywhere but here.

'No, you don't see, which is why I wanted to tell you this in person.' He took my hand in his.

I drew a deep breath. What could I say? 'You could have made a trip to London and told me there. Warned me before now.'

He looked down at his hands. 'I suppose, with hindsight, I could have.'

I pulled my hand from the comfort of his. There was nothing to say or do. This was what Ke wanted. Helston, home.

'Ke and Claire have been living in the shed cum cottage here in the garden, in order to save money for their new business, and their wedding.'

'Oh.' I swallowed. This was hard, harder than I'd ever imagined it would be. It was going to happen, though. Ke was getting married. I'd accepted that, but the reality was now proving far worse than any scenario I'd played out in my head.

'So when they asked me, and said they had a date with the church, and so many friends who'd be home for Flora...' His voice trailed away. Tony was a good soul. It was the right thing, but I didn't need to be here. In fact, I needed to be anyplace else but here.

I stood.

'Don't leave.' Tony got to his feet, stubbing out his cigarette. 'You need a drink. This has been a shock.'

I laughed. 'You of all people knew how this would make me feel.'

'That's why I'm the one telling you.' His hand rested lightly on my shoulder.

'How did you manage that?' I asked. How had Micki kept this news to herself? She could never keep a secret, and this wasn't even a secret, so maybe that was why. Mum may have sensed something, with my lack of enthusiasm to the engagement news.

Both Mum and Micki would be attending the wedding, I was certain.

'I lied and said I'd told you ages ago, and that you were fine with it.'

I turned to look at him. He needed to know I wasn't fine with it. 'I see.'

'You are fine with it, aren't you?' he said, studying my face.

'Ha, if you think that then I'm a better actress than my mother ever was.' I laughed bitterly.

'That's not what I meant.' He ran a hand across his bald head, as if he still missed the hair he'd long ago lost.

I looked at him closely, but I was none the wiser. 'What *did* you mean?'

'This wasn't the road you chose. Remember? You wanted something different, and you have a wonderful life.'

I swallowed. The truth wasn't always easy to hear.

'You are actually happy for Ke. I know that, and you do too.' He paused. 'It may not feel that way right now, but you are.'

Tears threatened. This wasn't fair. I shouldn't be here. This was the last place I wanted to be. Yet here I was, and in a matter of minutes the Midday dancers would appear in the garden, with Ke and Claire being two of them. Then tomorrow, probably dressed in the same morning suit, Ke would say 'I do' to the woman he loved, in the church he'd gone to intermittently during his life. Meanwhile, I would try not to meet them as I made my way through the garden and back to Mum's house, to return to the life I loved. My friends in Helston would think some crisis had blown up with an actor on set, which I had to deal with. That was all. And that would be the end of this chapter in my life, and an end to the quiet hopeful dreams I'd had of Ke.

Thirty-Eight
2025

8 May, 4:00 p.m.

The lager was cold and did nothing to soothe my anger at the reporter we'd just met. She'd been trying to dig for salacious stories, and twist what should be a positive piece on Helston's joyous celebration of spring. Outsiders didn't understand it. But they could respect it. If I'd had St Michael's sword with me, I might have run her through. Instead, I took a big gulp of lager and met Ke's questioning glance as I lowered my glass.

'Thirsty?' he asked.

'Apparently.' I drew a deep breath.

'That woman.' His free hand clenched.

'I know.' I shook my head.

'Thank you.' He smiled, and it reached his eyes this time. Something shifted inside me.

'No problem,' I managed to say.

'That's either the most interesting conversation I've ever heard, or the most boring.' Micki looked between us. 'Care to tell me what it was about?'

'No,' we said together.

'Nothing's changed I see,' said Wilf, half laughing. 'All for one and one for all... and all for the confusion.' He threw an arm around my shoulder and kissed my temple. 'Good to have you back Aramis.'

I looked up at him and smiled. He'd always been our gentle giant, never getting into the scrapes the rest of us did. He was not D'Artagnan-like at all – more Athos in truth, but as he'd joined us later, that had been his name.

'You survived your first Midday Dance.' Wilf tapped his glass against mine. 'No doubt, like Tony before you, you'll dance many more now that you and Lismore are a pair.'

'Lovely thought but I can't see that happening,' I said, in what I hoped was a polite and evasive way.

'But as the owner of Lismore, it's not quite your right, but almost,' he pressed on.

I looked down, not wanting to meet the glances of Ke, Micki or Wilf.

'Does this mean you're selling it?' Wilf waded in.

'Probate needs to be done before I can consider my options.' I drew a breath. 'The last thing Helston or Cornwall needs is another absent second homeowner.'

'But you're not like them.' Wilf took a swig of beer. 'You're from here. It wouldn't be a holiday home. I mean Lismore, come on – the house of dreams would be your heart home.'

I smiled. Heart home. I loved that.

'See, you just need old Wilf to set you straight.' He finished his beer. 'I'm off now. For some of us, the day isn't over yet. See you all later.' He grinned. 'It feels great to have the gang back together. I missed this.'

The three of us stood in silence as Wilf walked off through the crowds.

My phone vibrated again.

Ke held out his hand and took the empty glasses from Micki and me. 'Same again?' he said as he headed into the pub.

Micki looked at her phone. 'Vlad's worried you haven't been

reading his messages.' She looked up. My heart fell. Micki and Vlad had exchanged numbers. This was dangerous. 'He seems to think you should shag Ke.'

I choked.

'Not a bad shout, as someone needs to. I've heard his date didn't go well.'

'Dear God, give the guy a break. He can't go on a date without everyone knowing whether he got lucky or not.' I huffed. 'That's just not fair.'

Micki stared at me.

'It isn't. Some things should be private, and that's certainly one of them.'

She tilted her head and did her impression of Gran when she'd just heard a juicy bit of gossip.

'No, simply no,' I said, not budging on the right to some privacy.

'Well, I for one agree with Vlad. I totally take back my claim I staked earlier today, or in the past. I say go for it. It's time you guys made up.'

She'd done this before, and she didn't know the full details of our past. To her it should be simple. Ke and I had fallen out over something that had grown larger over time. And, in a way, she was right. That was probably what Ke thought too. That I'd just been messed up in my mind, no doubt because of the influence of La La Land, and had blown something out of proportion. As I'd said to Ke, it wasn't him; it was me.

But as all these thoughts ran through my head, another one landed.

'Micki, are you the one who put Ke's and my name forward for the Midday Dance?'

She looked at me, then away.

'You.' I stared.

'Don't say it like that...' She met my glance.

'What the–'

'It was for both of you.'

I closed my eyes and replayed the pain on Ke's face as we began the dance, and my own turmoil at having to face him. I opened my eyes and said, 'Micki, you may have meant well but you have no idea the hurt you've caused.'

'No, I don't, because you've never told me.' She stared me down, challenging me to blink first. 'You know, I was always jealous of you.'

'What?' I frowned. I'd expected anything but that.

'Yes, on so many counts.'

'That doesn't make sense.' I crossed my arms. Micki was the one at ease with herself, who was only ever relaxed about any mistakes she may have made.

'From your point of view, I had what you wanted... the complete family, the pretty face,' she paused and looked down at her chest, 'the tits. But you had the complete love of your mother and your Gran.' She drew a breath. 'They never compared you to your siblings, or judged you by how you looked, or by which boyfriend you had.'

'Micki...'

'No, you just don't get it.' She gave a dry laugh. 'You had brains, beauty, and ambition and could have had any man you wanted.'

I opened my mouth and then shut it.

'Yeah, I had to call dibs on Ke because it was the only way I had a chance. I had to get in there first.'

She stared hard at me, and I blinked, looking at my oldest friend, feeling like I didn't know her at all. Jealous of me? It had always been the other way around.

'Now you have nothing to say. Are you ever going to be honest about what happened between you two?'

Lismore, Cross Street, Helston, Cornwall

---

17 March 2017

My darling Flo,

This is just a brief note to tell you the sad news of Ke's mother's passing. I knew you would want to know. It was not a surprise to anyone and the unkind are saying they are surprised it didn't happen sooner. You of all people in Helston understood how hard this relationship was for Ke. He never spoke about it although I tried to encourage him to and I'm sure you did as well. He must have felt keeping the pain locked away was the best way to manage it. We all handle things in our way. Despite the difficulty, it is a terrible thing to lose your mother. When mine died, even though we hadn't spoken for years, something inside me died too. I can see he is feeling the same way.

I have been helping him with his business and seeing a fair bit of him, acting as a mentor of sorts. He's not showing the grief but it's there in his eyes. Maybe a note from you acknowledging his loss might not go amiss. Yes, communication between you has been limited, but I know I appreciated hearing from old friends when my mother died.

Otherwise, all is well here. The garden is eager this year and it's keeping me busy. I'll see you in London in two weeks, so I'll fill you in on everything then.

In haste and with love always,

Tony xxxx

Thirty-Nine

Flora Day, 2017

Saturday
Age: 30
Forecast: Light rain showers

My diary this year was golden. Tony's nod to my thirtieth birthday. Chronicling my thoughts in these beautiful leather notebooks over the years had ensured I not only could chart my life but also thought of Tony every single day, even if I'd only written one word, like yesterday.

Here.

I picked up my pen to write, then paused. What did I want to remember, think about or note?

Today marks the thirty-first year since I was conceived. Still no information about who my father is. The hole this has left still exists, but I've managed to push it down deep, so on most days it's no more than a small empty feeling. It's that sense that's never truly satisfied.

This was a milestone year. I'd initially celebrated my thirtieth in Vegas with Micki, who'd joined me with a few girlfriends from LA. The next celebration had been in New York with colleagues and clients, and the final one had been two days ago with Mum and Tony in London. The zero year had been well and truly marked. I was single, solvent and in love with my job. There wasn't much more I could ask for, except the one thing I'd used to want – a family. My current boyfriend wasn't family material, but he was fun, and that had many positives. Besides, with all the travel I did for my job, having a family would be very hard, if not impossible. There was no point in pining for something you wouldn't be good at – I'd come to this conclusion over the years.

Today, I was to meet Micki for coffee after the Hal an Tow. My heart was so much lighter than last year. I'd written to Ke on the loss of his mother. He'd been so quietly brave all these years about her when I would have raged. It felt weird that Claire was the one in his life to help him through this loss and not me. But it was good that he had her. I felt truly happy for Ke. Tony had explained that he'd been an angel investor in Ke's new business, to get the surf clothing brand off the ground. It was doing well from all accounts. They manufactured as much as possible on the industrial estate in Helston, and hired as many locals as they could. This was what Ke had wanted all those years ago. He was home, and part of the community that he loved. It made our parting all those years ago easier to accept. We'd both done well, and I was pleased for him. He deserved happiness.

The Early Morning Dance was a joyous affair, and I recalled all the years I'd done it, feeling more than a touch nostalgic. Weaving my way down to St John's for the first performance of the Hal an Tow, I felt the sun break through the cloud. This was the way it was supposed to be. As the words said, *And for to fetch the summer home.* The warmth of the sun brought all the good summers home to me. Peace. Although I knew it wasn't peace that Micki wanted to talk about.

Her marriage was in tatters. But as I'd told her at the time, and again in Vegas, the breakdown was two-sided. Both had cheated. And there was little hope that the marriage counsellor could bring them together again. No doubt today would be about the end, and a new beginning. Flora Day was about rebirth.

The whistles and drums heralded the pageant. I turned to the person next to me. We were both grinning.

'I look forward to this every year,' he said. 'I live on the Lizard and I love the day, but the Hal an Tow is my favourite.'

'It's wonderful,' I said. I loved the Hal an Tow too, but I think it was the Early Morning Dance that held my heart. It had been my first 'grown up dance', and with my first love, so it would always be my favourite in a day full of them.

'Oggi, oggi, oggi.'

'Oi, oi, oi.'

The cries rose, and the excitement in the crowd grew as the crier began the welcome. I scanned the faces, seeing so many I knew well, but also a fair few unfamiliar ones, such as the man next to me. Even in today's modern world, with so many pulls on our time, Helston's Flora still brought people from far and wide to welcome in the spring and summer.

The two people playing Robin Hood and Maid Marion were strangers to me. But even though my time away had left me a bit on the outside, I was still Helston through and through. It was in my bones, my blood and in my DNA. This became apparent as I belted out the words so familiar to me.

Hal an Tow, jolly rumble O.

The view of the English sailors seeing off the Spanish always made me smile. The Spanish hadn't come to Helston, but to Mousehole, where they were defeated, but what was the matter of a few miles when it made such a sight?

St Piran with his papier-mâché millstone paddled into the centre of the ring. Women dressed as waves moved fluidly about him. Ke's wife, Claire, was one of them. Her cheerful smile quelled the jealousy that rose in me. Of course I was allowed to feel it, but she made him happy, and that was what was important. She'd embraced Helston, despite coming from the other side of the Tamar.

I caught Mum's eye as she moved around the performers. This was all going well. The green men hadn't hit the spectators as they play-fought with sticks. The women dressed as hedges, covered in greenery, hadn't been knocked over as the performers entered the centre. This was the smoothest I'd seen it go, but it was only the first stop.

As I sang out the chorus with gusto, I saw Ke beaming at Claire. My heart then stopped as I noticed the baby strapped to his chest. How had I not known? My head span and I grabbed the arm of the man from the Lizard. It was too much.

We were in the garden of The Red when I finally caught up with Micki. She was drunk but still coherent.

'We started divorce proceedings on Friday,' she said flatly. Almost exactly four years to the day since she'd walked up the aisle.

'Are you ok about this?' I sipped my gin and tonic. It was doing a good job of numbing the emotions squirming within me. A potent mix of happiness for Ke and the past rearing up to stab me in the gut.

'There's no other options, and I'm only twenty-nine.' She rolled her head around, stretching her neck.

'For another two weeks,' I pointed out.

'Don't rub it in.'

I laughed. 'Thirty is good actually.'

'It is for you.' She sipped her pint. 'It is for Wilf and for Ke too, but what have I done, except marry the wrong guy?'

I put my hand over hers. 'Well, at least you realised it now.'

'You warned me.' She rubbed her neck.

There was nothing I could say to this, because I had.

'I should have stuck it out with Ke.' She looked me in the eye. Was that a challenge? She still didn't know Ke and I had slept together, unless he'd told her. Which was possible.

'He's happy with Claire.'

'And I wouldn't have made him happy?' she shot back at me. This wasn't a good conversation to have when she was drunk and I wasn't.

'Well, were you both happy together?' I asked, already knowing the answer.

'No, it just didn't work.' She took a big swig of beer. 'I tried but he... his heart wasn't in it. Nor, come to think of it, was his dick.'

I choked on my gin. I didn't want to know this; I really didn't. I'd tried to block their short time together from my mind. It had taken years.

'I guess he just wasn't as into me as I wanted, or thought he would be.' She picked at the grain of the wood on the picnic table.

I looked down. Her word choice was interesting.

'You know, I knew you had a thing for him too.' She took a sip. 'And I did wonder if something happened, before you two fell out.' She looked at me over the rim of her glass. 'But then I started to wonder if you fell out because you wouldn't let anything happen, because you were sticking to our deal.' She laughed. 'I never believed you would, though. I thought you'd ask me to give up my claim.'

I swallowed.

'I would have too. Because I knew he had a thing for you as well, and he was miserable after you'd gone to LA.' She shook her head. 'But I guess when you saw the bright lights of tinsel town, you realised he was a home boy and you were an away girl.'

I finished my gin, trying not to think of what a difference it could have made in my teen years if I'd known she would have released her claim. Ke and I might have gotten together sooner, which could have changed the course of everything that happened. The image of him with his child strapped to his chest, and his smile as he watched his wife, had nearly killed me. But it was the right thing. We were both on the life paths we were meant to be on. Micki had done me a favour, and Ke too.

Forty

Flora Day, 2018

Tuesday
Age: 31
Forecast: Overcast

It was eleven in the morning, and Micki had three glasses of champagne in her, which wasn't helping her to stand still while I zipped her into her dress. She was due to lead the Midday Dance. I hadn't planned on coming home this year, but this announcement had changed everything. Nothing would have made me miss watching my oldest friend in her moment of glory.

'Stand still or your dress will get hooked to your bra, then everything will be on display by the time you're half way up Meneage Street.'

'I can't.' She sighed.

'I know you're nervous but you've got this. You and Tom have danced together so many times before. All will be well.'

'But back then it didn't matter. No one cared if I got it wrong.' She took another swig of the champagne.

I laughed. 'They still don't.'

'Not according to Mum.' She looked over her shoulder at me.

'Really?' I stood up and tugged the dress into place.

'She keeps going on about how, in her day, they never would have let a divorced woman lead the dance.' She made a face of pure distaste, just like her mother.

'She's still cross about losing Carl as a son-in-law?'

'Yup.' Micki reached for her glass. I held her back from it.

'Well, I'm pleased you're shot of him, and I wouldn't want to live in a world that still frowned on divorced people. Time, thank goodness, has moved on.'

'True.'

I released her, and she topped up her glass.

I narrowed my glance, showing my disapproval. 'Just remember, as you're imbibing all that fluid, that you won't be able to use a loo until you reach Lismore.'

'Bugger.' She put her glass down. 'You know, I always thought it'd be you doing this first, not me.'

'Ha – until Mum danced with Tony, somehow making her acceptable, I don't think they would have entertained a cursed Richards woman.'

'True, children out of wedlock are worse than divorcees.' She took my hand. 'I'll be OK, won't I?'

'Of course you will, and you look amazing.'

'Thanks for the help, and for coming. At least you were only in New York and not LA.'

'This is very true, and I wouldn't have missed this for the world. Helston has bestowed its greatest honour on you.' Out of all those selected by ballot the committee chose four Helston born couples to lead the dance.

She grinned. 'They have!'

Micki was still wearing her gown. It was nine in the evening, and we were in the garden of The Red on our second bottle of rosé. We'd discussed her brilliance leading the dance, and how funny it was that Tom was now the respectable family man.

'I've never really forgiven him for pushing me over,' I said, topping up our glasses again. I already knew I'd regret the rosé in the morning, but I was past the point of caring. I think Micki had passed that point hours ago.

'I told him to,' she admitted, a guilty expression sweeping her face.

'You did eventually confess.' I ran my finger around the rim of the glass.

'God, forgot I had.' She shook her head. 'You never took it out on me.'

I laughed. 'Not my thing to push you back.'

'True. You were always the good one.' She tucked a loose strand of hair behind her ear. 'I was always the reckless one.'

'No argument from me on that.'

'Now, we are two old bags.'

'Speak for yourself.' I leaned back. 'Thirty-one isn't old. We're just getting started.'

'Hey, I'm still thirty!'

'For two weeks.'

She pursed her mouth in distaste then asked, 'Do you remember when Wilf asked us our plans for the future?'

I nodded.

'Well, I'm the only one who hasn't done anything.'

'That was your plan,' I said.

'Yeah, but...'

'No buts. You married a man who's left you pretty well off.'

She crossed her arms. 'That's not the point. I mean, I always thought you wanted a family more than anything else, even if you didn't say that when Wilf asked.'

I swallowed. This was a bit close to the bone.

'I mean, look at us. Me divorced and you never married, and currently not even screwing someone. Where have we gone wrong?'

I closed my eyes for a moment. I still longed for a family, but as each Valentine's Day rolled around, and I was another year older, that felt further and further away. But at least I wasn't a single mum of a daughter, trapped. 'Have we really gone wrong, or just gone our own way?'

She downed her glass. 'I like that. We *have* gone our own way. No kids, no men, but we have friends. Who needs anything else, except more wine?'

'We still have half a bottle.' I pointed to it, and she picked it up, emptying it into our glasses.

'Now we need another.' She stood, swaying slightly.

'Let's finish this, then why don't we move on to The Blue?'

'Good plan.' She sank onto the bench.

I just hoped that by the time she'd drunk her wine, and I had her out of the pub, I could then redirect her home, even if it was necessary to promise more wine there. I was at my limit, and I didn't want to think about what might be lacking in my life.

Forty-One

2025

8 May, 4:25 p.m.

It was strange to be standing on Church Street wearing a gown, facing a woman I thought I knew. It was like I was seeing everything for the first time just because I was in an evening gown in the afternoon. I'd watched women on Flora Day do it for years, but to be one of them was different. And to be here with the pint that Ke had just handed me seemed surreal. He looked like he was at the races, while Micki was the only one of us who appeared perfectly relaxed in jeans and a jumper, like she had it all together, and maybe she did.

It was nearly four thirty, and the party was just beginning, as people who'd been at work began to appear, and the crowds grew. But partying was the last thing I wanted to do. The Evening Dance would begin in less than an hour, and they'd be dancing through Lismore's garden. I intended to be out of this dress and out of sight when it happened. I'd met all the requirements for the day, except to greet the evening dancers, but Tricia was going to do it. Right now, I was exposed, and it wasn't comfortable.

Ke looked between Micki and me, and it felt like the way we'd been twenty years ago, when Micki had hatched a plan and I didn't think it was a good idea. I'd usually been right, but that didn't stop her from pressing the point. Was that what she was doing now? Had I misread her all these years?

Peter Johns came up to us. There was no escaping him today. He looked between the three of us, and as he did so, the thought again reared up that he might be my father. His features weren't so defined that I could see mine in them. He had children, and they looked nothing like me, although they resembled his first wife and not him. So if it wasn't him, then who?

'Ke, can you drop by the office on Monday?' Peter asked.

Ke shrugged. 'Sure, anything urgent? I could come tomorrow.'

'Not necessary. Monday will do.' He smiled at the three of us. 'Good to see you all back together.'

'Feels good too.' Micki raised her glass, and looked Ke and me in the eyes.

I met her glance, then watched Peter walk away.

'That's a funny look.' Micki tapped my arm.

'Just wondering if there's any chance he might be my father.' As soon as the words were out, I regretted them. It must have been the lager talking. I hadn't drunk this much beer in years.

'Still trying to figure that out?' She pursed her mouth. 'I thought you'd let it go.'

I laughed bitterly. 'I had, until I read Mum's letter.'

Both Ke and Micki stepped closer to me, their eyes on my face, alert.

'What letter?' Ke asked.

'Peter handed me two letters yesterday, then told me to read them when I was alone.' I rolled my eyes. 'In Lismore 'alone time' is rather difficult at the moment, but I read Mum's letter this morning.'

'And?'

I glanced between the two of them. What did it matter now if

I told them? It didn't. The only person it had ever truly mattered to was me.

'She wrote me a letter two days after I was born.' I drew a breath, seeing her words in front of me. 'In it she said she would lie to me about my father. She knew who he was, and she loved him, and he loved her.'

'The ever-living f...' Micki gasped. 'That's brutal.'

'Are you OK?' Ke asked.

'Short answer: no.'

'Oh, Flo, how, I mean, why?' Micki asked.

'I don't know. I've spent my whole life wanting to know who my father was, and finally managed to let go of that idea, then I'm given this letter.'

'Who's the other letter from?' Ke asked, looking into his glass.

'Tony.' I smiled. 'Probably full of life lessons he hadn't passed on yet.'

'You haven't read it?' Micki was never one not to do everything in a rush.

'After I read Mum's, the day went into full operation, so no.' I shrugged. 'I'll read it tonight, probably with a glass of Tony's favourite whisky.'

'Good plan.' Micki took a sip of her drink.

'Maybe now you can both see why this legacy of Tony's isn't the gift people think it is.'

Ke looked at me. 'It *is* a gift. He's given you a place to be at home.'

I shook my head. Neither of them would, or could, ever understand, because they both didn't have all the information. It was a waste of time to even try explaining.

'Daddy.' Matilda bolted towards Ke at full tilt. The look of love on both their faces filled my vision. Love. Love between a father and a daughter. One thing I'd never known. Why had my mother denied me that? Who had it been best for? Certainly not me.

I turned away. It was just too painful to watch.

'This is the lady you were dancing with,' Matilda said.

'Yes, Matilda, meet my old friend Flo.'

I put my best smile on my face and took Matilda's outstretched hand. It was warm and small in mine. 'Hello Matilda. What a pleasure to meet you.'

'Daddy, is she the girl with you in the picture of you dancing when you were my age?'

'She is.' Ke's eyes met mine. Everything in me tingled. Warning. He needn't worry.

'I'm a bit different now.' I bent down to her level.

'I like your dress.'

'Thank you. It's my favourite colour.'

'Mine too.'

'Bluebells,' we both said, then laughed together. When I stood, Micki was watching me closely.

'Right, time to head home so I can change,' Ke said, ruffling Matilda's hair.

'But I like you in that.' She looked him up and down.

'Thank you, but you know me.'

'Jeans and a jumper.' His daughter looked at him with a smile so like his own.

'Exactly.' He glanced at Micki and then at me. 'Take care.'

'See you later,' Micki said.

'We'll watch the start of the Evening Dance then head home, as it's a school day tomorrow.' He glanced down at Matilda, who made a face.

'Tina's mother asked if I wanted to have a sleepover.'

Ke took his daughter's hand, then waved to us, before walking down Church Street.

When I looked up, Micki was still staring at me. 'Why didn't you tell me?'

'About Mum's letter?' I asked, hoping that was what she was asking.

'No, that you got pregnant with Ke's baby. That's what

happened, isn't it? That's why you wouldn't speak to him after you left?'

I felt the blood leave my face. How had she guessed?

'The kid would have been a teenager by now.' She shook her head. 'It all makes sense now.'

I turned and walked with as much dignity as I could back to Lismore, neither confirming nor denying it.

Forty-Two

Flora Day, 2019

Wednesday
Age: 32
Forecast: Overcast

My flight had been delayed, I'd missed my train, and now I was driving to Cornwall jet lagged and somewhat delirious. Mum was performing in the Hal an Tow this year as Aunt Mary Moses. If Tony hadn't told me, I wouldn't have known, and I wouldn't have made the trip. But he'd said it was a big thing and hadn't needed to say any more. Mum was sixty-two, and she was handing over the reins of the pageant to the next generation. This was going to be the last one she was actively involved in. From here on in, she'd just be a bystander, lining the streets with the rest of Helston, and all the visitors who flocked to see the ancient ritual.

Sitting on the plane, drinking coffee, I'd glanced out the window and seen Cornwall below. In my diary I'd written:

The end of an era.

Nothing else. For it was, and I wasn't sure why she was stepping down now.

If I could stay awake and find a place to park, I should just be able to make it to the Guildhall in time to witness it. But it was just my luck to get caught behind three tractors making the best of the dry weather. Rain was forecast. My fingers were firmly crossed it wouldn't happen today, though. Not on the day Mum was actually performing. All these years, and she'd stayed behind the scenes, never taking a role, just making sure it went to plan, or as close to it as possible.

As I navigated the double roundabout by the Penryn campus, I thought about all the times I'd tried to encourage Mum back into acting or directing, or anything to do with theatre or films. She had Falmouth Uni on her doorstep; she could have taught if nothing else. But it had always been a no. Even now, I didn't understand. If it had been such a driving passion for her before, then why abandon it? Yes, there'd been me, but plenty of actors had kids and continued. She'd just let it go altogether.

The full-on argument I'd had with her before I left to go to Manchester Uni still rang in my ears. I'd said she was a coward, which was so uncalled for. She wasn't, but something had been keeping her away from it I couldn't work out. Nothing I yelled or pleaded, or even whispered, had made her open up about it, though. It was just the way she'd always been about the identity of my father, calmly shutting me down every time. Knowing my mother as I did now, I couldn't see her being reckless enough to shag an unknown bloke, no matter how drunk she'd been. It just didn't add up, and that alone still bugged the shit out of me.

But all of that stuff was the reason I'd needed to be here to see her Aunt Mary Moses. Not that the role took any acting ability. She'd be adorned with bluebells and greens, herding girls dressed in floaty frocks while the verse was sung.

God bless Aunt Mary Moses
And all her power and might, O
And send us peace in merry England
Both day and night, O
And send us peace in merry England

Both now and evermore, O.

It was a prayer, really. And mine, at the moment, was to go faster, or I'd miss her last performance. I'd already missed the one she would have done at eight thirty this morning. The Mary Moses verse was only performed at the first and the last.

Tapping the wheel, I debated whether to risk overtaking the red Fiesta in front of me. They were dawdling, and I didn't have time.

The crowds around the Guildhall were five and six people deep. I could hear the whistles, the horns, and the chants but couldn't see a thing, except the top of the banners. Helys bys Vyken. Helston forever. Maybe, but definitely not for me. Having worked like crazy, I'd been promoted to agent six months ago, and I was well settled in LA now, returning here three times a year at most, and less if I could get away with it. I really hadn't planned on being here this year.

'Flo,' Micki called from the front of the crowd. 'Hey, let her through.'

People obligingly parted, and she wrapped me in a massive hug. 'Glad you're here.'

I drew a deep breath. 'Yeah, me too.'

The opening words in Cornish were proclaimed, and something settled inside of me as the song began. As I watched it unfold, I saw not the current people playing Robin and Marion, but Ke and me. Back then there'd been hope, and there'd been promise.

Micki sang loudly and out of tune beside me, while the Archangel Michael slew the devil. I'd often thought of us this way. But, unlike the scene in front of us, with the angel and the devil, we were still the best of friends, despite our ups and downs.

Mum was beaming as she entered the centre of the circle to play her role, and the girls flocked to her. She looked up as she sang, and when she saw me she stopped for just a moment, although no one else would have noticed it. Tony clearly hadn't told her I was coming. Probably wise, as it turned out – I nearly hadn't made it. But the crazy journey was worth it for this moment to see Mum's happiness and to feel the Hal an Tow with her.

'Look at you and me crying.' Micki elbowed me. 'We're not six-year-olds, but you wouldn't know it looking at us.' She looped an arm around my waist. 'The question is, are we crying because of your mum, or are we crying because of the things we've lost along the way?'

I stared at her. 'That's rather profound for this hour of the morning,' I snuffled, then leaned in to smell her breath. 'Are you still drunk from last night?'

She laughed. 'I wish.'

Mum found us afterwards in the crowds and wrapped me in an enormous hug. 'You're here.'

'I couldn't miss your starring moment,' I said, stepping back.

She sent me a funny look, and I thought I'd overstepped the mark.

'It's always been the role I wanted most, except for the one of being your mother.' She took my hand in hers.

'I love you too,' I said, wanting to say more, but she was pulled along by one of the little girls who had danced around her.

'Let's go and find a pint.' Micki blew her nose. 'I need it after all that emotion.' She started towards The Angel, and I just had to pray Ke wouldn't be there with Claire. He was still the one person I didn't want to see, and yet everything in me called out to him.

Forty-Three

Flora Day, 2020

Friday
Age: 33
Forecast: Sunny

Cancelled.

Flora Day has been cancelled, thanks to the pandemic. Having tried so hard to come up with excuses not to go in recent years, I now yearned with all my heart to be on the streets of Helston. But I was on the other side of the world, locked-down on my own in LA. All day I'd been sitting watching YouTube videos of past Floras, hoping to glimpse my mother.

She'd died three weeks ago.

Those words still didn't feel real to me...

Bloody COVID.

Tony had rung to tell me. He had been barely able to speak. I kept telling myself it wasn't real. I couldn't go home, and I wanted to more than I'd ever wanted to. Mum was gone. How was that possible? She was a life force. She was everything. She was gone, and I couldn't bear it.

Micki, Tricia, Ke and Tony had been the only people in attendance at her funeral, such as it was. I'd watched it through the modern wonder and curse of the Zoom call. I'd wept, paced and raged, trapped so far away in LA.

Tony told me all her things were now in Lismore as he'd cleared her rented house and handled all the paperwork. It should have been me doing all that – instead I'd felt less than useless, stuck on the other side of the Atlantic. Unable to fly and in a way unable to grieve. None of the rituals that might have helped were allowed to me. And no one in LA had known my mother. Everyone was locked in their own small world during this time, which made everything worse.

I didn't know what to do with my pain or where to put it.

Lismore, Cross Street, Helston, Cornwall

---

9 June 2020

My dearest Flora,

Like you I'm struggling. I wake every morning looking forward to my chat with Maria, to talk about the glorious weather we're having, then the sad truth arrives and takes my breath away. I can only attempt to understand what you must be feeling out in LA.

I am trying to be gentle with myself. It's not something that I'm good at. But I know from having lost Angus it is the only way forward. Please, please try to do the same. With the world shut down this is harder than ever. The normal escape valves are closed. It is all too easy to let the pressure build up but please don't. Find a release. Run, walk, dance. Recite poetry. Watch favourite films. Call me and let's talk about her.

Each day it's the natural world that heals me. My roses have never been better. I tell her about them. This I know sounds strange or worse, but I still talk to her. It helps. She's listening somewhere.

I know you, like me, struggle with the fact that she was alone when she died. This cuts through me. When I'd dropped the groceries off for her, she'd said she felt like she had flu – a bad flu but not, she assured me, man flu. We'd both laughed until her coughing became too much. I am grateful that, despite the restrictions, I broke them and rubbed her arm. Her eyes smiled as they always did. It was enough to light up a city.

Yes, I can hear you say, she died alone in the house, only to be discovered by me when she didn't reply the following day. The doctor assured me it would have been quick or sudden. I know she would have been happy having those last moments in her own home in Helston and not on a ward in Truro. And it does no good to torture ourselves with what ifs.

Maria gave us all joy. She was the sun bringing everything into high definition. She loved you, and love that powerful remains. Wrap yourself in it. Grieve and above all be gentle with yourself. Call me at any hour. I am here for you and only wish I could be closer. I long to wrap you in my arms.

Love you always,
Tony xxxx

Forty-Four

2025

8 May, 4:50 p.m.

The walk back to Lismore had never felt so long or so lonely, despite the cheery waves from people. If I hadn't just had two pints, I would have driven out of Helston tonight, no matter what I was here for. It was now ten to five, so it was only a matter of hours before the house would be empty. By the time I rose tomorrow morning, this Flora Day would be nothing but a memory, and one that I wanted to forget. But thankfully, it would bring me closer to my goal of leaving.

Smiling warmly at whoever I saw in the house, I fled with as much haste as I could to my room. With care, I peeled off the beautiful gown and hung it up gently. It had done its job and provided a veneer of protection. But I'd lingered too long, and the magic and spell it cast had begun to slip.

Pulling my phone from my pocket, I saw the many texts from Vlad and Gina. I opened Gina's first.

Hope you wowed them and you're OK. Here's a pic of you dancing. You've never looked more beautiful. The old town suits you, as does the dress. Can't wait to hear all the goss. Love you.

Also, Vlad got pissed on the local brew while we were watching. Didn't know he was such a lightweight.

I snorted.

He must have been drinking the Extra Special, which is 7.4%

Sinking onto the bed, I peeked at Vlad's text.

Have you done it yet? Xoxox

I replied.

No, and I won't be. Love you.

I closed my eyes. The sun had gone from this side of the house, and the temperature was cold. Forcing myself up, I pulled on jeans and an old navy cashmere jumper of Tony's. It felt like a hug, and I needed one. Too many memories and too much emotion were associated with the eighth of May. It should have been the best day of the year, but for me it hadn't been for so long. I sat with the pain. Micki knew my secret, and that intensified it. My failure seemed even greater now that yet another person knew it. I could only hope that she'd keep what she'd figured out to herself. But truthfully, who else would care?

Ke.

Thankfully, he was now completely focused on Matilda, as he should be. The past no longer mattered, and something between us had relaxed today. For that, I was grateful. It would make leaving easier. Matilda was precious, and she was Ke's entire world. He would have to be both father and mother to her, while the community would fill in the gaps as best it could. It was good at that... mostly. Gran had had a different view, but her life had been difficult, and she'd worked hard to give Mum and me the best. Thinking of Mum's letter, I still didn't understand her choices. Why have me and then tell me a lie my whole life?

Leaving my bedroom, I went down the old servants' staircase to the basement. The stuff from Mum's house was all in boxes down there. Was the answer to my question somewhere in these? Where should I start? They weren't labelled, so it would be a game of guess the box.

The first one I opened contained framed photos. Each one told a story. My baby pics, school, me with Micki, me with Ke, Mum and Tony. Gran and Tony. For each one, I could remember exactly where they'd been in Mum's place. I closed that box and opened another. It was full of Mum's clothes. I lifted out a dress and held it to my nose. The scent was of must and damp, not her perfume anymore. Why hadn't Tony given these away, and why hadn't I gone through this all sooner?

I sank onto a box. She'd been gone for five years. Five years without her laughter. I'd never been able to say goodbye, and now here I was, crying in the basement of Lismore on Flora Day, clutching her old clothes. There was nothing right about this. Had I been hiding and ignoring the pain?

Yes.

There was no place left to hide anymore. I stood and put the dress back into the box, then put it by the door. I would wash it all and take it to a charity shop. Someone else could enjoy her things. They'd never fit me, let alone suit me. I stood a good five inches taller than Mum had. Once this had made me proud, as I used to rest my chin on her head. How she would laugh, and then she'd poke me in the ribs, telling me that just because I was taller didn't mean I could do anything better, except reach the high shelves.

The tall genes hadn't come from her or Gran. So they must be from my father, and it was because of him I was here in the basement. I pulled box after box open, and gasped. My journals. Of course, I'd left the old ones at Mum's because of all the moves. A rainbow of colours filled the box. I pulled a purple one out. Stamped in gold was 2009. My hand shook. I'd filled every page in that one, trying to figure out my own mind, and a way forward.

Breathing slowly to calm myself, I let the diary fall open.

It is done.

How many times had I turned back to that page to remind myself that the past couldn't be changed, no matter how much I'd wanted it to be?

A year of self-loathing. It was all in here. I should have destroyed it years ago, but I hadn't. I flipped through the pages. All my doubts, fears and love were written on them. Ink was smudged and almost unreadable in places. I hadn't known one person could cry so much.

What story had I told to reassure myself that everything would be all right? Was it as elaborate as the one my mother had created to cover her lie? I closed the diary and put it back as I heard someone on the stairs.

'What on earth are you doing here?' Micki stood on the bottom step with her hands on her hips.

I shoved the diary into my pocket. 'Looking for something.'

'You don't say.' She took a few steps towards me. 'You might be looking for new friends if you're not careful.'

'That's a low blow.' I walked towards her.

'Is it?' She didn't move.

'Yes.'

'Hey down there. They're about to arrive,' Mrs Wearne called.

Micki dropped her arms to her sides. 'Saved by the dance so to speak.' She walked up the stairs ahead of me, and I sighed with relief. When she reached the kitchen, I detoured into Tony's study and put the diary on the desk. Micki appeared at the door looking from me to the Gainsborough.

'You know, Tony said that painting always reminded him of you.'

'Yes, he said the same to me.' I studied the woman in a soft pink dress and matching bonnet. Her hair was in ringlets and darker than mine.

'At the time I couldn't see what he was talking about, but now I can, especially through the eyes and nose.'

I blinked. That was weirdly precise.

'He missed you,' she said.

'I missed him.'

'At the end, I meant.' Her glance didn't leave me.

'Oh.'

'A of lot us couldn't understand why you weren't here.'

'That's unfair. I did come.' I swallowed as her words hit me.

'Yes, but only at Christmas and New Year.' She crossed her arms.

'He said he had more time.'

'He lied, he lied for you.'

The sound of the music beat loudly in my head. I couldn't think.

'We best go and see the dancers.' Micki turned and left me standing, looking at the portrait. Tony had lied; Mum had lied. I hadn't lied; I just hadn't told people, and of course they'd come to their own conclusions. Even if they'd been told the truth, they would have come to their own conclusions anyway. Gran always said that. According to the town, Gran's mother had been shameless, and Gran had followed suit. Mum had just played right into the lie.

I'd tried to be different, but had that made me happier?

Forty-Five

Flora Day, 2021

Saturday
Age: 34
Forecast: Light rain

Cancelled.

Micki rang in tears, happy ones. The diehard Hal an Tow crew had gathered in the morning on Flora at the bowling green. They'd all stood the required five feet apart and began singing. She said she'd sung for my mother, and for me. The certainty of the coming of spring had never felt more needed.

A policeman had come to investigate the gathering. They were doing nothing wrong – they were following the law. He'd agreed. They had told him they wanted to walk up to Godolphin House care home and sing the Hal an Tow for the residents too.

Bless the man, he'd thought they should, and had said he'd walk ahead of them so that no one would stop them. So, Helston had celebrated its Flora Day with the ancient words of the Hal an Tow being sung.

I cried just thinking about it. Mum. God, I missed her. I hadn't been home for two years. As things were, I wasn't sure I'd ever go again.

The Evening Dance

HELSTON FLORA DAY

A band of music always precedes the select dancers, but they play only one tune, "The Furry dance" which is so short and simple that after a time one wishes to run away and hide, as it gets monotonous as the incessant ring of a door bell.

The dance is equally simple, but rather pretty, and the steepness of the streets makes the dancers blush like peonies. They first trip on in couples, hand in hand, during the first part of the tune, forming a long string of from thirty to forty couples, perhaps, the gentlemen leading his partner with his right hand.

At the second part of the tune, the First Gentleman turns with both hands, the lady behind, and her partner turns in the same manner with his own partner, and then they trip on as before: each part of the tune being repeated. The other couples imitate these movements.

The Cornishman – 9 May 1895

* * *

HELSTON FLORA DAY

I am sorry to say that a few little petty feelings rendered it impossible to form a second party; and, had it not been for the working class, there would have been an end to Flora Day at three o'clock. Therefore, every praise is due to those young men and women, who are the flower of the land, as Tennyson's Lord Ronald, in his beautiful poem of "Lady Clare" says. This party had no sooner finished than the rain set in, and the crowd made quickly as possible for their several homes, leaving the streets once more to the Helstonians. A great crowd, however, thronged round the "angel" Hotel door, to witness the arrival of the ladies for the ball, which opened at nine o'clock in the Assembly Room.

Royal Cornwall Gazette – 11 May 1877

Forty-Six

2025

8 May, 5:45 p.m.

I stood beside Micki and watched the dancers come into the garden. The wind had dropped, and the sun's warmth could be felt. The same couldn't be said for Micki. Her anger and disappointment hit me like an arctic freeze.

'I'm sorry,' I whispered.

'Thank you, though it's not really me you need to apologise to, but you know that.' She sighed. 'You'll have lived through the whole thing so many times you won't actually remember what happened.'

I frowned. That made no sense.

'Our memories are only of the last time we recalled something, so it changes over time.'

'Are you saying memories are false?'

'No, but they change, and the older they are the more they change.' She took the offered glass of Prosecco. 'Look, because you weren't here, you didn't see this side. You didn't see that Ke continued to be in your mother's and Tony's life. He was there for Tony at the end, and that had to be hard, really hard for him.'

I stepped back. 'No one told me.'

Micki shook her head. 'Why would they? You aren't.... You aren't Helston anymore.'

My mouth dried. *I'm not Helston anymore.* A sharp stab took my breath. This was what I'd wanted. It shouldn't have hurt, but it did.

She laughed. 'You know silly me, I thought I could wake the Helston in you and bring you back to life by throwing you into the middle of the day, your day. But I can see now the intervention was too late.' She took a sip. 'Can't say it doesn't hurt, because it does. You've forgotten who you are, and where you're from, and maybe that's ok in your world, but I can't see how it is. Because this place,' she spread her hands out, 'has made you the genius with actors that you are, and given you the skill to be one of the best casting directors in the business.' She paused and looked me up and down, leaving me wondering what she'd say next, because her face showed none of its usual softness.

'Helston made you, and you think you don't need it anymore. Well, I guess you don't.' She shook her head. 'That's the part I just don't get, and the part that hurts like hell. By turning your back on this, on us, you say something about yourself. You say that you're not worthwhile, but I know that inside somewhere you are.' She huffed. 'So, sell Lismore and walk away. Helston doesn't need you.'

Helston doesn't need me. Those words chilled me.

'The lights of the big city beckon, and who knows, you may just get an Oscar now that they're giving them to casting directors too.' She laughed bitterly. 'Being a casting director is just perfect for you, because it gives you control of things, to rehearse them so you can see what will happen. But you know, in real life that's not how it is. It only works like that in films.' She looked me in the eye. 'And you don't, and won't, take chances in real life. You're too afraid of making a mistake.'

I tried to speak, but she went on. 'I didn't think it was true, but you are dead inside, and I'm sorry for you, I really am. But now I'm glad that you're going.' She put her glass down and walked to the rope that separated the house from the spectators. With ease, she then swung her leg over and disappeared into the crowd.

The garden was full of happy people, and I was miserable. My best friend had just walked away after telling me she felt sorry for me. That I'd been so afraid of making mistakes, I wasn't actually living. Was she right? I wanted to shout no, but in my heart, if not in my brain, I knew she was. I was thirty-eight and had stopped living.

The urge to run away was huge. No one would care. Tonight, I could hide in my room and then leave first thing. Helston would go on, even if Lismore was sold to someone who didn't care about traditions and welcoming the spring. It was no different from the Whos in Whoville, who celebrated Christmas without the decorations and toys. Flora was embedded deep in the heart of all Helstonians. I took a deep breath. Even in me, although I'd done my best to kill it.

Tony had left Lismore to me for a reason. Maybe that was what was in his letter. In a few hours, the house would be empty, and I'd read it. Part of me was afraid of what it might say. Tony spoke his mind. He was full of advice. What would he tell me right now?

Enjoy Flora Day.

Live.

Love.

Laugh.

He'd done all of those things with everything in him. He'd loved fully. He'd lived until he couldn't anymore, and that still hurt. He'd laughed – even on my last visit we'd laughed. His laugh had weakened but had still been loud and irreverent. God, I missed him, and I missed Mum.

Her letter said she'd loved my father. Was that enough? Should I just let go, as they say? Micki was right. My fear of failing, and the need to rehearse everything, was holding me in place. But life was about moving forward. Mum had loved whoever my father was. That should be enough.

I glanced down the garden. My godmother Tricia and her husband Jack were with their children and waved to me, beckoning me down. Without thinking about it, I swung my leg over the rope and walked through the crowds. There was joy all around me. With a deep breath, I tried to let it lift me.

'What a day,' Bill said, handing me a glass of fizz. 'You remember the twins of course.'

'Babysat for them.' I smiled at both of them.

'Hey, Flo, great that Tony left you Lismore,' the darker-haired of the two said.

'Yes, yes, it is.' I let the words I'd just said sink in. He'd trusted me with it.

'It's so good to have you back,' Tricia said.

I smiled. She took my free hand in hers and said, 'Maria would have been pleased. She was so proud of you.'

I swallowed.

'You've read the letter?' Tricia fixed her gaze on me.

'I did.'

'And did it contain the one thing you've always wanted to know?' she asked.

'It didn't, and you played a part in Mum's lies to me.'

Tricia shrugged. 'Only a small part, as I don't know who your father is either.' She studied me. 'Today's been hard on you,'

I couldn't deny it.

'But maybe healing too?' She smiled encouragingly. 'Tony and I were your godparents, and he always took his role seriously, much more so than me, who relied on you to look after those two.' She nodded towards the twins.

'I loved doing it, and you paid me.'

'I always thought you'd have your own brood of kids, you were so good with them.'

I drew a breath. 'Well, I need those skills to work with actors.'

'Is that Chris fella as devastatingly handsome in person?'

'Absolutely, but he knows it, which ruins it really.'

'Shame,' she said, studying me. 'You know your mother wasn't happy until she came home.'

'What?'

'Not that she hadn't loved acting, but she said it left her too empty becoming other people all the time.'

I frowned.

'She told me having you saved her... It gave her a reason to let go of the dream.'

As Tricia's words sank in, a different vision of Mum began to take shape before me. Having me had meant she never needed to explain why she didn't want Hollywood, and that she didn't want the acting life, or shedding her skin to become another. If she'd told me this years ago – and she had tried to persuade me she was happy in her life – I'm not sure I would have understood. But I did now.

'She came home that Flora Day with her heart broken again by yet another man who hadn't been what he pretended to be... faithful. She longed for a different life, a truer one. And you gave her that.'

I swallowed. For years I'd always felt I'd held her back, but I hadn't. I'd set her free.

A shout was made for the dancers to reassemble, and the atmosphere in the garden changed. The band struck up, and they all lined up, then began to dance out onto the street again.

'Take all the time you need to think about what you've been given,' Tricia said. She looked around. 'This type of legacy is a big responsibility, and you have a big job too.' She gave my hand a squeeze. 'You'll make the right decision.'

Bill took her arm and their picnic basket. They were off to the

Guildhall to secure a spot there, while the dancers would make their way to Penhellis, then the bowling green, before finishing at the Guildhall.

In the distance, I spied Micki already on her way out of the garden. Peace would descend here soon, and maybe then I'd be able to think.

Forty-Seven

Flora Day, 2022

Saturday
Age: 35
Forecast: Overcast

The flight from LA to London had been sleepless, and on the train to Truro I'd stared out the window, watching the scenery without a coherent thought. No, that's not true. My one thought had been that I couldn't do this. How could I come back home when Mum wasn't there? Was it even home anymore? Was Lismore to be 'home' now? Tony had said as much, but it wasn't the same. It was too grand. Not that I didn't love it, and hadn't loved staying there, but it came with memories of things I'd prefer to forget.

I had no choice, though, other than to make this trip back for Flora Day. The grand celebration was going ahead again, and Mum was being remembered for the role she'd played in the town's day, and in the life of Helston. She'd been gone two years.

Today Tony would announce the acting scholarship he'd set up in her honour at Falmouth Uni. His generosity had left me sobbing for a day. Once I'd gained control of my emotions again, I'd written Tony a letter full of thanks and admiration. It was weird after all these years that he still preferred that form of communication. He'd replied that if he couldn't do good with his money, it wasn't worth anything. I loved him even more for that. A scholarship in Mum's name would have thrilled her. She'd loved seeing students with talent finding a way to follow their dreams.

I dressed, listening to the bells, and it was hard being in this room, here in Lismore. Last night I'd almost told Tony that I'd use another room, but it had seemed a childish thing to do. Facing your past was important, as all the self-help books said. Standing here now, I wasn't just facing it; I was immersed in it, and all I felt was loss. Loss of Mum, loss of innocence, loss of my first love, and loss of the Flora who'd existed loving this day more than life itself.

Looking in the mirror, I searched for the Flora of old. Was she there, in the thrust of the chin, or in the direct look of the eyes? Even if she wasn't visible anymore, she was in there, because she was whom I'd built Flo Richards, casting director, on. I was grateful to her. She'd taken her knocks quietly, and this made me more compassionate. She'd worked hard and taught me that nothing in life comes without a cost. She'd loved and lost, teaching me to value my friends, because they remained constant. Yes, Flora Portia Richards still lived inside Flo Richards, even though very few people would see that. My life here in Helston was invisible to most, except those who had known me then. Even Nick, who I'd let see the Flora side of me because I'd once thought he could become my life partner, had found the real me too much, too different. That was a sobering thought. Nick was long gone, and I was here alone to face this celebration of Mum.

Tony and I stood in the garden of Lismore with an invited gathering. It was four fifteen, and the next big event was at five. Over two hundred people were here to toast Mum. To survive this, I needed to call upon any acting skills I might have inherited from her. Standing in the crowd were Ke, his wife and his daughter Matilda. Ke had loved my mother, and she him. He should be here, as should Claire and her daughter, who'd come to know her. Mum had, over the years, I realised now, come to be a mother of sorts to Ke, especially after his own mother had paid the ultimate price for her years of addiction. He hadn't run away from here, as I might have done with that pain, but stayed and built something. Mum, I knew, had been proud of him, and pleased he'd found happiness despite all he'd suffered in his childhood home.

Micki was here with Malcolm, her current obsession. This too would pass, I hoped. There was no turning Micki from her plans, even if certain shipwreck lay ahead. In some ways, I admired her for that. I always stepped away from relationships before full damage was done, as I had done with Nick. I'd made it easier and said a farewell while we could still be friends and colleagues of sorts. Having said that, I hadn't been invited to look at his clients' new screenplays, and that stung.

'Thank you all for coming.' Tony spoke clearly. 'Everyone here knows how important Flora Day was to Maria, and how important she was to this day.'

'Hear, hear,' said Peter Johns.

'We all miss her. She was joy and energy and laughter.' He paused. 'She was my best friend, and the best friend anyone could have.' He turned to me. 'She was the best mother to Flo, and daughter to Jane.' He drew a deep breath, and I took his hand. I wasn't the only one overwhelmed with emotion. 'The pandemic took her from us far too soon. We all feel cheated – cheated of the years ahead filled with laughter and the Hal an Tow.'

'Does everyone have a glass?' I asked to give Tony a moment. Tears pooled in his eyes and in many others. I was doing all I could to keep it together.

'Good,' said Tony, giving my hand a squeeze before he continued. 'Maria was a brilliant actress. Her role as Portia was her finest and her last, except that every year she morphed into the magic that's held in the coming of the May, O.' He paused. 'I'm delighted that Maria's gift to us here in Helston will be spread a little wider to the rest of Cornwall, in the form of a fully funded scholarship in perpetuity to a promising Cornish student studying the performing arts. It's my hope that the Maria Richards scholarship will give many Cornish students the wings they need to fly. So please raise your glasses to Maria, the best of us.'

'Hear, hear,' the gathered crowd replied, raising their glasses.

I broke out in uncontrolled sobs. So much for acting ability and holding it together. Tony wrapped me in his arms and let the tears flow as he'd done once before.

Forty-Eight
2025

8 May, 6:15 p.m.

There was no reason I could find to explain to myself why I followed the crowds out of the garden. This was my time to be alone, and yet I was caught up in the mood of the people as some followed the dancers down Cross Street, and others went to find their spot to watch the dancers come up Coinagehall Street.

I didn't head there but walked to my old home. With everyone focused on the Evening Dance, this part of town was eerie in its stillness. Out of the wind, the sun was warm on my back. I stopped as I neared the little house that had been home for so many years. The door was still painted bluebell blue, and whoever lived there now had beautifully adorned it with flowers, just like Mum and I used to do.

I wrapped my arms around myself. The little plaque on the door with the number four still had the sprig of lily-of-the-valley on it. The paint had faded, but it was the same one Mum had done all those years ago.

Hesitantly, I stepped forward and ran my fingers over it as I'd done a thousand times. Mum had put the flowers there because coming home, she said, was the return of happiness, and making this a home for the two of us had made her happier than anything else.

Talisman. Like her, I'd touched it each and every time I came home, whether it had been months or just hours. Home. My home was mostly in LA these days. The flat I now rented in London, Soho, looked like a hotel, and to be honest so did my place in LA. This little two-up and two-down had never been like that. Everything in it had had meaning, from the photos on the walls to the fabric of the curtains. My mother had chosen everything with care. I had for my flats too, but not for what they reminded me of, or the joy they brought. The things in my life could have been chosen by a nameless designer who knew nothing of me and my life.

They didn't tell anyone anything about me. This was what I wanted. And yet, as I turned away from the house, I realised how empty that was. Everything in my homes was superficial and perfect. It hadn't the warmth that Mum had shown through her choices in decoration. It wasn't like Tony either, who filled his home with art and objects that brought him joy. He had dispensed with his painful past through his philanthropy. What had I done in my thirty-eight years?

I navigated the crowds around the Guildhall. Music filled the air. Helston was in party mode as people cheered. Instead of heading back to Lismore, I stood still as the dancers twirled past.

'This is so brilliant,' said the woman next to me. Her smile was wide, and I couldn't help but smile back.

'You're right,' I replied, spotting Tricia's twins dancing. Their partners were the ones their parents had arranged back in playschool. They were still dancing together after all this time. Their respective boyfriends were somewhere in the crowd, or maybe dancing with the partners they'd had at primary school. It was something rather special. Without thinking, I scanned the crowd looking for Ke and Matilda, knowing they would be here watching, not wanting to miss a minute of the day.

Out in front of 'Spoons, I spied them. Matilda was sitting on his shoulders. My heart clenched with sympathy at what they'd both been through. He was such a good man who had been through so much, and he deserved an apology and an explanation from me. It wouldn't happen today, but I'd make certain before I left that he had it. Only then would I be able to move forward. With that thought, something inside me settled.

Ke's glance met mine, and I smiled. He waved. Matilda grinned and pointed. She said something to her father, and he shook his head.

The last dancers passed and headed into the Guildhall. The crowd wouldn't let the band finish. Wilf was grinning as they played on for three encores. It was a good end to mark the eightieth anniversary of VE Day, and a Flora Day to remember.

After the chants of *Oggy Oggy Oggy, Oi, Oi, Oi,* I made my way through the crowds in front of the Guildhall. Everyone was in party mode, and I envied them. Not that I wanted to join in, for the bittersweet melancholy of the past surrounded me.

'Hey Flo,' Wilf called out as he jostled through people.

I turned and sent him a big smile.

'I think we need a drink and a catch up.' He placed a big hand lightly on my shoulder.

'Absolutely,' I said, while wondering where this had come from. Wilf had never been the complicated one of us. He was a 'what you see is what you get' type of guy.

Together we worked our way to the bar. I couldn't see over the people crowded around, but Wilf managed to order, and before long we were back out on the street.

'It's good you're home,' he said as we tapped our plastic reusable pint glasses. Mine was adorned with lily-of-the-valley, and Wilf's depicted the dancers in their finery for the Midday Dance.

'Why do you say that?' I studied his face. It had always been an open book. He was never one to hide his emotions, good or bad.

'One, because it is. And two, because you've been lost... Touching down here infrequently for short sharp visits hasn't anchored you.'

'I don't really fit here anymore.'

The corner of his mouth went up. 'I won't repeat what others have said.' He paused, and I could imagine it was things like 'too big for us now', 'flashy Hollywood style', and so on. 'I wasn't lucky enough to be born here, so maybe I have a different outlook.'

'I'd say you'd have that wherever you were.' I smiled at him.

'True.' He chuckled. 'But you *are* lost.'

'How am I? My career has never been better.'

'Won't argue with that, but there's no light shining in your eyes like there used to be, and I would guess that the road in front looks straight and clear.'

'It does.'

'But where on that road is there a place for you – for your heart?'

I shrugged.

'So I think by coming home, and spending time here, you just might find you again.' He took a swig of his pint. 'I said as much to Tony a few months ago.'

'You did?' I pulled my head back and studied him.

'Yeah, I was one of his carers.'

How had I not known that? 'Thank you,' I said quietly.

'He loved you.' He fixed me with his soulful eyes.

'It was mutual.' I sniffed. I didn't need to cry.

'He knew that, but he worried about you.'

'Why?' It didn't make sense. I was successful, solvent and independent.

'In his words, you were chasing your tail and not enjoying your success, or the life you'd been given. He felt you were too hung up on the past: one, not having a father, and something else that had happened.' Wilf paused. 'He wanted you to move on, and he felt to do that you had to come back.'

'That's why he left me Lismore?'

'Maybe. You were his goddaughter, so that's more likely the reason.'

I tilted my head. He'd had others; I could feel it.

'Just know you are here for a reason, so don't blow it by rushing away. Linger and let things unfold.' He laughed. 'You've seen the world, and conquered being in the film industry. Now see what happens here.'

Looking around at the crowds, I was an outsider in a place that I knew rock and stone from its history, its people, its folklore and its rhythms. I'd studied the stories behind this town and this day. Rebirth.

Forty-Nine

Flora Day, 2023

Saturday
Age: 36
Forecast: Sunny

I was here at Lismore because Tony had wanted me with him on Monday to award the first Maria Richards scholarship. Every year I didn't want to find myself in Helston for Flora, and yet I was like a homing pigeon, or maybe more like a moth drawn to the flame that'd kill it.

I opened my diary. A blank page stared at me. I wrote:

Flora Day again.

Not that I wasn't looking forward to presenting the scholarship to the young woman from Bodmin. Between the two of us, Tony and I had vetted one hundred applicants to find this year's successful candidate. It was both heart-lifting and heartrending. Each one had sent not only a statement on why they should receive the scholarship, but they'd included a clip of themselves performing. It was here I was in my comfort zone, but also out of it. There was so much talent in Cornwall, but so many without the means to nurture it. Of the hundred, I wanted to support them all, but there were twenty I saw who had something just that bit special, and who most needed what the scholarship offered to bring forth their talents.

Tony and I had spent hours on FaceTime talking through the merits of each candidate and their personal situations. Who would benefit most, and who would Mum have chosen? That had stopped us both in our tracks. Mum had a way with people, especially with the young she'd worked with. After her death, I'd received so many messages from people she had helped during their school years. She would have been so up for this scholarship in so many ways. Tony was generously paying tuition, living costs and a stipend. This would carry on for three years for each successful candidate. On the advice of the financial guru, who was working with the numbers so this could continue in perpetuity, Tony could only choose a candidate every other year. Not his original intention, but one we both accepted.

On Monday we were due to meet with Wen Hoskin, and hopefully her life would have the Maria Richards fairy dust to start her on her way. There were several candidates who'd just missed out, whom I would keep on my radar for upcoming projects. Actual time on set with professionals might also give them a break in a career that was hard enough if you had advantages, but near impossible if you didn't.

I was looking forward to Monday, but not today, although it was a joy to see the Early and the Children's Dances. I gave the Hal an Tow a miss. The Midday Dance was kicking off in moments. As I looked out on Lismore's garden, I saw Ke with his daughter Matilda. How heartbreakingly hard this day would be for them both, but especially for Ke.

Claire had died just two months ago of an undiagnosed heart murmur. She'd collapsed on the walk back from school with Matilda. It was beyond tragic. I'd written to Ke expressing my sorrow for his loss. There was no way I could have imagined it.

They'd been partners in life in every way... business, love and parenting. And poor Matilda.

Micki had given me a blow by blow of the funeral, while I'd been in Australia for a big film. There was no way I could have come back for it, but guilt covered my skin now. It felt cowardly somehow to be standing here when now was possibly the best time to go over and say something in person. But I didn't know how to, and what good would it do? I didn't belong here anymore, and I'd expressed everything in the letter of condolence. That had to be enough, even though I knew it wasn't. He'd been my best friend, and he'd just lost his wife.

Almost blindly, I walked out of the house and down to where they were standing by the pond. Matilda was watching the koi, whose bright orange bodies flickered in the sun breaking through the clouds.

Ke looked up, his eyes flashed, then an expression I couldn't read appeared on his face, before it became a polite smile. It was one I'm sure he used in business.

'Hi Ke.'

'Flo.'

Matilda looked up and smiled. She was missing a front tooth, and my heart broke in a thousand pieces. Poor Claire, missing all of this, and all that was to come. I swallowed before saying, 'Have you counted the fish?'

'I tried but there are too many.' She sighed. 'Tony lets me feed them.'

'I bet he loves that.'

She pointed at the fish. 'They do.'

I laughed. In the distance I heard the band. If I were going to say anything, I'd have to be quick. 'I'm so sorry, Ke.'

Matilda looked from me to her father. 'What's the lady sorry for?'

'Nothing.' He stroked his daughter's head, and the lead dancers appeared on the lawn. The moment had passed, and I'd failed to provide any comfort.

Fifty

Flora Day, 2024

Wednesday
Age: 37
Forecast: Sunny intervals

I had stated firmly that I wasn't coming to Flora this year. Tony, Micki and Tricia had all tried to convince me that I should – it'd be good for me, they said. But I'd dug my heels in and stayed in LA.

Of course, that didn't explain why I was up when the rest of LA slept, scrolling through social media and listening to BBC Cornwall's coverage. This wasn't helping anything. I didn't want to be there, so why was I sleepless and searching through every platform for a glimpse of the dances, the sound of the band, and spotting the familiar faces?

What did this say about me? That I should find a therapist. Which is what Gina and Vlad had told me repeatedly, as both felt I wasn't dealing with the loss of my mother. There was a sadness in my eyes that worried them both.

But I kept that loss buried with all the other losses along the way. They weren't a merry bunch, but they were what kept the inside of me full, if not whole. Take one piece away and I'd fall apart. And no one, least of all me, wanted that.

I turned my phone off, found a sleeping pill, and tried to drift off. Sadly, not the sleep of the virtuous, but of a woman who had a big day tomorrow. Then I remembered the voicemail on my phone I hadn't listened to because I'd been going from one meeting to another. I put on the kettle and looked at my phone. The message was from Tony. It was not like him. Curious, I pressed play.

'My dearest Flo.'

I smiled at his greeting.

'I had so hoped you'd come home for Flora Day, so that I could tell you this news in person.'

The kettle clicked, and my heart stopped. Nothing good had ever come out of a statement like that.

'My nightly trips to the loo became a little too frequent, so I went to the doctor. The long and short of it is I should have gone to him when those many nightly visits began, or the persistent ache that plagues my back became apparent. The pain was not from the gardening but from cancer. And this cancer in my prostate has escaped to find its way into my bones, and a few other places.'

I pressed pause, my heart racing as I tried to take it all in. His father had died of prostate cancer, so surely it should have been on his radar? Anger filled me. I went to the cupboard and took out the whisky Tony had brought me on his visit last year. I poured a large measure. Herbal tea wasn't going to help; nothing could. I should have gone home for Flora Day. With dread, I pressed play.

'It turns out that things are well advanced. I've always been one to be ahead of things... very avant-garde. It's stage four. So I've made some choices. I will only receive treatment that will ease things. There is no point in trying to save the Titanic that is me. I shall go down disgracefully.

'I know this news will upset you. You lost darling Maria far too early, and soon me as well. But you are made of strong stuff. Just think of your grandmother.

'I won't be fine, but I will be me. Please don't feel you need to hop on the next flight. They don't expect me to pop my clogs that quickly. I have months.

'I wish you were here for Flora Day, and I was telling you in person. I love you, my darling girl.'

I couldn't breathe.

Tony.

Despite his reassuring words, he must be terrified. I grabbed my phone to call him, but it was twelve thirty. Bang in the middle of the Midday Dance. He wouldn't hear his phone; he would be dancing. Was I missing his last dance?

Fifty-One

2025

8 May, 6:45 p.m.

Mrs Wearne was just locking up the house as I returned.

'There you are love. Everything is done for today. Tomorrow morning they'll be in to collect the portaloos.'

'Thank you for organising it all.'

'A pleasure, my dear. You take care.'

I watched her walk away, then I turned into the house, which was overwhelmingly silent after the noise of the crowds. Standing in the hall, I took stock of all the information that had hit me today. Too much to process. I hugged myself, feeling the softness of Tony's sweater.

'Well, Tony, you have surprised me,' I said to the portrait of him hanging on the wall. 'You must have had a reason for giving me all this, and whether it's the one Wilf said or not, you were never one to do things impulsively. Let's see what you have to say for yourself.'

After I'd made a cup of tea, I headed to Tony's study, my mind whirring with possibilities for what his letter might contain.

Hopefully, some answers. He could have left Lismore to charity, so why me? I'd forgotten I'd kept all his letters at Mum's, and amongst the boxes of her things there were years of weekly correspondence. He'd had so much he wanted me to know, to understand, from how to use words, to how to live life. In some ways he'd been a wise old man before his time, with his penchant for passing out advice.

Sitting at his desk, I stroked Gran's mended bowl, then unlocked the drawer and took out both letters. I put Mum's down and opened Tony's. At least I knew this wouldn't drop a bomb like Mum's had, but it would hopefully tell me what Tony had been thinking for the house and me. Wilf's words had disturbed me. Was I lost? I had everything, really. A job I loved and now three properties if I counted the rental in Soho, which was more than anyone needed. Looking up, I studied Tony's favourite painting. He'd said it reminded him of me. I suppose there was something in the eyes and the expression, a little defiant really. Her life as part of the landed gentry would have been very different from mine. She'd had money and status but no choice in what she did with her life, while I had a choice.

I opened the letter but hesitated. It was the last communication from Tony. More than anything else, this kicked me in the gut. Final. My hand shook as I unfolded the sheets. The aqua ink on them blurred, and I took a deep breath. I could do this. He wanted me to read these words.

My darling girl

As I write, I know the end is not far away. I treasure the time we had together over Christmas. I promised you I'd still be around for a bit longer, but I was lying, and I think you knew that. Over the years I have handed out advice to you whether you wanted it or not. Mostly not, I suspect. But being you, you would have read my letters carefully and at least considered what I said. I love this about you. But then I love everything about you. You know this. I'm so proud of all you have accomplished, and the woman you have become. I know your journey hasn't always been easy, but in truth, no one's ever is.

Losing your mother during the pandemic was brutal. Even for those of us who were close, it was impossible to accept. Maria was life itself. She gave her all to those she loved, and she loved you with everything in her. I was blessed that she felt the same way about me, despite my many faults. She taught me so much about what love actually means, as did your grandmother. They showed their love through their actions. If you were lucky enough, especially in your grandmother's case, to be theirs, then there was nothing they wouldn't do for you. But you know this.

Your mother did this for me.

I paused and glanced at the photo of Mum and Gran on the desk. It'd been taken on Tony's graduation day. The photo next to it was of Mum, Tony and me the day he was knighted by the Queen. I ran my finger over them, recalling the love in those captured moments.

What I am about to say next will unsettle you, and I have debated long and hard whether to say anything at all.

Oh my God, he knew who my father was. Of course he'd know. He and Mum were so close. They were platonic soulmates, really. I glanced at the photo of the three of us again. They'd both loved me so much. I was so lucky.

Flora Portia Richards, I am your father.

What?
Tony was my father?

I couldn't breathe.

We should have told you, I think. There were many reasons we didn't. Your mother and I were both at an all-time low that Flora Day. I thought Angus didn't love me when I asked to be exclusive and he said he needed to think about it. Something inside me broke, because he was my world. I couldn't understand. I'd arrived back in Helston distraught.

Tony was my father.

Maria had always loved me, as I had her. And she was fresh out of a relationship that she'd thought would last, until she'd found George in bed with her understudy. We reached out to each other, wondering if loving each other was enough. We knew at once it wasn't and didn't give it another thought. I returned to London, and Angus said yes. A few months later, your mother called, and we met. She told me her news. You were so wanted on both sides. But on my side, it was complicated. Angus wouldn't have understood. He would have seen what happened with Maria as a betrayal.

Your mother understood, and she was also well aware that in 1986 it would have been very difficult for you if people knew your father was gay. Children can be so cruel. So she created the lie she told you, and I went along with it. It killed us both to see your longing and your pain, but we felt this was best.

Another consideration was the way things were with my father. If he'd found out I had a child, that he had another heir besides his 'defective son' as he called me, then he would have tried to draw you in, to control you. Neither your mother nor I wanted that. We continued to talk about it after he'd died, and after Angus died too, but it didn't seem important then. You had stopped asking about your father; the lie was there, and everyone had accepted it. I'd always been in your life. Even if you had known, you would never have had the perfect nuclear family you dreamed of.

Tony was my father. These words kept running around in my head.

I hope that, although I was never your father in name, you felt as close to me. In fact, I hope that because you never knew of the connection, you could always say things to me that you would have held back had you known.

My dearest Flo, I love you and always have. You have given me more joy than I can ever explain. Being your father, even if the world has never known, was the greatest gift. Thank you.

My only regret, and the hardest thing in my life, has been watching your pain at the loss of Ke from your world. You did the right thing, but I wish you would have trusted yourself and him more. You have slowly closed yourself off from true joy. I wonder if you think it is only right because of your choices. When I've longed to talk about your pain, you shut down more, so I have left it. I shouldn't have. I should have pushed and poked more. It would have hurt us both at the time, but I think it would have been better out. Ke is a good man. He would understand. Above all, he was, and I believe still is, your friend. You need to move on, but you won't until you face your past.

By leaving you Lismore, I hope it will help you to see your past and find your future. I wish I were there to see it. But I am confident you will take the chance that is being offered to you to live, and to live fully, which means allowing yourself to make mistakes. There is no rehearsal for life. We only have one take, and the cameras roll from the start. But what you can do is say sorry, then move forward with your life. Enjoy the outtakes that happen along the way. Because of mistakes, like Maria and I trying things out, can bring forth something wonderful, even if they weren't planned.

As I write this, I know I should have told you in person. I almost did on Christmas Eve, but we were both sad and haunted by what was to come. I'm sorry. Please forgive me if you can.

Forgive him? My chest was tight. Forgive him for not telling me the one thing I'd wanted to know more than almost anything else. Why wasn't he still here? Anger filled me. This was wrong, so wrong.

Lismore. I know you'll see this as a puzzle, if not a burden. It is neither. You are my daughter and my rightful heir. The house is a special place. My godmother loved it. I love it. You, your mother, and I have had many wonderful times here. But that is not a reason to hold on to it. If you do sell, please consider the community that raised you. Do not rush any decision. What you are feeling at this moment I can only imagine but, like the sharp pain of grief, all emotions mellow with time, and we see things differently. As with grief, when it draws back a bit we see the love that caused the pain. So spend time with it, spend time in Helston. Remember what your grandmother always said... 'you can take the girl out of Helston but you can't take Helston out of the girl'. I would add, 'even if you think you might want to'.

I will leave you with the words of Shakespeare: 'It is a wise father that knows his own child.'

I have always loved you, and I hope that amid the confusion and anger you will be feeling right now, you can still remember that.

Love lives on,

Your father xxxxx

My father.

Love lives on.

Last year he was still here, dancing his final time. I should have come. God, I wish I could go back and do things differently. But he wouldn't want me to think like that.

Tony was my father.

My name, that's why he chose Portia as my middle name. Another quote from the same play came to mind. 'The will of a living daughter is curbed by the will of a dead father.'

Fifty-Two

2025

8 May, 7:15 p.m.

Tony was my father.

I looked at the portrait of my ancestor on the wall. There was no obvious resemblance between Tony and me except maybe in my eye colour. Tony, in his way, had tried to tell me over the years with things he'd done.

Mum.

My head hurt thinking about it all. I took my tea and walked out into the garden. Distant sounds drifted along with the breeze. I tried to let my thoughts go with it, but they circled, jabbing at me. All this time what I'd wanted was right there, and I hadn't seen it. It wasn't that I was blind, but when your godfather was gay and had a wonderful partner, it hadn't ever seemed to be an option.

Memory after memory rolled through my mind, then I thought of the infamous Star Wars scene when Darth Vader says to Luke, 'I am your father' and everything made sense in a different way. But unlike Vader, Tony was gone. Mum was gone, and I was left alone in this house to figure it all out. Who was I? A fatherless Richards woman, fated to be a single daughter of a single mother, or was I the daughter of two people who'd loved me? They'd loved each other, but not in the traditional way.

Strolling down the slope, I went through the garden to where Tony used to smoke in peace. Sitting on the bench we had shared on so many occasions, I let the brick wall cool my thoughts. There was nothing that could be done about the past.

Tears ran down my face, and I didn't stop them. Nothing had prepared me for this. There was no way it could have been rehearsed, because I hadn't ever pictured this scenario. I woke this morning certain of my path, and now, now I couldn't see a way forward.

Sell Lismore and leave Helston for good.

But that was the thing, was it for good, for my good?

Standing, I left the walled garden. Most of the evidence of the day was gone. In my head, I saw the spiral of dancers on the lawn in front of me. Echoes of the laughter and conversation hovered in the air, while the noise of the party taking place just streets away was a distant hum. A plan was what my head was calling out for, but Tony, my father – that still felt unreal – had said you couldn't rehearse for life. There was some truth in that. But now I was at a point where decisions needed to be made.

Turning and looking at the house sitting above the garden, I was, of all things, an heiress. The house my great-great-grandmother had been the housekeeper for was now mine. The wealth that Tony's family had accumulated from mining, and Tony's own, was now mine. It was an immense responsibility.

What would Tony have done? What would Mum have done? I wouldn't even contemplate what Gran would have done, although just thinking about her made me smile. This town was built on minerals and banks. And one way or another, my family had been a part of it. How did I leave all that behind? The funny thing was that at this moment I wasn't sure I wanted to.

My feet led me past the pet cemetery to the little chapel tucked away against the wall. I opened the door and was startled to see flowers there, along with memorial plaques to both Mum and Tony. My legs wobbled. Who had done this? Tony and I had popped in here many a time, including on my last visit, and there had been nothing here, only a simple cross on the wall.

Once my breathing had calmed, I said a sort of prayer, or maybe it was a plea. What should I do? And as I tripped slightly on the threshold leaving the chapel, it hit me. Could I make Mum and Tony's legacies bigger? Could I use my inheritance to focus on bringing Cornish talent to the fore?

This could work, but was it what I wanted to do? I drew a deep breath of the softly scented night air. With determined steps, I headed into the house to grab my diary. I needed it to sketch out my thoughts. As Tony had always said, it was a way for me to process them.

It hit me again that he'd been with me every step of the way. Each day as I wrote in the beautiful leather-bound notebooks, I'd thought of him. Most days it was first thing, but on some it had been my last thought. Maybe he'd thought that through.

Of course he had.

I stood in my bedroom looking at the photo of us taken on the red carpet the night a film I'd been very involved with was up for a BAFTA. Tears came again. He'd been there for every celebration, from my first steps into his arms, to graduation. How hadn't I realised? I scanned his face in the picture and mine, looking for something I'd missed in the past, like that I had his nose or mouth. At a push, I could see the angle of my jawline was like his: determined. But it wasn't obvious unless you were looking, and no one, including me, was ever looking at Tony as possibly my father.

Picking up the 2025 diary, I stroked the cover, telling myself not to cry as I walked to his study. Without knowing it, I'd had the best father anyone could ask for. He'd always been there to listen, to encourage and occasionally to scold. He was even doing that from the grave.

In his study, I pulled out his letter, almost afraid to read it again. Yet Tony's letters had sustained me my whole life. Boxes filled with all his early letters to me down in the basement were a testament to this. At times they had caused me such confusion – first about why he wrote to me all the time, but now it all made sense. Had he planned to tell me at some point later in life? Had Mum left that decision up to him? Neither of them should be gone. What I would have given to sit down with them both and ask them to explain, and so much more.

But I couldn't do that, so I picked up Tony's letter to see if there was anything else I'd missed.

Had he been right that I'd stopped truly living sixteen years ago? That was a frightening thought. I opened the 2009 diary and reread my entry for that fateful day. The me who went through it all, trying to figure out a way forward, had been so full of possibilities. Before the abortion, I'd been thinking of how to bring the film industry to Cornwall, because I'd wanted to be here and work in a profession I loved. Big ask. But as I leaned back in Tony's chair, I suddenly felt sure it could be done, and not in the way I'd thought then.

I opened this year's diary, running my hand over a blank page. Tony's yearly gift had been so much bigger than the A5 letter-bound pages.

The Cornwall Film Institute

With Tony's legacy, and building on the scholarship in Mum's name, I could slowly bring together the professionals based here, from Cornwall, and those wanting to be here. There were so many compelling stories set in this glorious landscape, from escapism to the reality of life in one of the United Kingdom's poorest counties. These stories needed to be told on film, and where better to do it than here?

At first, it could begin as a directory and slowly reach the point of studios in the heartland of Cornwall, bringing employment and full production to the Duchy. As this kernel of an idea blossomed in my mind, more plans and details began to take shape, and a thrill of motivation surged through me. I'd learned a huge amount over the past sixteen years, and all that could be brought to bear to make this a reality. I would help feed Tony's legacy back into the granite landscape and heart of the community that had moulded me.

Fifty-Three

2025

8 May, 8:00 p.m.

The tall clock in the hall chimed as I looked up from my notes. It was rough, but I had a tentative plan. Hope stirred. It was possible, and that was the key thing. It wouldn't be easy, but I could make it happen.

My phone pinged.

Still alive? Have you shagged him yet?

Vlad.

Always outrageous and he wouldn't give up. I typed back:

I told you, not going to happen.

After I'd sent that, I glanced out into the garden to see Ke walking towards the house. I shook my head to make sure Vlad's text hadn't caused me to hallucinate.

I left the study and walked through the drawing room and out, through the conservatory, not hiding my surprise. No rehearsal, and now was the time to apologise. If my plan had any chance of working, then I needed to make peace with Ke, and with myself. This wouldn't be easy, but it was important.

'Hi,' Ke said as he reached me, holding out a ring of keys. 'I thought you might need these.'

'I might,' I said, taking them from him. 'Matilda?'

'Convinced me that it was perfectly OK to have a sleepover on a school night.'

'Softie,' I said.

He nodded.

'Fancy helping me raid Tony's wine cellar? I've had quite a day.'

He sent me a look, slightly puzzled, then said, 'That sounds interesting and yes, I'd love to.'

'Good.' I looked at the keys on the ring. 'You probably have the key for it on here.'

'I do.' He picked up the keys from my open palm, then held up a skeleton key. 'It's this one.'

'Glad you knew.' I smiled.

'Until the week before he died, I'd come around with Matilda in the early evening, and we'd have a small glass of something.'

My heart swelled. 'Thank you.'

'No need to say thanks. It was as much for me and for Matilda.'

We passed the study on the way to the stairs to the basement. Tony's letter lay on the desk, and I noticed Ke glance at it.

'Have you read his letter now?' Ke stopped walking and studied me.

'I...have.' I drew a breath. Then, seeing his expression, I said, 'You knew?'

He nodded slowly. 'He told me just before he died.'

'Oh.' Tony had told Ke before telling me. Devastation hit hard.

'Not like that. He was trying to write to you as he always did, but he was struggling to find the words. There were maybe twenty crushed pieces of paper around him.' He took my hand in his. 'He was hesitating, and worried it would hurt you too much.'

I swallowed. This was too hard.

'I know he put his heart into writing it.' Ke's eyes met mine. It had to be hard to witness.

I drew a breath, thinking of how frail Tony had been at Christmas. It would have taken so much out of him. 'Did he show it to you?'

'No.' He searched my face.

'The letter explains so much.'

'Thirty-eight years is a long time to keep a secret. It had to be hard.' He sighed. 'It had to wear him down.'

I knew this too well.

'I miss him,' he whispered.

'Me too.' I reached out and touched his arm.

'He was so good to me, and believed in me when, to be honest, many wouldn't have. My background as a surfer with a passion for the ocean didn't necessarily make for a sound business plan.'

'I get that.' I walked to the door of the basement and flicked the lights on. Ke followed me down. I cast a glance at the boxes of Mum and my things. Talking to Ke about what had happened wouldn't be easy.

He stepped forward and unlocked the wine cellar.

'Red or white?'

I shivered in the dampness. 'Red, please.'

'Grape?'

I laughed. 'Once we wouldn't have cared.'

'True. The sickly white.' He chuckled.

'It took me years to get over that.'

'I remember.' He selected a bottle and handed it to me.

'I'll open this and meet you in the conservatory.' I stopped, thinking of what he'd said, about watching Tony agonise over composing the letter, and the loss Ke was feeling right now. 'His letter is on his desk, if you want to read it.'

He looked me in the eye. So much emotion was displayed there. 'Are you sure?'

I nodded.

'Thank you.' He gave a half-smile. 'See you in the study then.'

In the kitchen, after I'd uncorked the wine, I put together a plate of salami and cheese, along with some water. Carrying the tray through, I was surprised not to find Ke in the study.

I set things out on a small table and poured two glasses of wine, then walked to the desk. My heart stopped. My 2009 diary was there, open at the page where I'd poured my pain out. How had I forgotten I'd left it there, beside Tony's letter? I started shaking like a leaf. Closing the diary, I tried to still my racing brain.

I turned at the sound of footsteps on the gravel and saw Ke coming back inside. This was not the way I'd wanted to bring up this topic. I wasn't even sure I could go through with it tonight, feeling so unprepared. Part of the reason I'd been reading the diary before was to collect my thoughts, to plan out what I'd say.

The look of devastation on his face brought the pain of sixteen years ago rearing to the surface.

'I'm sorry,' I said, my voice shaking, which was so woefully inadequate it rang hollow.

He just looked at me with tears welling in his eyes.

'Ke, I don't know what to say except I am so sorry.'

'It's not for you to say sorry.' He shook his head.

'I should have told you.'

'I can't argue with that but...' He cleared his throat. 'I'm sorry you went through that alone.'

I couldn't breathe.

'You never should have carried this on your own.' He shook his head again. 'Didn't you trust me?'

I gasped. 'I did trust you, but not myself.'

'I don't understand.'

I put my glass down, trying to find a way to begin. 'Ke, I'm sorry.'

'You don't need to apologise for this.' He paused. 'It's clear that you loved me. If I'd had doubts before, your words have erased them.'

I ran my hand across my forearm, trying to find the words, but nothing was coming.

'I would have been there for you.' His eyes, those gorgeous sad eyes, fixed on me.

'I know and...' How could I say aloud what I hadn't been able to say at the time? It was sixteen years ago, but right this moment I was twenty-two and pregnant again, with the child of the man I loved. Words wouldn't come.

Ke stepped closer and took my hand in his. 'I can only try to imagine what you went through on your own in LA.'

I opened my mouth, but instead of words came tears, then loud messy sobs. Ke pulled me into his arms, where his tears mixed with mine. He too had lost so much.

My phone pinged in my pocket. Bloody Vlad.

'I need a tissue, and so do you.' I stepped back and looked at his poor reddened face, his blue eyes still glistening with tears. I loved him with everything in me. That had never changed, no matter how much I'd longed for it over all these years.

When I returned from the kitchen with a box of tissues, I found him in the study looking through the diary again.

'I know you've said it all here – the agony of your decision. I get it. But I still don't understand why, if you loved me, as these pages say, you didn't speak to me about it?'

'I tried calling but you didn't answer.' All the fear from that day settled on me now.

He frowned, clearly trying to remember. 'That last missed call I had from you? But I rang you back.' His words were only above a whisper.

'I'd had the abortion by then and I just couldn't talk about it, I couldn't tell you.' I closed my eyes, having so much sympathy for that young woman I'd been. 'In a way I was relieved you didn't answer because I might have changed my mind.' I gulped in air, needing to say these words, no matter how hard. 'We both wanted different things, and I knew if I'd let my guard down then both our lives would be ruined.' A strangled-sounding half laugh and half cry came out of me. 'My fear of being like my grandmother and mother.'

'Never, I would have...'

'I knew that, and I couldn't do it to you either.'

I watched his Adam's apple move up and down. 'But after?'

'I know.' I blew my nose. 'Looking back, it seems simple, but at the time I was an open wound, and I thought putting distance between us would be the best way to heal it.'

'But it didn't?'

'No, the opposite.' I paused.

'Tony knew, didn't he?' he asked, turning the diary in his hands.

'He did, and Micki worked it out today.'

'She didn't know before?' His eyes were wide.

I shook my head. 'I didn't want the world to know.'

We both laughed sadly.

'She was the one who put our names forward for this year's dance.'

'Doesn't surprise me.' He picked up his glass. 'Never has a glass of wine felt more needed.' He raised it and I did the same with mine. 'To Tony, your father, to your wonderful mother, and to our friendship finding its way again.'

'Yes.' I met his glance, the flood of emotions, long locked down, rippling the air between us.

Hope.

Epilogue

2026

8 May, 7:00 a.m.

Propped on the desk in front of me was the invitation. Today was the day.

7 PM
Flora Richards and Ke Dale
Invite you to their wedding
at
Lismore
A celebration to follow

I stroked the cover of my 2026 diary. Tony had put in the order for it before he died. He knew I'd need it more than ever to work out my thoughts and feelings.

Flora Day.
Flora's Day.

I wrote, thinking of the younger me.

And today is very much Flora's day.

It is my wedding day, to the man I've loved since I was eight. I am so full of happiness, yet it is tinged with sadness too, as Tony and Mum can't be here to celebrate with us. Their love is with me, though, and Tony's gift of Lismore has done just what he wanted it to. It has brought me back home in more ways than one.

I put Tony's pen down and closed the diary, for the church bells were ringing, rallying the residents of Helston. The dancers for Early Morning Dance would be gathering; the pubs were already serving their first pints. Helston had its party hat on, Lismore was ready for this Flora Day, and so was I.

Gina secured the last clip on the dress while Vlad took photos with his phone. The photographer was waving him away.

'See, I was right. You needed to shag him.' Vlad said.

Gina stepped back, and Vlad fixed the lily-of-the valley in my hair.

I laughed, filled with happiness.

Matilda poked her head around the door. 'Can I come in?'

'Of course.' I opened my arms to hug her.

'You look so beautiful,' she said as she stepped back.

'So do you. Blue is your colour.' She wore a dress the colour of bluebells, setting off her blonde hair.

'I feel like a princess,' she said, spinning around.

'I do too.'

She peered out the window. 'I can see Dad talking to the guests.'

It was ten to seven in the evening. The day had been kind weather-wise, and our hundred guests mingled on the lawn. Micki came waltzing in, clutching three bouquets – hers, Matilda's, and mine.

'Is she ready, or is she going to make the man of her dreams wait?' Micki asked with her hand on her hip.

I smiled. 'I think he's waited long enough.' Picking up my bouquet, I held out my other hand for Matilda's. Gina fussed with my skirt, and Vlad pushed the photographer out of the way to brush a tendril of hair off my cheek.

'I always knew you'd make the most beautiful bride.' Vlad stepped back, and Micki led the way down the staircase.

Today was the day, and my heart was overflowing with love.

Wilf stood at the bottom of the stairs, holding out his arm. 'Are you ready?'

'I am.'

'Good.' He grinned. 'This is a day I'd hoped for but never thought I'd see.'

'Neither did I.' I held his arm a little tighter.

In the conservatory, the Helston Town Band played. Wilf walked me through the hall and the door to the small salon. The doors separating the salons were open, linking the rooms. Ke stood at the far end. My heart swelled even more with love. Matilda tugged my hand, and I bent down to her.

'I'm so happy you're marrying Dad. He smiles again with you.' Her eyes sparkled.

'I've loved your father for so long.'

'I know,' she said. 'He told me.'

'And I love you too.' I kissed her cheek and then looked down the aisle between the rows of chairs filled with so many smiling friends. Ke turned, and my glance met his.

Home.

The walk down the aisle had its bittersweet moment as I thought of how Tony should have been by my side, but he would have approved of my choice in Wilf, and more than that he would have approved of the man I was choosing to marry.

Wilf gave my hand to Ke's.

Ke lifted it to his mouth and kissed my fingers. Looking at me, he said, 'I love you.'

My breath hitched. 'I love you too.'

He smiled, and in that moment all the broken bits inside me fused. I felt more whole than I'd ever been, with the mended fracture lines of past pain not hidden but glowing like the hues of rich Cornish copper holding together Gran's bowl.

Acknowledgements
& Author's Notes

First and foremost, thank you to my readers. I love sharing my stories, and I am so grateful to all who read them. Your enjoyment spurs me on to write more!

Those who follow me on social media will know that Mr Liz, aka my husband Chris, is my rock. Without his support and belief, none of my books would have happened. Now that he is retired, he has become my partner in crime, so to speak. He is my first reader, my research buddy, my proofreader, my photographer, my driver and my webmaster, not to mention being simply the best.

Although I live no distance from Helston as the crow flies, I have needed the knowledge of Gillian Geer for all things Flora Day. She has shared her love for the day, funny details, and sternly told me I couldn't write about Flora Day without taking part. I duly turned up at the rehearsal for the Hal an Tow the following Tuesday. Of course, she was right I was hooked and I loved taking part on the big day! Although my knees won't agree, it was brilliant fun and an honour to be a hedge in the joy that is the Hal an Tow. I am thankful for her expert information and, as always, all mistakes are mine.

Ginny Sealy of The Bookshop in Helston has been a star,

introducing me to Gillian, and Ginny has read an early draft of the book, checking my Helston details! I am so grateful to her, and I'm certain I've still managed to get things wrong.

My children, including my daughter-in-law Annabel, are my cheerleading department. When I say the story is terrible, they reply 'Oh, you're at that point again! Keep going because it's not'. My daughter Sasha has done a brilliant job in helping with my Helston research, including taking me on a pub crawl the night before Flora Day, introducing me to the owners of Lismore and creating the fabulous map of Helston in the front of the book.

Adam and Sarah Corbridge bought Lismore in 2021. When the previous owner, Michael Jay, put it on the market, he would only sell it to someone who agreed to keep the gardens open for Flora Day. I'd seen the articles at the time, and the seed of a story developed in my mind. Lismore is a magical spot, and Sarah kindly showed me her beautiful home and shared some of her memories of Flora Days past. She is an actress, and some of her stories of acting in the German adaptations of the Rosamunde Pilcher's work may have helped the story along.

Thanks also go to John Baker who spent time with me talking me through Tony's motivations so that they felt real and honest. As always, any mistakes are mine.

Writing a novel is a solitary role, but making sure the story is as good as it can be takes a team. My editor, Claire Baldwin, has taken Flo to her heart and made sure that this story sings the way it should. I am so grateful for her skill and patience. Huge thanks to Sarah Bauer for skills as a copy editor and proofreader. The hugely talented Berni Stevens has created a gorgeous cover, and we all know we judge a book by its cover.

As always, my Blessing of Writers – Brigid Coady and Deborah Harkness – keep me sane. Their support means the world.

My Cornish booksellers have been supporting my books from the start, and I love them for that and for so much more. Each shop is a unique hub in its community, offering so much more than books. Please support them and your own local bookshops.

As I mentioned above, the newspaper article about the sale of Lismore became the seed of the story but it was my daughter's friends always coming home for Flora Day that gave the story its meaning. Helston is a town with heart, and it truly shows on Flora Day. I hope I have in a small way captured a little of this in this tale of rebirth and redemption, even if just in a small way.

Finally, a note on Furry Day or Flora Day. I found myself down many a rabbit hole with the research, from getting lost in the town's history going back to its first charters to the tune of both the Hal an Tow and the one for the dance through the town. According to the blog of the Library of Congress, the Hal an Tow was sung to the tune used in the dance! If you like research deep dives, this one is interesting. They have a recording of a woman in the Ozarks singing the words to the Hal an Tow to the Furry Dance tune. It was recorded in the 1940s. How it ended up in the Ozarks isn't a mystery as Cornish miners travelled far and wide, but the change in the tune is. I leave this one to a historian or folklorist or musician to resolve!

About the Author

Called *'the queen of the contemporary Cornish novel'* by The Guardian newspaper in the UK, Liz is an award-winning author of ten books and two novellas, including the most recent *The Secrets of Harbour House* published in 2025. Originally from Massachusetts, she now lives with her husband and two mad cats near the Helford River in Cornwall, England. When not writing Liz is reading, painting, knitting and procrastinating on social media.

Her books are available in English, Swedish, Dutch, German, Portuguese, French, Estonian, Norwegian, Danish, Turkish, Latvian, Serbian, Czech, Hungarian, Italian and Finnish.

If you would like to subscribe to Liz's newsletter, sign up via her website at www.lizfenwick.com.

* * *

Follow Liz Fenwick on:

facebook.com/liz.fenwick
x.com/@liz_fenwick
instagram.com/liz.fenwick
tiktok.com/@lizfenwickauthor
pinterest.com/lizfenwick3